Colours of Magic
Next Chapter

Anna Novak

ISBN: 978-1-917778-46-6

Prologue

Love makes people do incredible things. There are no limits to how far one can go for those they love the most. They are ready to pay any price, make any sacrifice, commit any crime or even make a deal with the devil himself. And if it was up to you, would you go to hell and back for the love of your life? Would you do it for your dearest friend?

Chapter 1

Hayley was dead. Liam took her gently into his arms and lied her on the bed. He deemed the light, sat in the armchair by the window and patiently waited for her to come back to life. The crowd outside was celebrating New Year's Eve with loud music, dancing and fireworks. The streets of New Orleans always teemed with life as if there was always a reason for celebration so that night didn't seem unusual or special in any way for the locals.

Liam heard a heartbeat. Hayley was alive again but still unconscious, her breathing was regular and her heartbeat was getting stronger with ever second. Liam thought about the day when he woke up as a vampire for the first time. How everything was fascinating and terrifying at the same time. The sound, the light and the smell were overwhelming, attacking him from all directions. And the hunger - all he could've thought of was blood and how much he wanted it. The source did not matter, it was a pure primal instinct to survive at any cost. Somehow, it was the best and the worst day of his life and he cherished it and hated it simultaneously. The strength came with a face and a heart of a monster. What would he be now if it hadn't been for Leah? What would he have become? What kind of monster would he have embodied? How many atrocities would he have committed over those two hundred years? He sighed loudly and looked at his watch, it was quarter after midnight. Suddenly, Hayley opened her eyes and sat on the bed. Now, her breathing was rapid and shallow and her heart was beating fast. She looked at Liam as he was getting up from the armchair and walking towards her.

- Welcome back, Hayley - he said with a gentle smile - How are you feeling?

She looked around the room. Although the light was dimmed, she could see everything clearly. A small black spider running across the dark carpet suddenly caught her attention. Liam sat on the bed right in front of her.

- Hayley, talk to me, how are you feeling? - he sounded concerned.

- Everything is so clear and loud. Why is it so loud outside? - Hayley seemed annoyed.

- It's a New Year's Eve and people have a right to celebrate. Don't think about them, I'm here, focus on me.

Hayley looked at Liam's chest.

- I can hear your heartbeat... I can feel your warmth... I'm so hungry that I could swear my stomach hurts but it's impossible, isn't it? I should not feel any pain, right?

- You will feel pain. Even though a bullet cannot kill you now, you will still feel the pain of being shot. If you say your stomach hurts, it means it hurts indeed and you need to feed to feel better.

- Why is it so different to what it was like in my dream? I thought I would feel better or at least the same, but I am worse. Is this how my eternity is going to look like?!

Liam took a small vial of blood out of his pocket and handed it to Hayley.

- Take this, it will make you feel better.

Hayley reached for it and drank its content immediately. She didn't even care where he got it from. All that mattered was that the blood she desired so much was within her reach. She caught a deep breath and calmed down. Liam was right, it made her feel much better right away.

- Be patient, Hayley. It will get better and April knows the spells to help you speed up this process. I won't leave your side, you can count on me.

Hayley slowly got up, the carpet felt unusually soft under her bare feet. She looked through the window at the street full of people singing, laughing and dancing.

- Can we join them? Have some fun?

- I don't think it is such a good idea, you may hurt someone.

- Why would I? I just want to join them, not to kill them.

- You're not fully in control yet, you are not yourself Hayley and you can't be trusted.

- I will behave I promise so please let's go out, I want to go out - she sounded like a small child asking for a candy.

- Very well. But you cannot leave my side.

- I won't, I promise.

They put on their jackets and shoes and went outside. But Hayley's smile disappeared from her face the moment she went through the door. She saw everyone and everything clearly even in the darkest corners of the street. She felt the warmth of people passing her by, she could hear their heartbeats and their whispers. The air was full of smells so intense that it made her sick. She stopped and leaned against the wall.

- What is it, Hayley?

- I think I'm going to be sick.

- Let's go back to the hotel.

- No, I want to get through this and have some fun tonight. It's a New Year's Eve, we should celebrate.

- We will have fun, I promise, but now we need to go back, trust me.

She looked at him, sad and scared. He took her hand and slowly led her back to the hotel. He knew it was going to end that way, but he needed her to see it for herself. He didn't want to force her to stay in the hotel when she wanted to go out so badly.

When they got inside their room, Liam turned the radio on and got the champagne out of the chiller.

- Happy New Year Hayley – he said and handed the glass to Hayley.

- Happy New Year - Hayley responded with a smile but she sounded sad and disappointed.

They drank some champagne and moved the furniture so they could dance. Swirling around the hotel room took Hayley's mind off the noise outside and helped her relax. She felt much better in that room in Liam's arms than outside among strangers. A few minutes later, they landed on the bed laughing. They were about to kiss when they heard their friends on the hall. They got up quickly and turned the radio down. When Liam opened the door, everyone rushed inside.

- You did it! – Isabella yelled staring at Hayley.

- Did what? - June asked confused.

- Hayley's a vampire now.

April approached Hayley and took her hand. She could feel the difference. Hayley's aura was colder and darker and was rapidly changing for the worse. Suddenly, Hayley pulled her hand out of April's grasp and took a step back.

- Get away from me.

She stood behind Liam, holding his hand tightly. She remembered what he said to her earlier: 'you can't be trusted'. And he was right, all she could think of was blood and how much she wanted it. She was looking at April as if she was her prey and nothing more. She was ready to attack, her eyes turned black and her human part was quickly fading away, leaving an open way for her vampire instincts.

- April – Liam said quietly – do you remember the spell that Iris taught you today?

- Yes, I know what to do, I'm ready.

Liam turned around and looked at Hayley.

- Everything is going to be OK, trust me.

He was holding her gently by the wrists in case she totally lost control. April stood behind Hayley, put both of her hands on her sister's head and started chanting quietly, repeating the same two sentences over and over again: *'Tenebrae in te evanescant. Esto compos mentis tuae.'* There was a pale-yellow light between April's hands and Hayley's head. Everyone could see the magical power passing from one girl to another. A minute later, April let go of Hayley and took a step back.

- It's done. Hayley, how are you feeling now?

Liam let go of Hayley too. She slowly turned around and looked at April.

- I think it worked – she said and smiled.

Her eyes were green again, her aura was brighter and warmer so April hugged her relieved.

- I'm so happy you're OK, you really scared me.

- Thank you April, I don't know what I would do without you.

Everyone was looking at Hayley not quite sure what to expect. Even though she seemed herself again, there was something different about her now which was hard to explain or describe.

- So, are you tired or can we go and celebrate now? - asked Hayley.

- The night is still young. Let's go dancing!

They went to Frenchmen Street to enjoy live music and dance. The crowd was incredibly diverse as people from all over the world came to celebrate New Year's Eve in the most magical place on earth, where real witches and vampires blended in with the humans. The street was crowded but everyone seemed to have a good time. Every now and then, Hayley smelled blood. Occasionally, she saw some vampire feeding on someone who was too drunk or too high to notice what was really happening. Nobody paid any attention and only Liam, Isabella and Ethan knew that some of those happy and carefree people were never to return home from their very last trip to New Orleans and that their encounter with a real vampire would end up tragically with their demise. Their bodies would be left somewhere in the dark corner with no documents, wallet or a cell phone. The bite marks would magically disappear and it would look as if they were attacked and robbed so there would be no further investigation. Where there were crowded streets full of drunk people, there was always a victim or two, nothing unusual, nothing requiring too much attention. The life would go on for the others and the tragedies of New Year's Eve would be left in the past and eventually forgotten.

- Hayley, wake up - Liam whispered.
- What's going on?

Hayley sat on the bed and rubbed her eyes but then realised she did that only out of habit as she was not feeling sleepy as usual but was fully awake and ready to start the day.

- I want you to come with me.
- Where? What time is it?
- It's dawn, I want you to have a walk with me.

They went outside and started to walk along the street. The city was quiet and completely empty as all shops and restaurants were still closed. The sun was not up yet, but the sky in the east was clearly getting brighter. The streets were unusually clean considering how many drunk people were there that night. Either everyone knew how to behave or the witches of New Orleans had something to do with that and kept everyone in check using their magic.

- What did you want to show me? - Hayley asked confused, having looked around.

- Nothing, I just wanted to talk to you, find out how you feel. So, how are you?

Hayley sighed loudly.

- I must say it was nothing like I imagined it. It was completely different from Leah's version.

- You can't blame her. She wasn't a vampire, she couldn't possibly know what it felt like.

- I know, I just… I didn't expect it would be so intense. Everything seems too loud and too bright. I see all the smallest details and I hear all sounds. Constantly, something attracts my attention so it's difficult to stay focused. Yesterday, it was fun to go out and celebrate but I could barely enjoy the music hearing so many other things in the background. The flashing lights were getting on my nerves and people were incredibly loud. And I'm constantly hungry, I didn't expect the hunger to be so overwhelming. To be honest with you, I… I really thought about killing April yesterday. I know how it sounds and I am so ashamed but in that moment, she was not my sister anymore… I don't want to even think what could've happened if I had been there alone with her.

- Leave it in the past. You were not yourself then but you are now and your sisters are perfectly safe with you. You don't need to worry anymore.

- But how could I feel that way? How could I let myself think like that? It's terrible!

- Hayley, the way you felt yesterday is what it really means to be a vampire.

- What do you mean?

- I mean that you and I are different because the witches helped us let our human part be in control. We have human emotions and feelings but real vampires, in their pure form, are different and the only thing that matters to them is survival. They don't care about anyone. It doesn't matter whether the person they are about to kill is a criminal or a loving parent, whether they're old or young, people are just food. Vampires like to have fun and to enjoy their existence but they don't care about others, they are not capable of love or empathy. After transition, their vampire nature quickly takes over and everything that is human disappears. They become killers, monsters.

Hayley was looking at Liam with disbelieve.

- So real vampires are ruthless, heartless and soulless monsters, is that what you're saying?

- Yes.

They sat on the bench in an empty park. The sun was now up on a cloudless sky, the birds were chirping and the morning dew glistened on the grass like little diamonds.

- What are you thinking about Hayley?

- I'm shocked. I didn't know all that.

- I'm sorry we didn't have a chance to talk about this earlier, I just knew you wouldn't be one of those vampires and it would never be your problem. It doesn't concern you, never has and never will so don't worry about it.

Hayley didn't say anything and was just staring at the trees swaying in the wind.

- Out of curiosity – Liam started - if you had known all this, would you have chosen differently? Would you have stayed human?

- I don't know… Maybe... But it doesn't matter now, there is no turning back.

- Hayley, don't worry too much. You have me to answer all your questions and I will always be there for you. Forgive me for not telling you what to expect exactly. For some reason, I assumed you knew everything. That dream really messed with my head.

- That's OK Liam, I understand, it messed with mine too. But if you think of anything that I may still not be aware of, please let me know.

- Of course. Now come on, let's go back for breakfast. Others should be up now too.

Liam got up and reached out his hand, Hayley took it without hesitation and they started walking back to their hotel, enjoying the sunshine warming their faces. It was going to be a nice warm and sunny day, the kind of a day that they probably wouldn't see in Aspen for the next few months.

By the end of the day, everyone was back home apart from April who decided to stay in New Orleans. There was so much she needed to learn from Iris. Magic fascinated her and consumed her. She could already see her future in the French Quarter among people who understood her better than her own sisters. Magic was her whole life now and she wanted to embrace it completely. Iris suggested she could stay with her for a couple of days until she's found something for herself. She also promised to help her get a job and settle down. *'There is always a place for a witch in the French Quarter.'* - she assured with a smile.

April walked into Iris' small guest room but didn't unpack. Instead, she took out her laptop and started looking for a flat. She didn't need much, a studio or a one-bedroom flat would be enough. Hayley promised she would help if she needed money so she didn't have to limit her search to her own budget and it was a relief as April didn't have much. As a matter of fact, she has never lived on her own as Hayley has taken care of her and June since their parents died. Now, she needed to find a job and learn how to manage her money. She was in her early twenties and it was time for her to become independent and move on with her life. Contracts, agreements, bills, shopping, cooking, working - the more she thought about it, the more she got anxious. She took a deep breath to calm down, typed *'flats for rent New Orleans LA'* into her browser and started looking for her new home.

Hayley entered her house and had a look around. It was her home and yet everything seemed different. The colours seemed more vivid, the light seemed brighter and it smelled like dog so much that Hayley needed to open the windows and air out the house. Liam came with Lexi a few minutes later. They ate some takeaway and took the dog out for a walk. It was freezing cold and snowing but Hayley didn't mind, she was used to that kind of weather.

- You seem worried – Liam asked looking at Hayley who seemed lost in thought – What's wrong?

- I worry about June, I don't know if she's going to be OK without April being around. They have been inseparable and now they are so many miles apart. June has never lived alone and neither has April so I worry about them both, really. Not only am I their big sister but I'm also their parent in a way and they have counted on me since our parents died.

- I know it's hard for you, but they are big girls and they can take care of themselves now. I'm sure they are going to be just fine.

- I just need to get used to the fact they are not little kids anymore and this day had to come at some point.

Liam pulled his hat a bit more over his ears.

- Missing Louisiana weather? - Hayley looked at Liam and smiled. She knew how much he hated Aspen.

- I can stand the cold and the snow and that awful grey sky as long as I have you by my side – Liam smiled and squeezed Hayley's hand.

They walked in silence for a couple of minutes.

- Liam…

- Yes?

- Is that why you have never looked for a wife among vampires? Because all girls you met were ruthless killers?

Hayley surprised him with her question so he thought for a few seconds before he responded.

- The truth is that none of them truly cared about me because vampires don't love. They don't think about the future or the past, only now matters. I was never truly happy with another vampire. All those acquaintances didn't last long, there were no real feelings between me and any of them. I have never had a true connection with anyone, they meant nothing to me as much as I meant nothing to them. And before you ask, the answer is no, Leah couldn't have done her spell to make any of those vampires more human. That spell needs to be performed as soon after transition as possible, otherwise vampire nature takes over irrevocably. You cannot change anyone who's been a vampire for even a few days.

- What about Ethan? He's good but you turned him during the war, so who helped him?

- One of the nurses was a witch. She didn't like vampires but when I told her what's happened, she helped my guys, including Ethan. She knew the spell and performed it for us.

- So, if you couldn't change any vampire girl to be more human, couldn't you turn anyone like you turned me?

- No, there was nobody like you, Hayley. You have no idea how special and extraordinary you are in so many ways.

- That's sweet Liam, thanks. But can you still answer my question?

- I... I couldn't just turn some girl into a vampire without her knowing what she was getting herself into. Every human girl I ever loved trusted me and felt safe with me and I couldn't just... It's different with you because it was your decision, you knew what you agreed to. Every human who knew the truth about me despised me so if they perceived me as a monster, how could I turn them and condemn them to a life like mine?

Hayley didn't comment on that. She was wondering what she would be like if April hadn't cast that spell for her. She was a step away from killing her own sister that day and that thought was making her restless.

- I know that being a vampire has many perks and it should be fun but… I don't enjoy it. I hear too much and it annoys me, I smell too much and it makes me sick. I was far too sad when I was leaving April and I keep getting too angry without any good reason. My emotions are all over the place. How am I supposed to live like that? How can I face the eternity when I can't stand a few days?

Liam put his shoulder around Hayley to console her.

- It is not going to be like this forever, it will get easier. You will learn to ignore the noise and the smell and your emotions will normalize at some point. Don't worry Hayley. Maybe… Maybe we should take a trip somewhere to ease your mind? How about Miami? You liked it there.

- Is Amanda and Tom going to be there too?

- I'm sorry to disappoint you Hayley but I don't think they are anyway near America. But we can have fun just the two of us. We can swim in the ocean and jump off the cliffs. How about skydiving? Isn't it what you always wanted to do? Let's do something reckless, something that you were too afraid to do as a human. Maybe that way you can enjoy your new self.

- Maybe you're right… I could stand face to face with a wolf like I did in my dream. That was cool.

- You need to be careful when you want to try it yourself. It's more dangerous than you think.

- What are you talking about? Animals can't hurt me, I'm the stronger one, that's what you said.

- But not every animal is just a normal animal.

- What does it even mean?

- There is someone who we call a shapeshifter. It is someone who can change into an animal whenever they want to.

- Like a werewolf?

- Kind of. A werewolf could change only into a wolf, a shapeshifter can change into whatever animal they want.

Hayley got upset.

- How come you've never told me about them before?

- I don't know… Somehow, this topic never came up. But I am telling you this now because they are very dangerous and you need to be careful. It is very important that you don't come across these hunters when you're on your own.

- How come they can hurt a vampire?

- Magic. They are magical creatures with an incredible strength. Many years ego, witches created these creatures to protect people from vampires giving them an incredible power. As animals, they are very fast and strong. The spell is passed through generations, when one member of the family dies, the next one becomes a hunter and so on. Although witches and vampires are at peace now and don't kill each other, the spell is still alive and works. When a hunter comes across a vampire, they kill without hesitation. Vampires argued with witches to get this spell removed, dis-activated somehow, but the witch community declined their request. They claim that vampires need to know there are stronger creatures out there, they want them to be afraid in order to control them.

- How can I know if it's a hunter or a normal animal?

- You can't.

- Great. So now I have to stay away from the woods. I can't go hiking or skiing or…

- That's not true, don't be so dramatic Hayley. You can go hiking, you can do whatever you want, just stay away from big wild animals, don't approach them. And if they ever start chasing you, run and don't try to fight them. They may be strong and fast and scary but so are you. You are not totally vulnerable.

- Have you ever seen those creatures?

- Yes, once. I saw from a distance a bear killing another vampire. But I ran away, I was shocked, I panicked... I didn't even try to help as I wasn't sure I could... Please, promise me you'll be careful Hayley.

- I promise.

Hayley didn't say anything anymore and kept walking back home in silence. *'How come Liam has never mentioned anything about vampire hunters before? Or the fact that all other vampires were so different from him, Isabella and Ethan? Was there anything else he accidentally forgot to mention? Why am I finding this out just now?'* She was getting annoyed with her thoughts but then she calmed down reminding herself how much Liam loved her. There was no way he would hide anything from her intentionally or trick her into becoming a vampire. He was a good man and he wouldn't do anything to hurt her. She took him by the hand and smiled. She loved Liam too much to stay mad at him. At that point, she was sure there was probably much more she hasn't been aware of yet and that every now and then, Liam would surprise her with something new, unknown and unexpected.

- Anything else you'd like to share, Liam?

- Not at this moment, no. Hopefully, there is nothing more you need to know. But if something comes up, you'll be the first to know, I promise.

Chapter 2

First few weeks passed by incredibly slowly. Every day, Hayley was working hard on herself, trying to stay in control of her emotions and her actions. Whenever she felt she was getting angry, she closed her eyes, took a few deep breaths and counted to ten. She yelled at Liam a few times but every time, she apologised and explained she didn't mean it. Liam was very understanding and he patiently endured Hayley's screams and swearing, knowing it was just a phase that would eventually pass. After first four weeks, Hayley was noticeably better. She was not herself yet but clearly much more in control. The smell and the noise didn't annoy her that much anymore and her emotions were nearly back to normal. She felt ready to come back to seeing her patients, but before she scheduled the first appointment, she decided to fly to New Orleans to check up on April. She missed her sister very much and even though they talked occasionally over the phone, it was not the same as their Sunday meetings they had before.

Hayley packed her bag for her four-day trip to New Orleans and headed to the airport. She landed before noon and April was already waiting on the terminal to pick her up. Hayley was holding her winter jacket in her hand but was still wearing her winter boots. It was warm and sunny in New Orleans although the clouds slowly started to cover the sky. They decided to go to April's first so Hayley could leave her bag and change into something more suitable for the pleasant Louisiana weather.

Two weeks before, April has rented a small one-bedroom apartment on a St Peter Street by the river. She also has found a job in the House of Voodoo which was a walking distance from home. As the apartment belonged to one of the witches, April didn't have to pay much for it therefore she didn't have to ask Hayley for any extra money. She felt much better about herself knowing that she could afford to live on her own without asking her big sister for any kind of support. It made her feel all grown up.

Although the place was small, it was perfect for a single young girl. The kitchen was white and green with a tiny wooden table and two chairs in the middle. There was a double bed and a double-doored wardrobe in the bedroom and a nice three-seater sofa in the living room. April didn't need anything else. A few photos on the wall and a small fern on a windowsill made that place look homely enough.

- I like your place, April. It's very cosy – said Hayley having looked around the apartment.

- Thanks Hayley. It was very nice of the witches to help me like this. With this flat and the job I can now stay in New Orleans, I really like it here.

- I can't believe you decided to move in here so quickly. You didn't really know this city or those witches.

- I know it was a bit reckless… But those witches made this place feel like home. They understand me and my problems in a way that you and June never will. But I think you can understand my decision, Hayley. You moved in with Liam although you didn't really know him, only because it felt right. And my moving here felt right to me so you need to trust me that it was a good decision. I know I can be happy here, I already am.

- I'm glad to hear that. So… I'm ready to see the city now and meet your friends and see where you work. Take me everywhere!

They spent the rest of the day on exploring the city. Hayley met a few of April's new friends. Even though they hesitated at first, they agreed to at least say '*hi*' to April's unusual sister. After exchanging a few sentences, they have realised Hayley was nothing like any other vampire they have encountered in the past and her story was quite interesting and unique. They promised she could count on them if she ever needed help as, in a way, she was a part of a witch community.

The girls spent a nice evening in the pub. Loud music didn't bother Hayley at all. Although it was live music and not a karaoke evening, the girls had fun singing along and dancing around. They attracted a lot of attention being loud and foolish but they didn't care. Hayley was happy to see how much those witches cared about April and how much fun she had with them. She herself was having a good time too despite being the only vampire in the pub. Many people were looking at her surprised and confused, it was very uncommon for the witches to engage with vampires in any way. It was unusual to see these two fractions even talking to each other so seeing them dancing around laughing and clearly having fun was something extraordinary indeed.

It was already after midnight when Hayley and April were finally alone, comfortably sitting in April's apartment, eating ice creams and listening to jazz.

- So Hayley, how was your transition? We haven't really had a chance to talk about it and I'm sorry I haven't asked you earlier.

- That's fine April, you were very busy with your own life. To be perfectly honest with you, it was terrible. I thought it was going to be like in Leah's dream, that I would feel great but instead, I was annoyed and hungry and scared. After you helped me with your spell, I regained some control but it took me weeks to be where I am now. I'm glad I have most of it behind me now. It's still a lot of hard work every day but I see I am getting better. I just need to remember to keep my anger under control and be careful not to hurt anyone. Poor Liam, he was clearly sick and tired of me but he didn't say a word. He put up with a lot and I admit, I was terrible.

- I can imagine how hard it must have been and I'm glad you're better now. Hayley… I have been told a bit of this and that about vampires. When Iris was teaching me that spell for you she said you would be dangerous and unpredictable and that I should not trust you. Apparently, not all vampires are like Liam. Did you know that?

- Not until I turned. Apparently, once you're a vampire you're just…

-… Pure evil?

- Exactly. To be honest, I think if I had known this earlier, maybe I would've decided to stay human. I made that decision knowing too little.

- Do you regret it?

- No. But the truth is that my idea of being a vampire was quite different. I was so excited by the thought of being invincible and powerful and free. But it's not like that at all, at least not yet. Hopefully, at some point, I'll start enjoying my new me.

They sat in silence for a few seconds, stuffing their mouths with ice creams and letting their brains freeze.

- Enough about me – Hayley said - Now your turn. How have you been?

- I've been great. I love being a witch! I love the power that comes with magic and here in New Orleans it really feels like home. Iris was teaching me some simple meaningless spells so I could play with magic and learn how to control it. But with each day, the spells are getting more and more serious and complicated and I can't wait to see my full potential and what I am truly capable of.

- Go on then, show me what you can do.

April smiled, put her ice creams down and whispered some spell. A few seconds later a rose that she had in a vase on the kitchen table flew across the apartment and landed gently in her hand.

- Impressive - said Hayley.

- That was nothing! It was one of the simplest spells, I can move any object I want anywhere I want. All I have to do is focus. Now, look at this Hayley.

April grasped the flower head in her hands and whispered another spell. When she opened her hands, the flower was completely dead. The rose petals darkened and began to scatter in April's hands. Then, she grasped it again and a few seconds later, the rose was perfect again.

- Wow - Hayley said truly impressed – Can you do that to any living creature or just flowers?

- I can kill anything but the larger the creature, the more time and power it requires. Not quite sure if I can bring back to life humans or animals but I can definitely do that with flowers. I've had this rose here for nearly two weeks now and I don't have to buy a new one ever again.

- Amazing. I can't believe how much stronger you got after just one month.

- I didn't get stronger, Hayley, I have always been that strong. I have just learnt how to use my powers and there is still much more for me to discover. I know I can do more, I can feel it.

- I am very impressed little sister and I am happy to see you happy. Obviously, this is the right place for you. You really belong here.

- Thanks Hayley, it means a lot… How's June by the way? I mean, I have spoken with her a few times but how is she really?

- She misses you very much. You have lived together for so long that now she feels lonely without you. But she'll be fine. You couldn't live together forever, she needs to learn how to be on her own and to spend time her own way. She has been trying many new things, she's been out a lot meeting new people, discovering her talents, looking for a hobby. Don't worry about her, I keep my eye on her.

- I felt so guilty about leaving her. It was such a spontaneous decision and she was not ready for it.

- She is a big girl, April and she can handle being on her own. You need to sort out your own life and focus on your magic. Besides, she could move to New Orleans too if she wanted and you could keep seeing each other.

- You're right, she could move here, nothing keeps her in Aspen. I mean, I know you are there but it's not like you need her to be there for you.

- Exactly. But you already know who you are and June still needs to discover herself. Her older sister is a vampire, her twin sister is a witch and she is just an ordinary human. She must be disappointed to be so normal.

- Maybe she's not supernatural be she definitely isn't normal.

They both laughed.

- So April, did you find out anything interesting about vampires that I don't already know?

- Nothing more than what I have already told you.

- Has anyone talked to you about shapeshifters?

- About what?

- Liam told me about them only recently. Apparently, these are some magical creatures designed by witches to kill vampires.

- Are you serious?

- Unfortunately, yes. Maybe your friends will know something more.

- I will talk to them in the morning. I am really interested in what they have to say.

- Great. I will let you do your witch business and in the meantime, I will pop out for a cup of coffee and wait for you in the park. I got the impression that witches are not big fans of vampires.

- They're not, but you are an exception, Hayley. I think they really liked you.

- Look at the time! It's three o'clock already. Maybe you should have some rest?

- And waste my time with you on sleeping? No way! I'm staying awake. Do you feel like having some hot chocolate?

- In the middle of the night? After this huge amount of ice creams that we have just finished?… Sure, why not.

The next day, April left Hayley at Cafe Du Monde and went to talk to Iris who was waiting for her tour to start. She was one of the tour guides. It was funny to listen to her talking about magical New Orleans, the vampires, ghosts and witches. She was telling nothing but the truth and the tourists had no idea that their own guide was a real witch and everything she said was something much more than just catchy stories.

- Have you ever heard of shapeshifters? - April asked bluntly, pulling Iris away from the crowd.

- Where did you hear about them?

- Who are they, exactly?

- They are people who can turn into animals. They have been created by the witches over a century ago. Their sole purpose is to kill vampires.

- Why do they still exist? I thought witches and vampires are at peace.

- Not really… Vampires are destructive and merciless creatures, they kill people who witches try to protect. We decided not to hunt them down as we were afraid too many of our own could die in the process. If vampires knew we were after them, they could start attacking witches. As strong as we are, we would be able to win the war eventually, but many witches would die and we don't want that. Nobody wants to risk their lives, especially that vampires don't kill witches so we don't have to be afraid of them. But we let the hunters exist. Vampires are not happy about it but there is nothing they can do. Let's call it 'population control'. But April, you didn't answer my question, where did you hear about them?

- My sister told me.

- Right, your sister, the vampire.

- But she is one of the good ones, you know? And she doesn't deserve to be killed by some vampire hunter. She has never hurt anyone, she's not a threat to anyone. Why can't we just stop the spell and make all the hunters disappear?

- This is not an option, April. We need them to protect people from vampires and we cannot stop them all only because there is one or two good vampires in this world.

- Can I protect my sister with some spells?

- No, there is nothing you can do or any of us. I'm sorry April… I need to go now.

April started slowly walking back to the coffee house. She knew many powerful witches and she couldn't believe that none of them could do anything to help Hayley. She got the feeling that Iris was not completely honest with her and she decided she would dig deeper to search for the spell that could protect her sister.

Hayley patiently waited for April to come back. She was sitting outside, drinking an exceptionally good coffee and enjoying the sun. It was only an early February, but it felt like May. She wouldn't see that kind of weather in Aspen for at least another three months. The streets were crowded but the atmosphere of the city was still enjoyable with jazz from the Jackson Square quietly heard in the background. Suddenly, Hayley saw April coming back and she didn't look happy. Hayley took the last sip of her coffee and got up to meet April halfway.

- So, what did you find out?

- This is not something we can discuss here, Hayley. You never know who might be listening.

They walked back to April's place in complete silence. When they got into the apartment, April answered Hayley's question.

- It's not good. Iris says that there is nothing we can do to protect you from the hunters but I think she's lying.

- Why would she lie? I thought she was your friend.

- She is, but I don't think she likes vampires very much.

- So you think she could lie to you and put my life at risk because other vampires are cruel and deserve to die?

- As a matter of fact, yes, I think she could do that. Hayley, I know it sounds terrible but I have been around witches for a month now and I see how they protect their community at any cost and how much they care for one another. They all go by the same rules and they all have the same believes. If all their ancestors thought it was OK to let the vampire hunters exist, they all will believe that too. But I don't believe that there is nothing that can be done. I just think that nobody wants to do anything and Iris didn't want to tell me that because you're my sister… But I will find out.

- How? If Iris is really lying to you I don't think any other witch would tell you the truth.

- There is one who will.

- Who?

- Leah.

- I think if Leah knew what to do, she would've done it long time ago.

- Maybe, but I need to hear it from her.

April started moving her stuff around, making space on the floor in the middle of her living room.

- What are you doing?

- I will talk to Leah, but I need to prepare first.

She took a handful of soil and formed a circle on the floor. Then, she put four white candles inside that circle and lied down, having each candle by her feet, head and both hands.

- OK. I will fall asleep now and you can just wait here for me.

- How long are you going to be like that?

- I don't know, a few minutes. Don't worry, I'll be fine.

April closed her eyes and started saying the spell: *'Accipe me videre maiores meos, relinquam corpus meum.'* She repeated it three times. Then, all four candles lit up and she fell asleep.

April woke up in the middle of the New Orleans and it didn't feel like a paradise or heaven. It felt like dawn or twilight, the sky was grey and covered in heavy clouds and the fog was floating around. Dead witches were walking around, some were visible to April and some were not but she could still feel their presence and hear them whispering. They talked to each other or cast some spells for those who were still on earth. They didn't look either happy or sad, they looked emotionless and unfriendly like ghosts or zombies from the horror movies.

- Leah!

April yelled having looked around. Leah showed up in front of her, out of thin air.

- Come with me April, we cannot talk here.

She led April aside and cast a spell. A small wooden hut appeared in front of them in the middle of the Jackson Square and they walked inside. The hut was cramped and there was only one room in there with two chairs and a small fireplace. It was much warmer and pleasant inside than out there.

- No one can eavesdrop on us here so we can talk freely. What brings you here, April?

- I need your help. Is there anything that can be done about shapeshifters? As far as I know there is nothing that witches can do, there is no spell I can use to protect Hayley, but I think witches are lying to me.

- The vampire hunters… Yes, I have tried to get rid of them when I heard of them for the first time but I was not strong enough and nobody wanted to help me. These are incredibly powerful creatures. The spell that was put on them has been cast by dozens of witches many years ago therefore it's incredibly strong and I don't think there is anything we can do. Getting rid of the hunters would be very dangerous and I can understand why witches are unwilling to help you. Besides, French Quarter witches are not strong enough to stop the spell anyway, I'm sorry to disappoint you April. But remember that Liam and Isabella have been vampires for over a century and nothing happened to them. Hayley is safe with Liam and you don't have to worry about her. She's not truly immortal but she has never been. She just needs to be careful. I'm sure Liam has already told her about all dos and don'ts and he can take care of her just as he has been taking care of himself all these years.

- Thank you anyway, Leah. I just wanted to make sure witches are not lying to me. I was afraid they were hiding something from me and I needed to talk to someone I could trust.

- Of course. I understand how difficult it is for you, I have been there myself. You feel connected to the coven and you want to perceive the witches as your family but on the other hand your sister is a vampire and you are somewhere in the middle, between fighting fractions, unable to choose a side.

- No Leah, I am able to choose a side. If I needed to, I would always choose Hayley. It doesn't matter how much witch community means to me, I would always take my sister's side. But I hope I could count on the witches if I ever needed their help. Despite being a vampire, Hayley's mind and heart are still human and she's nothing like all the other vampires.

- I know. And whatever happens, remember I'm here for you.

- Thank you, it means a lot… I should go now, Hayley is waiting for me.

April whispered the word that would bring her back to the world of the living, the candles extinguished and she woke up seeing Hayley walking nervously around the room.

- Finally, you're back! I thought you would never wake up. Did you talk to Leah?

April got up and started tiding up the room.

- I did and she confirmed what Iris said that there is nothing we can do.

- OK… so what's next?

- You just need to be careful, stay away from the woods and try to avoid any big wild animals. Liam and Isabella survived nearly two hundred years so I think you will be fine too. Try to relax and stop worrying. When you were human there were countless ways to die and now there is only one danger out there so I think we can handle it.

April moved the furniture back and cleaned the room.

- Now, let's go out eat. Practising magic makes me hungry.

Chapter 3

April has been working hard learning as many spells as possible. She has also been thinking what she and Leah could do about the vampire hunters. She couldn't really understand why they were so important. It looked like they were only dangerous as large wild animals but how many vampires were walking around the woods those days. She decided to talk to Leah again and try to find out more. It was the middle of the night and she was feeling tired but she knew she wouldn't be able to fall asleep. She prepared the spell and visited Leah and exactly like last time, they were having their conversation inside the wooden hut so nobody could hear them.

- Leah, I just keep thinking why it is so important to let the shapeshifters be… I mean… Vampires don't go to the woods that often, so what's the point?

They both sat down by the fireplace.

- It's not like that at all April, you're clearly missing a lot of information. These hunters are something more than just a bear or a wolf walking through the woods. They live among us and they can recognise a vampire from the distance. When they are in their human form, they follow the vampires around, trying to find out where they live and they wait patiently for a perfect moment. They can kill anywhere. They can slip through the door as a mouse and then change into something more dangerous. Many vampires nowadays die inside their houses or hotel rooms. The story about the hunters being in the woods is true but old. Vampires used to hunt in the forest and live there too as many of them were not capable of living peacefully among people. But that changed throughout time.

- How did Liam and Isabella manage to stay alive all these years? From what you're saying it looks like they can be easily killed at home or even on the street - April started getting nervous.

- There is a spell to prevent the hunters from entering the house and it can be put on the house itself or on any item inside. I put that spell on a few items for Liam and Isabella and they have carried them around every time they moved.

- So Hayley is safe when she's home, that's good, one less thing to worry about.

- Yes, and also the hunters won't attack when there are people around as there cannot be any witnesses. As you know, vampire body turns into ashes after death so no human can witness that. Hayley is safe among people, nobody would attack her on the street during the day. She's also safe if there is another vampire around because one hunter cannot kill two vampires at the same time. My advice is that if she wants to go into the wild away from the city, she should go with Liam - Leah took April's hand and smiled - Don't worry April, she's safer than you think. Usually vampires don't stick together, they are loners, having no real homes or friends or family so they are an easy target. Hayley is not alone, she has Liam to protect her and he knows how to survive any danger. It's going to be OK, April. Don't lose sleep thinking about it.

But despite her conversation with Leah, April didn't sleep that night, going through different books and journals, trying to find anything helpful. But with every next page, she was losing hope. Getting rid of the hunters seemed as impossible as getting rid of vampires. There was a reason why witches haven't killed all vampires or turned them back into humans, the spell was simply too strong and the same was with the hunters, there were too many of them around the world and the spell has been active for decades. It looked like there was nothing more she could do beyond what has already been done. April closed the journal and sighed with exhaustion. She closed her eyes and fell asleep leaning her cheek against a pile of books, feeling too tired to get up and go to bed.

As time was passing by, April's life has reduced to working, learning and sleeping and she started getting tired of it. In spite of being surrounded by friends, she started feeling homesick and lonely so she decided to take a week off and visit her sisters in Aspen. June picked her up from the airport on a Saturday morning in the middle of an exceptionally cold March. She had the whole week planned to make sure April wouldn't be bored. Dancing, live music and karaoke were on top of her list but for June the most important thing was for her sister to meet her new friends. She wanted to show April what her life was like now and to make sure that she didn't feel sorry for moving out and leaving her alone.

They were out all days and talked all nights. April used her magic to sustain them so they didn't have to waste any time on sleeping. It was good to be together again, carefree and silly. Although they missed each other very much, April didn't want to come back to Aspen and June didn't wish to move to New Orleans. She felt too normal to join her witch sister in that magical city and she knew it was not a right place for her. At the same time, April felt too unique to live in Aspen and she was sure that the French Quarter was her true home.

They had a great time together feeling like children again, having their secret conversations under the duvet. All problems were gone and it was all about having fun. They were so disappointed when that one week quickly passed and it was time to come back to reality. The last day before her flight back to New Orleans, April visited Hayley to say goodbye.

- How was your week with June? - Hayley asked pouring down coffee.

She didn't spend much time with April as she wanted the twins to have fun without feeling that their older sister was watching over them.

- Very intense. We talked constantly about everything, as if we haven't seen each other in years. This one week made me realise how much I've missed her.

- I can't believe she actually found any free time for you, she's been so busy since you left.

- But she seems happy, that's all that matters to me. I was worried about her and wanted her to move to my place but now I see she has been building her life here and it looks pretty good. I met her friends and they seem fun. Apparently, June has a boyfriend. I was supposed to meet him but something came up and he couldn't see us. Have you met him?

- No, I haven't and this is the first time I hear about him.

- She didn't want to say too much but she promised that if everything goes well, she will introduce him at some point.

- Interesting… I will try to get something more out of her next time I see her. We haven't spoken much recently as she's been very busy with her new lifestyle. But enough about June. How have you been April?

- I'm OK but I don't have any good news for you, I'm afraid. I've talked to Leah and read many journals and spell books and unfortunately, it looks like there is nothing we can do about the vampire hunters. I'm sorry, Hayley.

- That's OK April - Hayley said that with a note of disappointment in her voice - I appreciate you tried.

- I know this is not something you wanted to hear, I'm sorry to disappoint you.

- Don't worry April, I know you've done everything you could so thank you and don't think that you disappointed me, you are a very powerful and smart witch and I'm so proud of you.

- Thanks. Maybe at least you have some good news for me. How have you been, Hayley? Are you any better?

- Yes, thank you, I feel better every day. I came back to seeing my patients.

- That's great. So you're back to normal?

- Well, if being a vampire can be classified as normal. But at least now, I can take Lexi out for a long walk and she is the only one coming back home tired.

- Lexi! I completely forgot! - April started going through her backpack - I have something for her. That spell that has been put on the rings for me and June to keep us young and healthy, well… I put the same spell on a collar for Lexi.

She took a red leather collar out of her bag and handed it to Hayley as Lexi was out on a walk with Liam.

- That's so great! Thank you very much April. I didn't even know it was possible.

- Why not? Lexi is just another living creature. Now she can be your loyal friend for eternity.

- You have no idea how happy I am.

- I'm glad I could do this for you - April got up from the sofa - I will be going now, I promised June we would spend these few last hours together. Take care Hayley. I miss you and I love you.

- I love you too - Hayley gave her sister a hug - Have a nice flight back and I hope to see you again soon. Don't be a stranger.

- You too. You're always welcome to visit me any time you want. There are so many cool spells I could show you. It's getting more and more fun.

- That's great, I can't wait to see what you can do. Have fun with June, I know it will be difficult to say goodbye again.

- We promised to see each other more often. I wish I could teleport, that would make my life so much easier.

- Maybe one day you'll come across a spell that would make it possible for you.

- There isn't one, I've already asked around. How disappointing.

- Don't stop hoping, you're a witch now so you of all people should know that there are very few things that are truly impossible.

June came back home from the airport. Her home seemed so empty and quiet now without April. She missed her twin sister very much and she would do everything to have her moved back in. But it was clear that April was not interested in coming back and June needed to accept the fact that their paths have now separated and they needed to move on with their lives. When April moved out in January, June decided to throw herself into extra activities to keep herself busy. She was intensively searching for new friends and a hobby to the point that she didn't remember what boredom was anymore. When she was not working, she was taking French lessons, guitar lessons or dancing lessons or reading books for her book club meetings. Losing her twin sister was like losing a part of herself and she was doing whatever she could to fill that void.

June reheated her dinner from the previous day and turned the radio on. She didn't like eating in a complete silence and that radio has been her only company since April moved out. Suddenly, her cell phone made a sound and she received a text message:

-How are you?

It was Jack, he knew April was leaving that day.

- Eating dinner all by myself. Have just come back from the airport. House's so empty.

A minute later she received another message:
-Want me to come over?
It made her smile. She liked Jack. She met him when she was having one of her guitar lessons a couple of months ago. He couldn't be more than twenty-five-year-old, handsome, smart and funny. Short blond hair, blue eyes and dimples made Jack very attractive and charming. They talked in the hall often and after a few weeks, Jack asked June out. They have been seeing each other and texting since then. It's been a month now and June really enjoyed his company. She hasn't introduced him to her sisters yet because he seemed so normal and she wanted to keep him away from anything magical afraid that it could scare him away.

- *I could use some company* - June eventually replied with a smile on her face.

Jack came over thirty minutes later. He brought some popcorn, crisps, chocolates and ice creams. June was waiting for him and although she was wearing sweats and her hair was simply down, she sprayed herself with perfume and put some make-up on to make sure she looked nice but casual.

- I wasn't quite sure what would make you feel better so…

- Good choice. Thanks, Jack.

Without hesitation June reached for the box of chocolates and quickly kissed Jack on the cheek.

- So how are you? How was your week with April?

June couldn't reply straight away as she had her mouth full of chocolate already. She opened the box before they even sat down in the living room.

- It was great! - she finally said - We had so much fun. I really miss her and it was breaking my heart to see her leaving again.

- I understand she had her reasons for moving to New Orleans but why didn't you follow her there?

- Because she already had her new friends there and her job and she was doing very well without me. She didn't need me anymore and so I decided it was time for me to move on too. It was hard and it made me sad but I got through it eventually.

- Are you happy now?

- I am… Kind of… I still miss her very much and I wish she was here… But I met some cool people. I met you - she smiled - And I think I would've never met you if April hadn't left.

- Why do you think so? If it's destiny, we would've met one way or another.

- Destiny? Do you really think you can turn my world upside down?

- I'm sure I can give you many unforgettable moments. I'm pretty cool, you know?

- Of course I know you're cool, otherwise I wouldn't get interested in you. I don't waste my time on just anybody.

They spent the evening talking and watching movies. They were cuddling on the sofa under the blanket and the fire was burning in the fireplace across the room. It was a pleasant evening although the weather was frightful outside. June enjoyed the idea of having someone. She was afraid of loneliness and she needed someone who would console her and be there for her in her lowest moments. And Jack seemed to be the right person for that job, she liked him very much and hoped that their relationship would become something serious.

Jack decided to leave shortly before midnight when it was still heavily snowing. June didn't want him to go but she was very tired after April's magic stopped sustaining her a few hours earlier.

- Are you sure you want to walk home so late? Why won't you call a cab? It's freezing out there.

- Don't worry June, I'll be fine, trust me. The weather doesn't bother me. See you tomorrow?

- Maybe. Ask me tomorrow.

They both smiled. Jack kissed June goodbye and left. She worried about him and asked him to let her know once he's home. She was afraid of the evil hiding in the darkness but Jack was not afraid. Once he disappeared around the corner, he had a look around to make sure nobody was watching. He took a deep breath, closed his eyes and turned into an owl so he could quickly and safely get home. He flew through his open window and turned into his human form in his bedroom. He didn't text June right away as he shouldn't be home for at least another twenty minutes. He grabbed a bite, took a shower and then finally sent a message to June before she decided to call and check up on him.

-You can relax now, I'm home. Goodnight June.

The next day Jack had his usual walk around the city searching for vampires. He stayed away from the city centre, pubs and hotels and decided to walk through the parks instead. It was pleasant and sunny outside and even though a thick layer of snow was covering the ground, it didn't stop people from going outside. There were many people around jogging, walking their dogs or pushing prams. Having walked deeper into the park, Jack found a vampire sitting on the bench in the park. It was a girl in her thirties looking quite ordinary, even friendly, watching a dog playing in the snow. It was clear that the dog belonged to her. *'A vampire with a dog. That's something new.'* - Jack couldn't hide his surprise. Vampires didn't care about anybody else so it was truly extraordinary to see a vampire taking care of another living creature. Jack swept the snow off a nearby bench and sat down watching the girl from the distance. Occasionally, the girl threw some snowballs and laughed every time her dog tried to retrieve them. She looked very human and behaved like everybody else. If asked, nobody would believe she could be a ruthless killer. After about fifteen minutes, the girl took her dog on a leash and started leaving the park so Jack got up and followed her, keeping a safe distance. He couldn't attack her on the street, there were far too many people around so when the girl walked inside her house, he turned into a bee and tried to fly through slightly open kitchen window but he couldn't. Some unseen force was preventing him from entering the house. He had a flight all around the house, looking inside through the windows, watching the girl playing with her dog in the living room. Then, he noticed a sign by the door saying *'Hayley Anderson – psychologist'* Still as a bee, he flew back home.

- A psychologist with a dog… This is very intriguing – he thought aloud, walking around him room in his human form - And why couldn't I get inside her house? She's clearly protected by magic, but why? What witch would cast a spell for a vampire? Why would anyone protect her? She behaves like no other, that's true… But she's still a vampire and witches don't cast spells for vampires...

He couldn't stop thinking about Hayley. He had many questions and lack of answers nearly drove him crazy so eventually, he decided to get to know her better to see what was going on. She was not like the other vampires he killed before so he decided to take his time with her and postpone killing her by a day or two. He searched her online, found a phone number and called her without hesitation.

- Hayley Anderson.

- Good afternoon Ms. Anderson. I am interested in having a session with you.

- OK… Let me see… Would you like a one-to-one session or a group one?

- One-to-one please.

- Very well… I see someone cancelled their meeting so would you like to come over this afternoon?

- Sounds perfect.

- Five-thirty?

- Great, I'll be there.

- Can I take your name, please?

- John Smith.

- OK Mr. Smith. I'll see you later.

Jack couldn't wait to meet Hayley and talk to her. He needed to know why she was protected by the spell and why she seemed so different. He couldn't just kill her right away, having so many unanswered questions. Hunting vampires was exciting at first but now it felt more like a job, a duty. But that particular case made hunting exciting again and he couldn't wait for the deadly game to begin.

Jack knocked on Hayley's door five-thirty sharp. His heart was beating fast with excitement as he didn't know what to expect. He has never spoken with a vampire before but he was not afraid.

- Mr Smith? - Hayley opened the door smiling gently - Please, come in.

Jack entered the house without any problems and sat on the couch in the living room as instructed. The house looked ordinary and cosy.

- So – Hayley started - Can I call you John?

- Sure.

- Good. So John, tell me, what brings you here?

Jack thought for a moment not quite sure how to respond. He clearly didn't think that through. He was so excited about talking to Hayley that he has forgotten to prepare his part of the conversation.

- Lack of self-control – he finally responded.

- OK… tell me more about it. What makes you lose control?

- Bad people. I have no tolerance for evil, I want to bring all bad guys to justice.

- A vigilante?

- Something like that. I like punishing people for their atrocities. I can't stand that there are real monsters among us and nobody is doing anything about it.

- Do you truly believe that? We have police officers and judges and they bring bad people to justice.

- You're right, they do. But there are those who cannot be caught by the police. The best killers stay out there, they know how to hide.

Jack didn't want to say bluntly that he was a vampire hunter, he wanted to build the tension and see how Hayley would react. She didn't scare him.

- And I assume you know how to find them?

- I do, yes.

- So how do you find them?

- I can't answer that.

- OK… So what do you do once you find them?

- I kill them to make sure they won't hurt anyone else ever again - he said that looking Hayley deep in the eye.

She didn't comment on that. She didn't know whether it was a real killer she was talking to or someone with a vigilante complex who just wanted to believe he was doing something good when in fact he was not doing anything at all.

- Do I scare you? - Jack asked as Hayley didn't say anything.

He didn't want her to know who he truly was yet as he was interested in what she had to say and he wanted to continue their conversation that he started to enjoy. But on the other hand, he wanted her to know the truth so he could see fear in her eyes.

- No, you don't scare me. From what you say I understand that you kill only bad people and I am not a bad person so why should I be afraid?

- You're right. Forgive me if I made you feel uncomfortable.

- You didn't. I am just trying to understand you better, so John, tell me, do you have an alias and a cape like every other hero?

- I don't, the world doesn't need to know about me. I am not looking for fame, I don't need anyone to recognise me on the street, I just want to make sure I eliminate as many monsters as possible so humans can be safe.

- Humans? - Hayley repeated surprised - So the monsters you hunt are not human?

- They're not. They are real monsters, creatures created by magic to kill people as they feed on them.

- Like vampires? - Hayley began to feel anxious.

- Exactly.

- Do you truly believe in vampires, John? - she asked with a vague smile, trying to make it sound ridiculous.

- I do. Don't you, Hayley?

- I think vampires are a product of a very vivid imagination and nothing more. Books, stories and movies with no reflection in reality… Aren't you afraid that you might have killed ordinary people? Humans?

- I am sure the creatures I killed were not human. But there is no point in explaining this to you if you don't believe me.

- I am not saying I don't believe you. I believe that you are sure you killed vampires to protect people and that whatever you have done was in good faith. I am sure you are not a bad person and you don't kill just random people.

- I'm glad you understand that, Hayley.

- Do you consider yourself a hero?

- Yes, I am a true hero. Not like a batman or a superman but a real hero.

- Will I ever see you on TV?

- Definitely not.

- How can you be so sure?

- Because when I kill I make sure nobody sees me and there are no witnesses. I don't want other monsters to go after me, I need to stay anonymous.

- Is that why you introduced yourself as John Smith? Because you don't want me to know who you are?

- That's right. You don't need to know my real name.

- Why are you really here, John? You said lack of self-control but obviously you are satisfied with what you do and you want to continue your work. So what do you really expect from these sessions?

- I think I… I just wanted to tell someone about me, to see their reaction, to be appreciated. I wanted someone to thank me for protecting people.

Jack was telling the truth. He really wanted someone to know who he truly was and even though he was not looking for fame, at least once, he wanted to be appreciated for his devotion and dedication.

- Very well. Thank you John for protecting people. I just want to be sure that you know what you are doing.

- I know exactly what I'm doing. My father and his father and all fathers before them, they all did what I do.

- So this is then a family tradition to protect people.

- You may say that, my family has been chosen for this. This is my duty, my life purpose. I move from one town to another and search for monsters. Once I have made sure the town is free of them, I move on to the next one and so on. I don't have a place I could call home, I'm a traveller.

- Has any of your murders been on the news?

- No, I leave no trace behind, there is no blood, no body. The monsters I kill don't have families or friends.

Nobody looks for them, nobody asks about them, nobody misses them. I'm doing world a favour.

- So there is no sign of a crime that police could follow?

- No. And what I do is not a crime, I don't hurt people. Monsters don't have a right to live among us... Can I ask you a question, Hayley?

- Go ahead.

- Why are you a psychologist?

- Same reason as yours, I like helping people. It brings me joy knowing that someone sleeps better at night and is happier because they talked to me and opened up to me.

- Interesting...

- Tell me about your parents and your childhood.

Jack told Hayley about his growing up and his family. One hour of their session passed very quickly and Hayley needed to ask Jack to leave. He didn't schedule another appointment but he said he would get in touch in case he needed to talk to Hayley again. For some reason, he didn't want to kill her just yet. It fascinated him how well Hayley hid the fact she was a vampire and how normal her life seemed to be. Once he has left, Hayley locked the door and made sure all windows were closed. She went upstairs and let Lexi out of the bedroom. There was nobody else scheduled that day and Liam would be home soon. She was walking nervously around the living room, biting her nails and thinking what to do. Suddenly, she heard the key turning, the door opened and Liam came in.

- Hi Hayley... Are you OK? You seem scared.

- I think I have just met a vampire hunter.

- What are you talking about? Where?

- He came here.

- Inside the house?

- Yes.

They sat on the couch. Hayley's voice was shaking and she was nervously playing with her fingers.

- He called me today, he wanted to talk to me professionally. When he came over, I invited him in. He says he kills monsters to protect humans. He also says it is something all his ancestors did, that his father taught him how to hunt and kill vampires.

- Did he really say that? Did he mention vampires?

- He did. And I don't know whether he is a real vampire hunter and he came over here because he needed to get inside the house, he needed me to invite him in, or he is just delusional and made it all up.

Liam took Hayley's hand to comfort her.

- Hayley, if he was a real hunter, he would've killed you already. Why would he just sit here for an hour and talk to you? It doesn't make sense, this is not what hunters do.

- But all those things he told me… He sounded like a real vampire hunter to me, Liam. He really scared me.

- I can see that. Call April and tell her what happened. Maybe there is a way to keep him away although you already invited him in. Are you going to see him again?

- I hope not, he didn't schedule another appointment. When I asked him why he came to me he said he wanted me to know the truth about him and thank him for keeping people safe. He wanted me to appreciate his work. This is what confuses me, he could've killed me but instead he wanted me to admire him… That's why I hope he is nobody but a guy with mental issues and a vivid imagination. Maybe he really saw a vampire once, maybe this is how his father died and now he tries to convince himself that he can kill vampires to protect other boys from losing their fathers too. Some people with trauma do that, they create a new image of themselves so the past doesn't hurt that much. Or maybe he met a real hunter once and now he tries to be like them. I don't know Liam, but he was very confident that he was telling me the truth and he sounded very convincing.

- Call April. See what she can do.

Hayley told April about John Smith but they both agreed that he couldn't be a real shapeshifter. A real vampire hunter would use every opportunity to kill without wasting too much time. He wouldn't play with Hayley like that, he wouldn't want her to suspect anything. After all, Hayley could've killed him if she had really believed he was dangerous and he couldn't have risked that. They all decided though that it would be better if Liam was home when Hayley was having her sessions with anyone new. It would be difficult for a hunter to attack two vampires at the same time. That day, Hayley put an information on her website saying that she was unavailable to anyone new and that she could continue seeing her regular patients only. She didn't want to risk inviting in anyone who could potentially harm her. John really frightened her and for the first time since she has turned into a vampire, she was truly afraid she could die.

Jack went to June straight from his meeting with Hayley. He was intrigued and Hayley made a huge impression on him but he still hasn't figured out why she was protected by magic. He didn't want to kill her yet but he knew the longer she lived the more people died. He decided he would pay her another visit soon and end her meaningless life like he did so many times before with other vampires.

He spent a nice evening with June. She was such a lovely girl, so unaware of the evil around her, but she didn't mean much to him. He moved to Aspen only for a few weeks and he was not ready for any long-term relationship. His meetings with June brought a bit of joy into his dark life but she could never be a true part of it, she could never know who he really was, nobody could.

June looked at Jack quietly watching the movie. He seemed miles away.

- Are you OK? - she asked - You seem off.

- Something happened today… I discovered something very unusual and unexpected.

- What was it?

- Let's say… All my life I was told that my neighbours living across the street were pure evil and I should stay away from them. But today, I discovered that they were in fact different and not all of them seemed so bad.

- OK… - June looked confused - And taking all metaphors aside, what did you really discover?

- It doesn't matter, I can't tell you.

- Why not?

- I just can't. You wouldn't understand.

- Alright, so what are you going to do with that discovery then?

- I don't know yet… I mean… How come my family was so wrong?

- I think that there are two options here. One is that even though they all live together, they are not the same and you may be right. The other option is that they are all the same pure evil but some of them hide this fact better than the others. Some may pretend to be good but it's all just an act.

- You're right… They may pretend to be good for their own safety…

- So what are you going to do?

- Never mind. Let's don't talk about it anymore, it doesn't matter.

When Jack came back home later that evening, he sent a text message to Hayley asking for another meeting. Having spoken with June, he decided it was impossible for a vampire to be good and caring and Hayley was just like the others. There was no such thing as a good vampire and he shouldn't be fooled by Hayley's acting skills. She was just another monster that he should eliminate and it was exactly what he intended to do.

Hayley read the text message she has just received. Mr Smith wanted to see her again.

- Liam, what should I do? - she asked with a note of fear in her voice - Should I tell him that I don't have time?

- No, tell him you'll see him again. I will be here and take a picture of him. We will ask Isabella to check him as she has access to all kinds of databases. Maybe she can tell us something more. Don't worry Hayley, he won't try to hurt you if I'm here, he wouldn't be able to fight both of us. We can protect each other, trust me.

- I hope you're right. I haven't thought about dying since I willingly died on New Year's Eve… I thought death was not an issue anymore but clearly I was mistaken. As a matter of fact, I feel even more in danger now than ever before.

Liam put his arm around Hayley.

- Hayley, everything is going to be OK, don't panic. Me and Isabella survived many years and no vampire hunter has ever come after us. The same will be with you, nobody is going to hurt you, I give you my word.

But Hayley didn't sleep at all that night. The idea of letting Mr Smith into her house again frightened her. She felt better knowing that Liam would be in the next room, ready to protect her but she was unsure how that meeting would end and she didn't want to die. She was listening to the clock ticking and Lexi's rapid breathing. Through the window, she could see how with every minute the full moon was slowly moving across the night sky finally completely disappearing to make way for the morning sun.

The session started at five as agreed. Mr Smith came on time and sat on the couch, ready to talk. He wanted to exchange with Hayley a few more sentences, make sure she was completely off guard before he decided to attack.

- What did you want to talk to me about this time, John? - Hayley started with a bit of tense in her voice.

Suddenly the door opened and Liam walked in.

- Don't mind me – he said – I just need a glass of water from the kitchen.

He was holding a cell phone by his ear but that sentence was clearly directed to Jack who was now looking at Liam shocked as he didn't expect anyone else to be there.

- I apologise – Hayley said – He will not interrupt us again.

- Who is he?

- He's my husband.

'Husband? Vampires don't build relationships, they always live alone' – Jack was confused. Was it possible that Liam and Hayley put so much effort into making everyone believe they were good and nothing like typical vampires?

- So, where were we? - Hayley asked, trying to get Jack's attention again.

Jack was watching Liam coming back from the kitchen, completely distracted. *'Maybe they really are different and that is why their house was protected by the spell?'* Jack had so many questions but he couldn't ask any of them.

- How long have you been together? - he asked looking at Hayley.

- This is a personal question John and we are here to talk about you, not me. So let's go back to you. What did you want to tell me?

It was clear now that he couldn't kill Hayley as planned. Not with another vampire being in the house. He couldn't risk being killed.

- I… I begin to suspect that my parents have been lying to me. But I think they didn't know they were wrong, maybe they were lied to as well.

- What are you talking about?

- Monsters. They categorised them all as evil, ruthless and stupid… But I think not all of them are like that.

Suddenly a cell phone rang in the next room and Liam answered it.

- Sister, what do you have for me?

'Sister?' Jack thought – *'how's that possible?'*

- Are you going to stop your hunting quest then? - Hayley asked to get his attention back.

- No… I still think these creatures are evil I just realised they are smarter than I thought.

Liam opened the door and entered the room.

- So, Jack Watson, why are you really here? What have you planned?

Jack looked at Liam shocked.

- How do you know who I am?

- I know more than just your name.

Jack didn't respond.

- So what was the plan? To get inside Hayley's house and kill her? But you didn't expect I would be here and now what? Will you give it another go tomorrow or a day after that, waiting for a perfect moment?

- Jack – Hayley started quietly – you don't have to do this. I am a psychologist, helping people coupe with their emotional problems. I have a husband, two sisters and a dog. We are good and we don't deserve to die. Leave Aspen. Hunt the real monsters someplace else and let us be.

Jack was looking at her thinking what to do. He has never talked to a vampire before, he always observed them from a distance so then he could kill them without a single word. But it was different now. These vampires were unusual, they were a family with a seemingly normal life.

They didn't seem aggressive or out of control and they were nothing like other vampires he's met before. They could kill him within a blink of an eye but instead they tried to make an agreement and let him go. He was thinking intensively on how to respond as that whole situation distorted his perception.

- I will leave Aspen – he eventually responded.

- Good – Hayley said relieved - You made the right decision. Thank you, Jack.

He got up and left without a word as Hayley followed him and locked the door.

- So – she said to Liam – do you trust him?

- No. He said what we wanted to hear because he was afraid that we would kill him otherwise, but he is not going to stop, this runs deep in his blood, this is what he has been taught all his life and he won't just change overnight. He doesn't believe we're good and he will come back, I'm sure of it. He has access to the house now so he can appear in front of us anytime, in any form. I think you need to leave this house for a while, Hayley and move in with June. I will look for Jack with Isabella and Ethan.

- You're right, I should go to June at least for a few days. I will ask April to come over too and put a new spell on the house, we need to be sure Jack can't get inside..

- Don't worry Hayley, it will be OK. Go and pack your bag and I will call June.

June welcomed her sister with open arms. She hasn't seen Hayley for a while, busy with her new life. Hayley unpacked her stuff in April's old room and they both lied in bed ready for an all-night-chat like when they were younger.

- So what brings you here? - June asked - Don't get me wrong, I am very happy you're here but it is a bit unexpected. Liam hasn't told me much but he sounded concerned. Should I worry?

- I'll be honest with you June, I'm in trouble. I thought I didn't have to worry about death after my transition but…

- Death? - June sat on the bed looking at Hayley shocked - What are you talking about?

- Has April told you anything about the vampire hunters?

- Yes, she told me a bit of this and that but apparently there is not much she can do about them. But I didn't know it was that serious, after all, Isabella and Liam survived decades.

- One of them was in my house recently.

- How come? I thought your house was protected.

- It was but I invited him in, he was one of my new clients. He came to talk to me about his problems and then he started talking about vampires. I didn't believe him at first but then Liam confronted him and he didn't deny anything. We asked him to leave Aspen and he agreed but we think he was lying. As we are not sure what he would do or who he really is, we decided it would be better if I moved here and Liam with the others would try to find him.

- Wow. Who knew your life could get so complicated.

- I know… But I don't want to think about it anymore, let's talk about you. It feels like we haven't had a proper conversation for ages. So, what's up?

June was worried about Hayley and didn't feel like talking about herself but that was what Hayley wanted as she needed to keep her mind off the great danger that she was in.

- I'm fine. It was difficult to get used to an empty house and April not being around. I quickly realised I had far too much free time that I didn't know what do with, that's why I decided to try new things. And it was a good decision, I met great people and had so much fun. French didn't go that well so I switched to Spanish and it seems much easier. I like playing the guitar but my fingers hurt, they were really red and sore at first but once I have passed that phase, playing became quite enjoyable. And I love dancing! I am not very good at it yet but I am slowly getting somewhere. I feel the rhythm and apparently this is a good start.

- That's good. I'm glad you're happy.

- I am… And I met someone. There is this guy I like - June blushed - We kept seeing each other for over a month now. He's handsome and smart and funny and very easy to talk to. Maybe he's the one?

- I'm happy you found someone. So when will I meet your prince charming?

- I don't know. I thought it was too early to introduce him as this is nothing serious yet.

- It could seem too early to have him meet the parents but I think there is no rule when it comes to the sibling. Invite him over for a dinner tomorrow. April will arrive in the afternoon, it will be fun.

- You're right, it may be fun. I will let him know.

The next day the girls were preparing for a party. June's boyfriend was supposed to join them for a dinner and for later, they planned a night out so June could practice her dancing. Hayley was happy being with her twin sisters again under one roof. They promised there would be no talking about vampires or witches and that night would be perfectly normal with no magic involved.

June rushed to open the door the moment she heard the doorbell. She was wearing her rock 'n' roll polka dot dress, white trainers and a red ribbon in her hair.

- Hi Jack, come on in, everyone's in the kitchen. You're going to love them.

She marched into the kitchen with Jack by her side.

- Ladies, this is Jack.

- Oh my God – Hayley said and dropped the plate she was holding.

- It can't be - April said and raised her hand to cast the spell.

But before she managed to say anything more, Jack ran out of the kitchen and left the house. He turned into a sparrow and immediately flew away. June ran after him but before she reached the door, he was already gone. She had a look around completely confused and then locked the door.

- What the hell has just happened?! - she said when she came back to the kitchen.

- A shapeshifter – said April – He was a vampire hunter.

- Moreover – Hayley added – He was THE hunter I've been hiding from.

All three were standing in the kitchen, looking at each other without a word. Finally, June sat down at the table and started to cry.

- I can't believe this is happening. And I thought he could be the one and instead he's a murderer trying to kill my sister.

- So what do we do now? - said Hayley terrified - The whole point of me being here was that he couldn't get close to me but now he obviously can so I need to go someplace else.

- Stay – April said – I will put a spell on this house to keep him away.

- Good. Can you do that to my house too? Liam, Isabella and Ethan are there now.

- Of course, I will. Don't worry sisters, everything is going to be OK, we can handle this. There are six of us and together we are invincible, we just need to stick together.

April quickly cast the spell, they took June's car and were at Hayley's within a few minutes. When they went inside, Isabella and Liam were sitting at the kitchen table with a laptop and Ethan was sitting on the couch, petting Lexi.

- What are you doing here? - He asked surprised to see girls walking through the door.

- That vampire hunter showed up at June's.

- What?! How's that possible? Did he follow you there?

- No, he turned out to be June's boyfriend.

- Wow, what were the odds – Isabella said - Great choice, June. Anyway, we were waiting for a confirmation on where he is renting but maybe you know where he lives?

- Yes, he lives by the Triangle Park, I know the address.

- Great! That makes it so much easier then. He probably won't be home but he would have to come back at some point to pick up his stuff so we can wait there for him.

- I can cast a spell to prevent him from turning into an animal inside his house – April said.

- That would be very helpful – Liam admitted - OK, June April and Ethan, come with me. Isabella, stay with Hayley in case he showed up.

Isabella nodded without a word of objection. When they left, Hayley locked the door and sat down on the sofa with a loud sigh.

- Don't worry Hayley, everything is going to be OK.

- Everyone keeps saying that and I appreciate you want to calm me down but you don't know what's going to happen. Who knew that guy would be the one seeing June? I was supposed to be safe in her place but she invited him for a dinner! I became a vampire to eliminate the ways I could die. Liam worried about me every day before transition but I don't think he's any calmer now. This is not what I wanted for myself, I didn't want my life to look like this. I was supposed to be strong, invincible, forever young and free. Instead, I am constantly suppressing my emotions feeling either angry or sad, I can't sleep at night and I don't feel strong when I need to run and hide from a magical serial killer. Most of all, I don't feel invincible or free. I don't enjoy this life, Isabella. I wish it was all just a dream and I could just wake up and be human again and normal. How can I go back to my old life when clearly I'm a completely different person now? Can I just simply go back to where I have left before I died? Can I continue my human life when I'm not human anymore?

Isabella was surprised by Hayley's unexpected outburst. She thought Hayley was doing fine and everything was OK, but obviously, she was mistaken.

- I know this is not your dream come true yet. I have been where you are now and I know exactly what you are going through. I remember it has been hard at the beginning when I tried to adjust and it took me more than just a few months to do so. You need to be patient Hayley and it will get better eventually. You have the whole eternity in front of you and you cannot give up now. You will never be alone, you will always have Liam and your sisters and now, apparently you also have an immortal dog. Life of a vampire is not all rainbows and unicorns. You just swapped some of your human problems for different ones and you need to accept the fact that life will still be hard and complicated but in a little bit different way now. I think you should take some time off and go on holiday with Liam. Do something crazy and dangerous, enjoy your new self, have some fun! Life is not all about survival, you know? And you can't just keep thinking everyday about death. Take small steps and focus on going through today. Try to enjoy some moments of happiness, even the shortest ones and try not to waste your time on worrying. Play with your dog, enjoy Liam's company, have fun with your sisters, help people with their human problems or just simply relax in front of a TV or with a good book, listen to music, watch the sunset. Life can't be all bad, whether you are a human or a vampire.

Hayley calmed down and wiped away her tears.

- And I thought I was the one with a degree in psychology.

They both smiled.

- Well, I based all my knowledge on my own experience and I have nearly two hundred years of it.

Suddenly, they heard their friends parking outside. They were already back from their trip to Jack's place.

- What are you doing here already? - Isabella asked when they walked in - What's happened?

- Nothing – Liam said angrily. - We were too late, he has already taken all his stuff and disappeared.

- Maybe he was still there?

- No – April said – I used my magic and didn't locate anyone or anything apart from us.

- So what's now? - Hayley asked with a note of fear in her voice.

- Don't go anywhere alone, always in twos - April said - Your house is safe, he won't be able to get in neither here nor June's.

- That's good, thank you April.

They all looked at each other not quite sure what to do next. It was not how they imagined that evening would look like. Sad faces didn't match girls' dresses and they were no longer in a mood for a party.

- As I'm the only human here – June said - excuse me all but I need to go to sleep now. I am really tired, I barely slept last night.

- I will go with you – April said – You will drive me to the airport in the morning.

They both said their goodbyes to the rest and left. Isabella and Ethan decided to go back to Rockford too, they could still catch their night flight home. Isabella approached Hayley and gave her a hug.

- Call me when you need to talk – he whispered into her ear and left.

Liam locked the door behind them and looked at Hayley.

- Are you OK? - he asked concerned.

Hayley sighed loudly and started walking upstairs.

- I'll take a long relaxing bath and try to erase this awful day from my memory.

Jack was in a motel room by the road eighty-two just outside Aspen. He was nervously looking through the window and checking the door lock.

- This is impossible – he kept saying to himself out loud - Vampires don't work together, they don't protect each other so how come these vampires are completely different? And now I know why they are protected by the spell, June's sister is a witch. I can't beat them all, especially with that witch being around, unless… Unless I surprise them one by one. They will stick together for a while afraid I may come back, they will carefully watch their back. So let's leave them for now, I'll go hunting someplace else and come back here in a few weeks or months. They can't be on their guard forever. I will get them sooner or later I just need to plan it well… Maybe I can bring more hunters into this town… Yes, that could work. They're not invincible, I just need the right approach.

April was sitting in an armchair in the corner, watching June sleeping. The mixture of mascara and tears left a few black lines on her cheeks and her red ribbon was now lying loosely on the pillow. April was worried about her sister. Poor June, she was so happy with Jack and now she's all alone again. How could she possibly know he was a vampire hunter? April didn't want to leave her sister now knowing how much her trust has been shattered and she really wanted to help her. She was deep in thought for a few more minutes and then got up and quietly left the room. In June's jewellery box on the stand in the hall, she found a silver necklace with a small ruby stone that she gave her last year as a birthday gift. She clasped the pendant in her hands and started chanting: *'Dic mihi quando magicae adest.'* Then, when she opened her hands, the pendant was glowing red. She put it on the kitchen table and took a few steps back. The pendant slowly stopped glowing. When she started getting closer, it started glowing again. *'Perfect.'* she thought with a smile on her face and went to sleep.

Hayley couldn't fall asleep, thinking what Isabella has told her. She was thinking about all the places she could visit and things she always wanted to do. She was lying in bed and browsing the internet on her cell phone when Liam woke up.

- What are you doing Hayley?

- I can't sleep.

- What are you thinking about?

- I want to go somewhere for a week or two. I want to live a different life for a bit.

- Any particular place in mind?

- I'm thinking… Cuba?

- Interesting. Tell me more.

- I want to lie on the beach all day and dance all night. I want to enjoy the ocean. I want to dive and swim with the dolphins and sharks. I want to see the underwater caves and jump off the cliffs… I even want to smoke a cigar and see what all the fuss is about.

- Cigar? - Liam laughed – Sure, why not? We can do that, we can do everything you said. Prepare a list and I will book the flights and the hotel. When do you want to leave?

- Today? Tomorrow?

- So soon? What about your clients?

- I will tell them I'm having a family emergency and I need to leave for a few days, they will understand. I need to go somewhere Liam, I need to relax. Being a vampire appeared to be quite stressful and I think I'm more anxious now than when I was a human. Let's visit Cuba and forget about the rest of the world.

- Let's do that. It sounds like a very good idea.

The next morning, June woke up shortly before nine. She found April already awake, preparing coffee in the kitchen.

- Good morning sis – April said - I have something for you. It's on the table.

- This is my old necklace, isn't it? Or did you buy me the same one again?

- Yes, that's the old one but I upgraded it for you.

April started slowly coming closer and the stone started to glow.

- Oh my God! What have you done? - June grabbed the neckless and started looking at it carefully.

- It will now show you whether the person next to you is in any way magical. It is glowing now because I'm a witch. It will also glow with Hayley or Liam around. So next time you meet a nice guy you can make sure he's not just another vampire hunter.

- This is going to be very helpful, thanks April. It's exactly what I needed.

- Don't worry sister, you will find someone sooner or later. That witch from New Orleans told you about your mysterious man and your two twin girls so he's definitely somewhere out there, you just need to be patient.

- I wish she could've told me more. I wish I knew his face or his name. Can you tell me that?

- Unfortunately, no. I don't have a gift of foresight.

- Do you know what gift you have?

- I haven't discovered it yet. Everything I can do, other witches can do as well.

- I bet you can do something really cool. Let me know as soon as you find out.

- You will be the first to know, I promise.

Chapter 4

After a twenty-hour flight with one stop, Hayley and Liam were finally unpacking in their hotel room in Havana. It was a late evening and yet only a few minutes after sunset. The sky was a bit cloudy but it was not supposed to rain that night. It was still very hot and Hayley wanted to go out so they went to the city centre. The streets were as crowded at night as during the day as everybody wanted to experience Cuban atmosphere and feel real Havana spirit. They went to La Casa de la Musica for dancing. It seemed awfully loud to their vampire ears but the music was great and Hayley wanted to stay. They ordered some drinks and decided to watch the crowd before hitting the dance floor themselves. There were a few very good dancers but the rest were amateurs, swinging the way they felt was right, trying to keep the rhythm. Hayley quickly drank her tequila shot, took Liam's hand, smiled and started leading him towards the dance floor.

- Come on, let's have some fun.

They were dancing for hours. Other couples around them were coming and going but Hayley and Liam were the only ones who didn't need to rest. Hayley completely switched off, it was only her, Liam, music and the dance floor. She didn't care where she was and who was around her. She danced with her eyes closed smiling as Liam was holding her close. She forgot about her problems, about Jack. The whole world shrunk to that club only and it felt perfect.

When the club closed at three in the morning, they went to the beach. There were still a few more hours till sunrise so they went to the Morro Castle to jump off the cliff. It was closed for public but not for Liam and Hayley. They got through easily and jump off the cliff a few times. Then, they spent a few hours on swimming and diving and lying on the beach. The ocean was warm and pleasant even so late at night and it was so peaceful with nobody around. When they noticed the sky was getting a bit brighter on the east, they climbed the lighthouse and waited for the sunrise. The sky slowly changed from dark blue and black into purple and red. The sun was slowly rising, reflecting on the surface of the water in orange and yellow, creating a spectacular, breath-taking view where the whole ocean looked as if it was made of pure gold.

The next day, Heyley and Liam travelled to Varadero for skydiving. It was something Hayley always wanted to try but never had guts to do. Now, knowing that she couldn't die, she was very keen to try it. They got to the skydiving club early in the morning for their twenty-minute training about positions, signals and equipment. Shortly after, they boarded a small plane with a few other people. Everyone was excited and couldn't wait for their time to jump. They were looking through the small windows, watching beautiful Cuba from a bird's eye view. A few minutes later, one by one, they jumped off the plane. It was the best thirty-five seconds of Hayley's life, she loved the free fall. For the first time, she felt truly free and invincible. She watched how the beach and the ocean were rapidly getting closer, she could feel the strong warm wind brushing her face. Then, for a few more minutes, she could enjoy the beautiful view slowly parachuting down. The water was incredibly clear and see-through and people on the beach were standing with their heads up pointing at the parachuters and waving. Five minutes later, they all finally landed on the beach.

In the afternoon, Hayley and Liam rented a boat to swim with the dolphins and sharks and enjoy the peace and quiet of the Atlantic Ocean. The weather was amazing, thirty degrees Celsius, cloudless sky and warm breeze. They couldn't ask for more. When they came back to Havana, they bought the cigars at the local store and went to the beach.

- And? How's your cigar? - Liam asked.

- Well… It's definitely not for me. I don't understand why it is so expensive and so desired.

- I like it. I don't smoke cigarettes but there is something enjoyable about smoking cigars.

- Does it make you feel like you are an Italian Mafioso?

- A little – Liam smiled - Apart from the cigar, have you been having a good time so far?

- Very much, yes. It is exactly what I needed, to switch off, to forget about everything, to have fun.

- I told you, life's not all bad.

- You're right, it's not so hard to be happy. I'm glad you're here with me.

- Me too.

Liam put this arm around Hayley and enjoyed his cigar looking at the ocean and amazingly red sunset.

It was an incredibly relaxing two weeks. Hayley tried everything she had on her list, having so much fun, away from her regular life. The real problem started on their way back home. As they haven't taken any blood with them, they were famished when they were entering the house. Liam coped with it much better than Hayley. He has been hungry many times before but she has never experienced anything like that. The last twenty-four hours of their journey were nearly impossible to stand. Hayley couldn't focus on anything other than all those people around her so for their flight back, she took some sleeping pills and slept through both flights and the waiting time between them. Once she's opened the front door, she ran straight to the kitchen and started drinking voraciously living the fridge door open. Her hands were shaking as she was squeezing the bag.

- From now on, all our holidays will be one-week max - Liam said - I have forgotten you could feel so unwell.

- I have never been that much hungry in my entire life. My stomach hurt, my hands were shaking and I swear I could smell blood in the air.

- I'm so sorry Hayley.

- But I survived. And the most important thing is that everyone else survived and I haven't killed anyone on the plane. That was the part of the adventure. I feel much better now so it's all just a memory. I will be more careful next time, but if I'm that hungry ever again, I will not take that risk and just feed on a stray cat.

Liam started to laugh.

- I'm serious!

Hayley threw away empty blood bags and closed the fridge door.

- You don't have a heart to kill an innocent poor kitty.

- If my life or life of those around me depended on that, I would kill a cat without blinking.

- I don't believe you.

- It just means that you don't know me that well after all.

- I think that you'd rather die than hurt a fly.

- Well… You're probably right.

- So, how did you like Cuba?

- I loved it! The music and dancing and happy people everywhere around day and night. It was so nice and sunny and hot. I liked the dolphins and the sharks and the caves and the skydiving… Can't wait to print out the photos and put them on the wall.

- I was really surprised you wanted to swim with the sharks, I thought you didn't like them.

- True, but it was only because I was afraid of them. But now, I am not afraid anymore and it was a nice experience to see them so close. It was fun, the whole trip. And now, it's time to come back to seeing my clients and living my ordinary life.

- Ordinary? - Liam laughed again - You are a vampire, living with your vampire husband and your immortal dog. What exactly is so 'ordinary' about that?

Hayley laughed too. Liam was right, her life was many things but for sure it was far from ordinary.

Hayley was sleeping like a baby that night with her head filled with happy memories of the past two weeks. It was an amazing unforgettable journey and she couldn't wait to tell her sisters all about it. Although the danger was still out there and the risk of dying was still very real, she didn't worry that much anymore. She was mortal as a human and she was still able to enjoy her life so why should it be any different now? She decided that the fear of death would not overshadow the pleasure of life and she would still live her life as if every day was the last.

Chapter 5

April came back from work and went straight to shower. It was the first hot day of the year and the sun was mercilessly burning, leaving everyone sweating and annoyed. When she came out, she noticed there was a voicemail left by Hayley: *'Hi April, I'm at June's now and... Oh my God... Don't hurt her! Stay away from her! No!'* April heard a sound of a fight and someone screaming. Then, there was a moment of silence but the message was still being recorded. She heard footsteps and someone picked up the phone, said *'three more to go.'* and hung up. April started nervously dialling Hayley's number but there was no signal anymore.

- No, no, no, this is not happening. Come on Hayley, pick up. Pick up!

Suddenly, April woke up in her bed covered in sweat and breathing heavily.

- Thank God – she said relieved – It was just a dream. What a bloody nightmare!

She couldn't shake it off though. She sat in her bed for a few more minutes, wondering why she had that dream and what it meant. Curiosity didn't let her rest so she put the code in for past voicemails and discovered the voicemail from Hayley was there. It sounded exactly like the one in her dream but it was dated sixth of May, exactly a month from now. April quickly dialled Hayley's number with her shaking hands and breathed a sigh of relief when her sister answered the phone. She couldn't comprehend what was going on, something like that has never happened before. Without much thinking, she called her work saying she wouldn't be coming that day, then she packed her backpack and reserved same-day flight to Aspen.

- April! What a surprise, come on in - Hayley let her sister in and hugged her tightly, so happy to see her.

- Hi… I'm sorry I'm coming unannounced but I really need to talk to you. To all of you really… Do you have any more clients now?

- No, I'm done for the day.

- Good. I'll call June.

- April, what's going on? Is something wrong?

Liam and Hayley were now both looking and April impatiently awaiting some explanation.

- Let's wait for June to come over. Liam, could you please call Isabella too? I would like her and Ethan to listen to what I have to say.

Within the next fifteen minutes, they were all sitting at Hayley's kitchen table with Isabella and Ethan on the speakerphone. April has extracted the voicemail and everyone listened to it carefully, shocked and confused.

- I don't understand – Hayley said furrowing her brow.

- Neither do I – said April – I have no idea what is going on. This message is dated sixth of May which means, technically, it hasn't happened yet. I had a dream that I was listening to this recording and then when I woke up I discovered the message was real. I don't know what it all means.

- I recognise the voice – June said – It's Jack.

- But how would he get into your house? - Liam asked – April put a new spell and you wouldn't invite him in again, would you?

- Of course not!

- Exactly! So how would he get there? And why would he hurt June? She's human, it doesn't make any sense.

- I don't know what to think about it – April said - Nothing like that has ever happened to me. I would understand the dream was some kind of a warning or premonition but the fact that this message is real… It's insane!

- So what do we do?

- Just be careful. Jack may not be acting alone so we need to avoid strangers. Don't let anyone unknown in. No plumbers or electricians, nobody gets in, understood?

- Of course, what about the sixth of May?

- I think we should all be together. I suggest we all meet here. Be on your guard, all of you. And look out for each other. I will talk to my friends and see if they had ever come across anything like this before. There must be a reason why I had those glimpses of future and I need to be sure we can prevent it from happening.

- I have a better idea – June said unexpectedly – We should let it happen.

- Are you insane?!

- No, hear me out. If we try to prevent it, be someplace else that day, Jack may try to strike again another time and another place and what if you don't see that coming next time? I think we should use this opportunity that we know where he's going to be that day and we should fight back. I suggest that I let him in if he ever shows up and let him prepare that ambush for Hayley. But we will be prepared, we will make the first move, attack with all the strength so he can't stand a chance and we can finish him once and for all.

- This may actually be a good idea – Liam agreed - June is right, we don't know where he is so we can't stop him but as we already know his whereabouts that day, we can confront him.

- And then what? - Hayley asked - Are we going to keep him in the basement for the rest of his life?

- I will figure something out - April responded – if I could stop him once and for all from changing into an animal, he wouldn't be a threat as a human. He's got his powers only when he turns, otherwise, he is just normal.

- I think this is crazy and being a bait puts June in an extreme danger - Hayley was getting nervous.

- I'll be fine, you all will be there waiting for him. You will make the first move, it can't go wrong.

Hayley realised everyone wanted to go ahead with June's plan and she was the only one having doubts.

- Very well - she eventually agreed - Let's do this, we have a month to prepare, we can't make any mistakes. I don't want to see June get hurt so we need to do it right.

- We will – April assured her – Don't worry, it will work.

It was very intense four weeks as everyone was impatiently counting days till the big day - the sixth of May. They wished it never came but at the same time, they were tired of waiting and wanted to have it all behind them. They were sure everything was perfectly planned and nothing could go wrong.

From the first of May, Jack was watching them all from the distance, either as a bird or a cat. Hayley and Liam were always going out together when walking out the dog or shopping. Liam's sister has never showed up and Jack didn't even know where to look for her. He figured out that June's house would be an excellent trap. He could make her invite him inside and lure Hayley in. April was clearly still in New Orleans and June was all by herself.

On the sixth of May, Jack was following June everywhere. He watched her at work inputting data into the system and answering the phones for most of the day. Then, he watched her playing the guitar and trying hard to memorize a few new sentences in Spanish. Then, he followed her back home and it was already seven o'clock in the evening. In the meantime, everyone else was in June's house preparing for Jack to show up. April was working on the spell preventing Jack from turning into an animal inside the house. She also put another spell so he could get in but couldn't get out. She scattered the ashes on the doorsteps and windowsills. They stayed visible, forming perfect thin lines but nobody could break these lines without using a proper spell. They all were trapped inside the house as long as the spell was active. All five of them hid in June's bedroom and impatiently waited for her to come back home.

Shortly after seven, they heard June opening the front door with the key. Jack appeared suddenly right behind her and grabbed her with one hand, pressing a knife to her back with the other.

- Invite me in – he whispered angrily.

- Come in.

The moment they crossed the doorstep, Jack stabbed June with the knife and closed the door. June fell on the floor and screamed in pain. Everyone jumped out of the bedroom and saw June curling up on the floor in pain and Jack standing over her, holding a knife covered in her blood, looking at them, scared and surprised. Without much thinking, Hayley got to him first, before anyone else. She hit his face a few times, breaking his nose and his jaw. Before he passed out, she lifted him up with just one hand and broke his neck without hesitation. When she let him go, Jack's body dropped on the floor with a loud thud. Hayley was standing over the dead body, breathing calmly as if nothing had happened, her eyes were black. She looked at Jack's body lying on the floor, his face was covered in blood and slightly disfigured. Hayley looked at the others afraid of what they would say but nobody was looking at her, everyone was gathered around June. She was lying on the floor in a puddle of blood and April was kneeling next to her, repeating the same words over and over again, keeping her hands over June's body. Hayley was watching them from the distance, and it all seemed like a dream. She didn't care what she did, all she cared about was June. Suddenly April's nose started to bleed and June stopped breathing.

- No! - April yelled - No! Please! Come back!

She started chanting again nervously: *'Ad corpus redeat spiritus.'* Her voice was breaking and her hands were shaking. After a few more attempts, she stopped the spell and just started to cry feeling completely hopeless. Hayley was looking at June's dead body, numb and speechless. Nobody said a word for a couple of minutes, looking at June and hoping she would still wake up. But she wasn't unconscious, she was truly gone. April's magic didn't work.

- I will get the car – Isabella said quietly – We will get rid of Jack's body. April, could you let us out?

April swung her hand to break the line by the door so Isabella and Ethan could leave. Liam got some sheets from the wardrobe and started covering Jack's body. Hayley approached April and hugged her tightly. She wanted to say something but the words got stuck in her throat.

- How did that happen? - April asked through her tears – We were all here. We were supposed to protect her! Everything was planned! I tried to save her, I tried so hard! But it was too late, the wound was too deep and I couldn't...

Hayley helped April up off the floor, she wiped the tears and the blood from her face and hugged her again. They were heartbroken. There was nothing anyone could say to console them. Their world shattered into pieces as their beloved sister was gone.

- This is not happening – Hayley said with tears running down her face – I can't believe we let her die… I knew it was a bad idea! We should've never...

All of a sudden, June sat on the floor, struggling to catch her breath. She looked around the room while sitting in the puddle of her own blood.

- Oh my God! - She said with her eyes wide open - What's happened?!

June got off the floor, her hands where shaking, she was terrified.

- You… died - April said confused furrowing her brow.

- Am I dead?!

- I'm not sure - April replied and took June's hand, it was warm - I think you're alive.

- Was it your magic?

- Maybe… or maybe it was the ring.

- The ring? - June asked looking at her covered in blood hand - It was supposed to protect me from death, not to bring me back to life.

- Maybe it was me then…

Hayley and April captured June in a tight embrace so happy to see her alive. They stood like that for a few minutes, with tears of happiness running down their faces.

- The most important thing is that you're OK - Liam said - You are covered in blood, go and take a shower and we will clean this place.

- Right… Where's Jack?

- Don't worry, he's gone.

- Did you kill him?

- I did – Hayley replied.

Her face was serious, she was neither sad nor frightened.

- Right… So what do we do with the body?

- Don't worry, I will take care of everything.

April knew all the right spells. She turned Jack's body into ashes and placed him in a small glass jar that they buried in the garden behind the house. She also got rid of the blood on the floor and on June's clothes. By the time June came back from the bathroom, everything was as if nothing has happened. The house looked perfect.

- June, do you want me to stay with you tonight?

- That's OK Hayley, April is going to be here. I'm fine, don't worry, you can go home, it was a long day.

- It's good to have you back. You really scared me.

- You were right, that bait thing was not a good idea. But thankfully we have a super witch in the family.

- Yes, April saved the day and we're very lucky to have her. Have a good night June. Call me if you need anything, OK?

- I will. Hayley, I'm OK, you don't need to worry about me anymore.

- I will always worry about you, you're my little sister.

- I will keep an eye on her – said April – have some rest Hayley.

- What about you? You look tired.

- I have my magic, I'll be fine.

- How are you Hayley? – Liam asked when they were already in bed, ready to go to sleep.

- I'm OK. I'm happy June is alive.

- Do you want to talk about Jack?

Hayley was lying quietly for a moment. She didn't want to talk about what's happened. In fact, she didn't know how to talk about it and how to be honest with Liam. She wasn't sure if she should tell him the truth.

- Hayley, you can talk to me, I'm here for you.

- I don't think you want to hear what I have to say.

- You can tell me anything. I'm your husband, you can trust me.

Hayley got out of the bed and started walking around the room nervously.

- I killed someone today. A human being, a young man… I took his life and I didn't even blink… For the first time since I turned, I've felt nothing. I was completely emotionless about what I've done. And the worst part is that… I don't feel bad about it. I don't feel guilty or remorseful. Since I turned into a vampire I have been struggling with sadness and anger and fear and all emotions were overwhelming and out of control but now when I should feel bad I feel nothing! Nothing at all! I am a murderer and I don't care. There is something seriously wrong with me Liam, and I don't know what to do.

- Hayley, you killed someone but he was not a good man. As long as he was killing ruthless vampires it was fine but he came after June. He didn't have to hurt her but he did. He took her life and if it hadn't been for April's magic, she would've stayed dead. You took a life of a killer that's why you don't feel sorry. I am sure that under any other circumstances, you would feel guilty.

- I hope you're right… But the truth is that tonight, I was truly a vampire. For the first time, I acted like a real vampire… Without thinking, fearless, merciless… No guilt, no remorse… I took Jack's life so easily and now it scares me.

- Don't worry Hayley, you did the right thing and to be honest, if you hadn't killed him… I would've. I bet April would've too.

Hayley came back to bed and cuddled up to Liam. She closed her eyes, took a deep breath and tried to convince herself that everything was OK. She hoped that Liam was right and she didn't feel guilty only because the person she killed that night hurt June and not because she was slowly changing into a monster she never wanted to be.

April was lying in bed with June, squeezing her hand to make sure she was really there, afraid that if she let her go, June would disappear.

- April… I need to tell you something. When I died, I was surrounded by darkness, there was nothing around me. And then, I saw a beautiful green meadow under the perfectly blue sky. There were many colourful flowers and trees all around with birds singing and butterflies flying above my head. Far on the horizon, I saw a sandy beach and the crystal-clear sea. There were so many different people smiling and laughing, interacting with each other. In the middle of that meadow… I saw our parents. They were holding hands, looking at me, smiling. I started walking towards them and mum reached out her arms to greet me but then, I felt some unseen force pulling me back. And then, there was darkness again and next thing I know, I'm lying on the floor in my house… Did I see heaven? Is this where you talk to Leah?

- No, I meet Leah in New Orleans and it doesn't feel like paradise, it all looks rather normal even gloomy I would say. So yes, I think it could've been heaven, a place where all non-magical people go.

- I hope you're right as it was such a lovely place. - June smiled - And it was nice to see our parents again, I miss them. It's good to know where I would go once I'm dead. It looks like there's nothing to be afraid of. Death is just a doorway to a better world.

- I'm glad you're back with us though and heaven needs to wait. You're safe now and I will look after you tonight.

- Thank you for bringing me back. I told you your special power would be awesome and I was right. - June said with a smile, closed her eyes and immediately drifted away. She has never felt more tired in her entire life.

The next day felt unusually normal after what has happened the day before. June was sitting at the kitchen table with April, eating breakfast and talking about their parents who died when the twins were sixteen. They had many nice memories of their childhood and the time they spent together on trips and games. Suddenly June stopped talking and was just holding her cup of tea, bluntly staring somewhere over April's shoulder. She didn't say or do anything, as if she was paralysed.

- June? What's wrong? - April asked.

June was looking at their mother standing right behind April, smiling and looking very much alive.

- Can you see me? - mother asked surprised.

- Yes! – June replied – How can you be here? What's happening?

Her mother approached June for a hug but her hands went straight through her. They couldn't touch each other as if the mother was just an illusion.

- June, what's going on? - April was looking at her sister as if she was crazy.

- Mum is here – June finally replied - I can see her, we can talk.

April got up and took June by the hand. Then, she saw their mother too.

- O my God! - She said with tears in her eyes – Mum!

- Hi baby, I missed you so much.

- What are you doing here?

- I'm always here whenever you think of me. I've watched you so many times before, wishing we could talk again but you've never seen me. What's changed?

- June died – April said without much thinking – And then she was brought back to life, maybe that's why she can see you now.

- Then how come you can see me too? Did you die too?

- No, I'm channelling June so I can see what she sees. Mum, I'm a witch.

June summoned the spirit of their father too and asked both parents to sit in the living room and wait for Hayley so they could have a proper family gathering.

The family reunion lasted till midnight. They talked about everything that happened in the past six years but Hayley didn't mention the fact she was a vampire. They went through the photo albums, reminiscing, laughing and having a great time. When the spirits of their parents disappeared, the girls got off the sofa and stretched after sitting the whole day.

- This was unbelievable – Hayley said – How's that even possible?

- It's June, she died and came back to life with a gift. She can talk to the dead now.

- Amazing, and I thought nothing could surprise me anymore. That's the only weird thing this family was missing, a true connection to the world of the dead.

- Hayley, would you like me to contact Bradley? - June asked unexpectedly.

Hayley didn't even think about that. She has made her peace with her husband being gone and she has started building her life with Liam now. She was not the same Hayley he used to know and she was afraid he wouldn't want to talk to her, disappointed with what she has become.

- No… Not yet. I need to think about it.

- OK, no worries, whenever you're ready. Goodnight Hayley. Pop in whenever you want to talk to mum and dad, and thanks again for everything you've done yesterday. I know it must have been a hard decision to make.

- I did what had to be done. I would do everything for you June, you know that. Now cheer up and leave the past behind, you have a brand-new life ahead.

- And now our parents are back too. It was definitely something worth dying for.

- But don't do that again hoping you can get some more cool gifts in return. God knows how many times April can bring you back.

- I know, don't worry Hayley, I won't do anything silly, you know I'm a smart girl.

- Of course you are, that's why I trust you. Thanks again for a lovely day. It was truly amazing.

- Do you want me to drive you back home?

- No, that's fine, I'll walk. Don't worry about me, I'll be careful.

Hayley was walking back home slowly, taking her time, thinking whether she should talk to her dead husband or not. Without June around, she didn't even know that Bradley was walking right beside her, looking her deep in the eye, trying to decode her thoughts.

- How was your day with the twins? - Liam asked when Hayley finally got back home in the middle of the night.

- Magical… I've talked to my parents. It looks like June can talk to the dead now after she died and came back to life yesterday.

- That's amazing! You can talk to your parents now whenever you want to.

- June can. I could see them only because April was there with her spells. Liam… There is one more thing I wanted to discuss with you… And I want you to know that your opinion really matters to me and I won't do anything that you say 'no' to.

- What is it, Hayley?

- June asked me today if I wanted to talk to Bradley, my ex-husband.

- And do you want to talk to him?

- I'm not quite sure. Would you be OK if I did?

- Hayley, you don't need my permission. He died unexpectedly and I understand there might be something you wish you would have told him. If you want to talk to him then do it. It's one hundred percent your decision. So, how was it to see your parents again?

- Weird... I still think this was just some kind of an illusion and it didn't really happen.

- You need to start getting used to unexplained and impossible things being part of your life. You are a vampire, April's a witch and now June can talk to the dead. What a trio!

- Don't forget about the magical collar my dog wears.

- Right, and that of course.

- I think we are slowly running out of anything new that may still happen to this family.

- Believe me, whatever happens next, I won't be surprised.

Hayley didn't sleep that night, thinking what she would say to Bradley. She still loved him and missed him but she already closed that chapter and he was a part of her past now. How could she talk to him? What would she say? Losing her parents was painful but it didn't impact her as much as losing her husband. She was struggling with her decision, lying in bed, next to sleeping Liam. Bradley was sitting in the armchair in the corner, wondering what Hayley's decision would be and what he would say to her if she ever decided to see him. He didn't know she was a vampire. All he has witnessed after his death was Hayley's depression ended with a suicide attempt and then her wedding day. He hasn't visited her since that day and was completely unaware of what has been going on in her life. But she seemed different and although she looked exactly the same, she was clearly not the same Hayley anymore. She seemed happy though and it was all that mattered to him. He was in heaven now so he couldn't be jealous or angry. He really wanted to talk to her and hear her laughing at his jokes and spend at least a few minutes pretending he was not dead. But how could he do it to her? After that, he would go back to heaven, to his everlasting paradise and she would continue living on earth without him. She tried that once and it didn't end up well so how could he expose her to the same pain again? Maybe it's time to leave the past behind, to come to terms with the fact that what was once, would never come back. Maybe it was time to finally say goodbye.

The next day, early in the morning, Hayley took Lexi for a walk and went straight to June's. After a sleepless night, she decided she would talk to Bradley after all. When she knocked on the door, June opened still dressed in her pyjamas.

- Hayley, what are you doing here? It's six o clock!

- I know and I'm sorry to wake you up so early but I really needed to see you and I couldn't wait for you to come back home in the evening.

- You want to talk to Bradley.

- Yes, was it that obvious?

- Kind of... I mean... he came here with you... Hi Bradley, nice to see you again.

He smiled but didn't say anything.

- Great... - Hayley was a bit embarrassed knowing that her dead husband was following her around.

- He's here because you think of him, Hayley. It's not like he's around all the time. Come on in and let's sit down.

- June – Bradley said quietly. He sounded sad. - I have a different idea. Take a piece of paper and help me write Hayley a letter. I think it would be better that way.

- What are you doing? - Hayley asked confused seeing June walking around and obviously looking for something.

- I am looking for a notepad and a pen. Bradley wants me to write you a letter.

Hayley got a bit upset, afraid that Brad didn't want to talk to her.

- OK, I'll make myself a cup of coffee and wait in the kitchen, let me know when you're done. Take your time.

Hayley waited impatiently, sitting on the kitchen floor and petting Lexi. Thoughts were running through her head and she was feeling restless. She was sure Bradley didn't want to talk to her because he hated her for being with Liam. June came five minutes later and handed over Bradley's letter.

- Should I read it now or should I take it home?

- He says you should take it.

Hayley left holding the letter tightly in her hand. She took a few steps and sat on a bench. She didn't want to read it at home, she couldn't wait to see what Bradley had to say.

'My Dearest Hayley, I wanted to say that you cannot imagine how much I miss you but I think you are quite familiar with that feeling. I saw you losing your mind when you found out I was gone and it was breaking my heart to see that my death left you so damaged. I was with you every day and every night, watching you slowly sinking into the abyss. When I saw you trying to take your own life I felt so helpless like never before and it hurt me that there was nothing I could've done to help you. Then, I stopped seeing you because you stopped thinking about me. I don't know what has happened but something changed inside of you and you were not broken anymore. When I saw you again, you were wearing a wedding dress, ready to get married again. You were happy, no longer fallen into pieces but complete, no longer dying but full of

Hayley read the letter a few times, leaving more and more teardrops on the paper. She was relieved Bradley was at peace now and not angry with her or disappointed. She looked around to make sure nobody could hear her.

- Bradley, I know you're here… I just wanted to say thank you for telling me all this. I really wanted to see you again and hear your voice but you're right saying that it would just bring back the pain and open old wounds. I want you to know that I am happy now and you don't have to worry about me. I love you and I always will. For eternity, in this life or another. Goodbye.

Hayley wiped the tears from her face, smiled and started walking back home to join Liam for breakfast. It was the closure she has been missing. Now, she could finally let Bradley go.

Chapter 6

Weeks were passing by and life was getting back to normal. June was enjoying her new life, talking to her parents often. She has put the past away and tried to forget Jack and the fact that she has died because of him. She sold her guitar and decided not to play ever again. Now, she was more into dancing than any other hobby, spending most of her free time on the dance floor. That's where she met Oliver, a twenty-six-year-old guy from New York who moved to Aspen three months earlier. Oliver was extremely charming and easy to talk to so June was smitten instantly. He seemed too perfect to be true, messy blond hair, green eyes, tall, well-built, a James Dean style, some could say. They have talked for hours right after dance classes and then again over the phone at night. June liked Oliver very much but didn't have high hopes after what has happened with Jack.

After six weeks of daily talking, she finally invited him over for a dinner. She decided to take things slow and to make sure she really knew Oliver, before she let herself fall in love again. One broken heart was more than enough.

On Saturday late afternoon, June had a dinner ready on the table and her fancy red dress on. She sprayed herself a little bit with her favourite Versace perfumes and reached for her magical ruby necklace. As she was putting it on, she realised she has never worn it around Oliver before. Every time they spoke, they were right after classes, still in their dancing clothes and her necklace was hidden in her bag. *'Don't be ridiculous June.* - she thought looking at her reflection in the mirror - *Not every guy walking this earth is a monster, this one is perfectly normal and you're going to have a lovely dinner.'* She heard the doorbell and started walking joyfully to open the door. When she was about to press the handle she noticed her necklace was glowing red. *'Oh no... Not this one... Why does it keep happening to me?! Are there any humans left on this planet or am I the last one?!'* The doorbell rang again. June took a deep breath and opened the door.

- Hi Oliver, change of plans, let's eat something out.

- Hi, no problem Love, but I don't know any good restaurants here so I'll let you choose.

They went to White House Tavern. It was crowded and loud but the food was good so they decided to stay. Oliver was even more talkative than usual and June tried to listen but she was deep in thought the whole evening, unable to focus. When it was nearly nine o'clock and the restaurant was about to close, they started slowly walking back home.

- June… I don't mean to sound too nosy but you seem to be very far away today… Is everything OK?

- Yes, I'm fine, why?

- You've been very quiet. As a matter of fact, I think I was the only one talking. It was our first official date and I really hoped you would have a good time today with me.

- So did I.

- Well… Did you have a good time?

- Not really, no.

- Oh… I'm sorry to hear that, I thought we have been getting on quite well. What's changed?

June stopped and looked at Oliver. Her face was serious, even worried.

- Oliver… I like you… I really do… But we need to talk and I want you to be honest with me. So if you don't want to tell me the truth just be blunt and admit that, but don't lie to me, OK?

- OK… - Oliver looked confused - June, what's going on?

They sat on the bench, away from anyone else. The streets seemed empty, it was not a nice evening for a walk so everyone was either home or travelling by car. It has been raining the whole day and the temperature dropped to twelve degrees Celsius that evening. June was getting a bit cold but she didn't pay much attention to it. She thought for a moment what to say to Oliver and how to get the answer that she needed but didn't really want to hear at the same time. She wanted him to be just a normal regular guy, a simple human being. But her neckless was telling her something else and she was afraid that whatever Oliver would say next was not going to be anything good.

- June? - Oliver was getting impatient.

- What are you? - she finally asked bluntly, looking Oliver right in the eye.

- What do you mean?

- I know you're not human, so what are you then?

- Are you serious June? What kind of a question is it? - he started to laugh but June was deadly serious.

- OK… Then let me be honest with you first.

June took her glowing pendant out and showed it to Oliver.

- This thing glows only when a magical creature is around, that's how I know you're not human.

Oliver didn't say anything. First, he looked at the pendant, then he started staring at the pavement, thinking what to say.

- My twin sister is a witch – June continued - My older sister and her husband are vampires and I can talk to the dead so I don't think there is anything you can say that may still surprise me. So what are you, Oliver? A vampire? A witch?

He got up and looked at June.

- I can't answer that question.

- Why?

- I just can't. But if you can't accept this and just keep insisting on an explanation then I think we will have to stop seeing each other.

They were looking at each other without a single word for a few seconds.

- I need to know the truth, Oliver.

- Right… I'm sorry, June.

Oliver looked at June one last time and started quickly walking away. June was sitting on the bench, watching how her pendant was slowly dimming as Oliver was getting further and further away. She got up and started walking back home alone. She has suddenly realised she was having shivers and her fingers were getting numb. She was not dressed properly for such a cold evening but she had too much on her mind to remember to take a jacket.

Oliver came back home angry, shocked and disappointed. It was not how that evening was supposed to look like. He really looked forward to his first official date with June and he truly cared about that girl. But he has never expected she could be anything more than a normal human being. At first, he thought it was a shame that June knew about his magical side but then, he started to believe that maybe it was actually something good. He could be completely honest with her, for the first time in his life, he could finally tell someone the whole truth. June was no stranger to magic so maybe she could let him be a part of her already magical world. It was worth giving a go, she was worth taking that risk. All his life, he was afraid of only two things: loneliness and rejection. But unless he risked rejection, he would always be alone.

Two hours later, when June was mindlessly watching some movie, someone knocked on her door. She got up with hesitation and slowly approached the door. Through the peephole she saw it was Oliver but she decided to open the door anyway. She was very curious what he had to say and she felt safe knowing that he couldn't come inside without her invitation.

- Forgive me June, I shouldn't have walked away like that, I owe you an explanation. May I come in?

- No – she responded instantly - This house is protected by a spell so you can't come in. I don't know what you are and I can't trust you so…

- I understand. But what I have to say cannot be heard by anyone else so do you know where we can talk privately?

- I suggest you come back tomorrow morning and we can talk in the park. I don't want to walk around the city so late at night.

- OK, I will come back tomorrow then. Goodnight June.

- Goodnight.

June locked the door and went straight to bed but she couldn't fall asleep with so many thoughts running through her head. '*He wants to be honest with me and that's a good start. But why couldn't he tell me straight away? I wouldn't mind if he was a witch, I even think that would be cool... I also would be OK with him being a vampire, we could work it out like Hayley and Liam did... If he's a vampire hunter then we have a problem, that'd mean he's a threat to my family... He can't be anything else, can he? Any other unknown kind of monster... Why couldn't he be just a normal guy? I knew he seemed too perfect. Where are all the humans? Is it really so difficult to come across a normal regular human being?... All teenage girls of this world would kill for a cool magical boyfriend and they can't find one but when I look for a simple human, he's nowhere to be found. Is it me or has the whole world gone crazy? Maybe I should fly to Mars if I can't find any humans on Earth... Looks like I haven't found my mister right after all.'* June has been rolling from side to side all night, looking at the clock every now and then and getting annoyed by insomnia. It was already nearly dawn when she finally fell asleep.

June woke up after only a couple of hours of sleep. She was full of energy though and her emotions were all over the place. She ate breakfast and stared at the TV for an hour before Oliver finally knocked on her door. She put on her trainers and a jacket and left, walking in silence all the way to the park. They sat on the bench away from the path. The park was nearly empty at eight o'clock on Sunday and only a few joggers and dog walkers passed them by not paying any attention to them. June looked at Oliver clearly waiting for him to start the conversation.

- I'm sorry June. I didn't know how to tell you this as I have never said that to anyone before.

June didn't comment on that. She couldn't wait to hear what he had to say but she didn't want to put any more pressure on him.

- You're right - he continued - I'm not human, I am a witch... In a way... Kind of.

- What does it mean?

- I practice magic.

- Like my sister?

- Not exactly. You see... your sister made that pendant for you and put a spell on your house to protect you, well... I don't do that. I practice only black magic.

- Like what?

- Well... I can curse someone, make them sick... Or dead.

- Why would you do that?

- This is just what I do. I don't create and protect, I can only destroy and hurt. But I use my magic only against bad people, I punish them for their wrongdoings and I give them what they deserve. I am a punisher… Sort of.

- So you punish bad people for their sins. Are you a devil?

June's heartbeat was getting faster as fear was gradually taking hold of her.

- Not an actual devil like in the Bible or something… But my job is pretty much the same. I have been selected for this task, we help purify society.

- 'We'? So you're not the only one?

- No, people like me are everywhere around the world.

June was sitting quietly, processing what Oliver has just told her. She didn't expect to hear anything like that and he managed to surprise her after all. Oliver was looking at June, trying to guess what she was thinking. But seconds were passing by and she hasn't said a single word.

- Is there anything you'd like to say, June? I bet you didn't expect I could add something new to your already weird world.

He smiled but it didn't make June any less nervous.

- I really don't know what to say… I think you were right earlier and we should stop seeing each other, like you suggested yesterday… At least for now.

- Is that what you really want?

- No… But I know this is what I should do.

Oliver got upset. He really hoped she would react positively and appreciate his honesty. He told the truth to someone first time ever and he was instantly rejected. That truly hurt.

- You are already a part of the magical world June, so why can't you have me in it? Why can I not be a part of it? You say your sister is a vampire so if you can accept her being a monstrous killer why can't you accept me? I'm a good guy.

- It's not like that, she's not like that. It doesn't matter, you're something completely different, unknown and I should stay away from you until I talk to my sister.

Oliver stared at June as she was struggling with her decision.

- I know you've started having feelings for me June, I can feel it. I know I am more to you than just 'someone you know' and I think you should listen to your heart instead of your head. We can be happy together, Love. I can make you happy if you give us a chance. You are the first to know about me and with everything else going on in your life if you, of all people, cannot accept me then no one can. I will tell you everything you want to know, I promise, I won't have any secrets and I will never lie to you. You can trust me.

June listened to him, wondering what to do. She couldn't stand his green eyes staring at her, awaiting a response.

- I can't make this decision right now. Let me think about it but for now, stay away from me, please.

Oliver didn't say anything. He was clearly disappointed and sad.

- Goodbye – June said and walked away without looking back.

She went straight home and cried as she really cared about Oliver. After what happened with Jack, she was very untrusting and it took her a lot to trust Oliver and invite him over. He completely turned her world upside down and she really hoped they could be soulmates. But with his every word, the vision of them being together has been slowly fading away.

In the evening, June prepared two beers for herself and Hayley and called April. She needed to discuss her love life with her sisters, expecting some piece of advice. They waited impatiently for June to start talking. They knew something was wrong as she looked sad and nervous.

- So… - June started – I've met someone.

- Another vampire hunter? - April joked but June remained serious - Sorry, go on.

- I've met him at one of my dancing classes. We had a really nice time and after a week or two, I gave him my number so we've talked every night since then. Yesterday, I decided to invite him over for a dinner and that's when I noticed my ruby pendant was glowing, before I even opened the door. I didn't invite him in, we went out instead. He was perfectly nice and funny and I would've had a really good time if I hadn't thought so much about what he was. So I asked him directly and after a while he admitted he was a witch.

- That's good – April interrupted again – Witch is good, you shouldn't worry.

- But he's not just a witch, apparently he practices black magic. He's some kind of a punisher. Have you ever heard of anything like that, April?

- I have… These witches have been trained only to hurt and kill. They are still witches but most spells they know is black magic related. They are called Daemon Maga which means a demon witch. They punish people, purify society.

- That's what he said.

- I think you should stay away from him. – Hayley sounded concerned.

- April, and what do you think? - June asked with a note of hope in her voice.

- I can't tell you what to do, June, I don't know too much about them. I can ask around, see what other witches think.

June sighed with frustration.

- Why does it keep happening to me?! First Jack and now Oliver.

Hayley hugged her sister to console her.

- There will be someone else.

- Who? Who else is left? What another weirdo will I attract next?

- Come to New Orleans – April said unexpectedly - In here you'll meet either a regular witch like me or a human. I haven't seen any vampires or hunters living here.

- I think this may be a good idea, actually. - Hayley said - You can move at least for a couple of months, see if you like it there. I will look after your house here so you can always come back if you want. Just give it a shot.

- What about my job?

- I'll help you get something here – April assured her – and you can live with me, this place is big enough for two of us. It will be fun, just like old times. Come on, June, what you say?

June thought for a moment.

- OK, why not, let's give it a go. I will give my one-month notice tomorrow but I have some holidays left so I may be ready to move in about three weeks.

- Great! Can't wait to have you here! - April was very enthusiastic - It will be fun, you'll see.

June disconnected and sighed.

- Everything is going to be OK, June. - Hayley said - New place, new friends. April already knows many people there, she will help you find someone nice.

- I hope so. Thank you Hayley for being here for me.

- No problem at all, you know you can count on me anytime.

- I know and it means a lot.

- So you really like that boy, don't you?

- I really do, but I also liked Jack and that didn't end well for me.

- Not everyone is going to be like Jack.

- I hope so.

- Would you like me to stay over?

- No, you can go home now, I'll be fine. Thanks Hayley.

June took a shower and went to bed as she was exhausted after one sleepless night. She checked her phone but there were no messages. Oliver did what she asked of him but she was a bit disappointed that he followed her request, she got used to their conversations ending with 'goodnight'. She put her phone aside, closed her eyes and fell asleep feeling sad and disappointed.

The next three weeks have passed by extremely fast. It was a mid-July and the weather was very nice. Twenty-seven degrees Celsius in Aspen was a lot so everyone was happy that a proper summer has officially come at least for a few days. June has attended only her Spanish lessons and completely resigned from her dancing classes. She didn't want to risk seeing Oliver, although she missed him very much. The idea of him being in any way magical frightened her, especially that he was something completely unfamiliar and new. But she knew him, she knew he was smart and funny and good and compassionate and she couldn't picture him as someone evil. She couldn't understand why anyone would create someone like that to simply hurt people, it sounded so cruel and unfair. Sometimes she thought that she should give Oliver a chance but there were moments where she truly believed there was someone else right for her somewhere out there and she should keep looking for him. That's why she agreed to move in with April; New city, new friends, it all sounded very exciting and June wanted to give love another chance. She packed her clothes leaving everything else and was on New Orleans airport in the evening when it was raining heavily but was still very warm and pleasant. She was glad April picked her up and she didn't have to walk in the rain. April prepared a proper 'welcome party' for June and they went to the pub to meet her witch friends for a long night of karaoke and dancing. It felt like old times, when the twins were studying and living together in Aspen, having parties with their classmates nearly every weekend. Those times were so magical for them although there was nothing truly magical going on in their life back then.

The next day, June got a job as one of the performing witches. She was the one talking to the dead and that was a huge attraction in New Orleans. People were paying her a lot for a chance to talk to the ones they loved and lost. Some people came just for fun not believing it was real, but some people ended up leaving hundreds of dollars, sitting there for hours, crying and asking more and more questions, truly believing June was talking to their parents, partners, children or friends. And she really was. She started to enjoy that job although it was very sad to see people heartbroken and crying. But she brought peace to many, letting them deal with their unfinished business. In that job, June could eventually earn more money than she has ever had in any of her previous jobs. It was a good place for someone like her, she could use her gift to help people and she could earn more than enough. She worked as a medium for the whole day every day and went out with April and her friends nearly every evening. New Orleans never slept and the city was full of strangers. June met a few nice guys but nobody charmed her like Oliver has. She kept thinking about him and missed him very much and it was driving her crazy.

One night, when April was already asleep, June decided to message Oliver just to see what his response would be. She was wondering how he felt about her now, after those few weeks. On one hand, she wanted him to hate her and be with someone else as it would make things easier for her, but on the other hand, she wanted him to still be the same Oliver she loved so much. She wrote a few different messages but deleted every single one, unable to make up her mind. Nothing seemed right, after all, what could she say? That she was sorry? That she missed him? That she regretted moving out?

- Hi.

That's all she finally sent. Although she had so many questions running through her head and so many stories that she wanted to share with Oliver, first she wanted to see if he's keen to talk to her. She didn't need to wait long for an answer.

- Hi.

'That's a good start' – June thought with a gentle smile.

- How have you been?

- OK, but I've been better. I'm glad to see your message. How are you?

- I've been better too. Can't get you out of my head. Is that some kind of magic? Did you put a spell on me?

June didn't know why she said that, it didn't sound good. He could think she got in touch only because she was angry with him. But she really hoped it was magic and the reason she felt so miserable was because she was hexed with some terrible heart-breaking spell.

- Of course not! I deal only with bad people and there is no bad bone in your body, June. I'm happy to hear you think about me though, I have been thinking about you too. I miss you, I miss our night talks... Would you like me to come over?

In that moment June truly regretted moving out. She would do anything to see him now, to see his charming smile, to hear his voice, to look into his amazing green eyes.

- I'm not in Aspen anymore. I moved.

- Because of me?

- Yes, but I also wanted a change. See new people.

- And how did that go? Did you meet someone?

- I've met dozens of people and had lots of fun.

- Good... So why are you still thinking about me then?
'Good question' – June thought.
- Because I haven't met anyone like you.
- Isn't that what you wanted? Someone NOT like me?
- In a way – yes. But nobody made me feel like you did.
- And how's that?

June's heart started beating faster - *'He's so mean!'* – she thought - *'he knows how I feel about him, he just wants me to say it.'*
- It doesn't matter. I need to re-think some decisions.
- Can I help you with that?
- Go on.
- I can make it very easy for you, Love. Come back to me. Give us another chance. Come back to Aspen.

June thought for a moment before she replied.
- Not yet.
- Still listening to your head then?
- But I wouldn't mind if you stayed in touch. That would mean a lot to me.

Oliver didn't know how to respond to that request. He was happy to see June's message and he really missed her but the last thing he wanted was to be put in a friend zone. He didn't want June to treat him as a friend, as someone she could turn to with her broken heart. But she obviously needed time to figure out what she truly wanted and the time was all he needed to win her back.
- Let's stay in touch then. It's good to talk to you again but it's getting late and it's long past your bedtime. Have some rest, June. Goodnight.
- Goodnight.

June put her phone aside and fell asleep with a smile on her face. It was exactly what she needed and what she missed so much. Although she was the one asking Oliver to stay away, she was relieved seeing he wasn't angry with her. *'It doesn't matter what he is –* she thought *– it's just texting, a*

Oliver messaged June every evening for the next two weeks. They talked about their day-to-day life and the past. Nobody talked about the future and Oliver didn't put any more pressure on June to move back. He suggested he could come over to visit her in New Orleans and she eventually agreed. June took a half a day off on a Sunday afternoon and waited for Oliver on the Jackson Square with April. She wanted her sister to meet him and to say what she thought about him. It was a cloudy summer day and they were glad the sun was not burning and they didn't have to desperately seek shade. Oliver was approaching them quickly, wearing a plain white t-shirt, a pair of jeans shorts, a baseball cap and sunglasses. He was over six-foot-tall so it was hard not to see him in the crowd. Even though June and April were twins, they were easy to differentiate. April wore make-up and her hair was much longer, usually in French braid. She loved skirts and dresses, always looking stylish and elegant. June was more laid-back, wearing loose sports clothes and a short ponytail. They were so similar and yet so different.

Oliver stopped in front of them and took his sunglasses off.

- Hi June and you must be April. – he said with the most charming smile.

- Hi. - April responded and reached her hand out to greet him.

Oliver hesitated for a second and then shook April's hand. She immediately stopped smiling feeling shivers all over her back. The aura surrounding Oliver was dark and unpleasant and it was clear that he brought suffering and death to many people.

- April, are you OK? - June asked concerned, seeing April all serious and frightened.

- Yes, I'm OK. - she said and pulled her hand back.

- She's afraid of me – Oliver said - I suggest we stop torturing your sister and let her go now. April, you know I wouldn't hurt June, she's perfectly safe with me and you don't need to watch over her.

April hesitated with her decision. She felt very uncomfortable in Oliver's presence but she didn't want to leave June alone.

- It's OK – June said – you can go if you want.

- I'm sorry June. I just… I can't be here.

- I understand. Go, I'll be fine.

April gave Oliver an apologetic look and left quickly, nearly running across the square without looking back.

- Wow – June said – That was very unexpected.

- In contrary, this was very expected. To be honest, I was surprised she wanted me to shake her hand, most witches want me to keep the distance.

- Why is that?

- Apparently, they can feel my dark aura and it makes them uncomfortable. They know I am not a bad guy but I still repel them, for some reason.

- Interesting… And I wanted to suggest you find a girl among witches. You say no one could ever accept you and you can't be honest with anyone so I thought maybe a witch would be a good match but obviously I was wrong.

They took a slow walk along the river enjoying a nice cool breeze from Mississippi.

- How can you even suggest that?

- What?

- Looking for a girl. I don't need to look, I've already found one and she's perfect, she just doesn't want to admit it.

June blushed.

- OK then. You promised you would be honest with me, no more secrets, so tell me what I don't know yet.

- Very well… Let's see… I can teleport. As a matter of fact, that's how I got here today.

- Really?! Wow! That's cool. What else?

- That's it really. I don't know what else to tell you, you already know I do magic.

- If you're not the devil… - June started unsure - Are you a demon or something?

Oliver was clearly amused.

- No, June, I'm not a demon. Just like you, I get happy or sad and these are human emotions, right? I can even get hurt and die so doesn't it make me human?

- I guess it does.

- Anyway, this is a beautiful day that we can spend together and I don't want to ruin it so no more talking about me. You know everything already so don't ask me any more questions. For the rest of this day, I am just a normal guy, deal?

- Deal.

They spent the rest of the day on exploring the city and enjoying a nice weather. June saw a few witches looking at Oliver suspiciously every now and then but he didn't pay any attention to them. She really enjoyed his company and hoped that day would never end. Despite everything she knew, being with Oliver made her feel great. She hasn't been that happy in a while and all she wanted to do was to pack her bags and come back to Aspen.

It was already long after sunset and it was getting chilly. They couldn't stay outside any longer and June didn't want to drag Oliver to a pub or restaurant where he would be devoured by curious yet unfriendly witches.

- I need to go now - said June – it's getting late.

Oliver approached her slowly and brushed her face with his fingers. Her heart skipped a beat and her mouth was getting dry.

- Come with me, Love. Come back to Aspen.

- I can't.

- Why?

- It's… Complicated.

- Is it really? - Oliver hesitated for a moment - I love you June. And I know how you feel about me, I know you have feelings for me so don't try to deny it.

This was the first time he said that honestly to anybody and saying these words aloud suddenly made him realise how much he truly cared about June, especially in that very moment when they were about to say 'goodbye'.

- Can you read my mind too? - June said embarrassed and took a step back turning her face away.

- No, but I can read your emotions. Just like I knew how much April was afraid of me I know how much you want me to be close.

He took another step closer and kissed her.

- I need to go now – June said blushing. Her heart was beating fast.

- Why?

- Because I don't trust myself when I'm with you.

- You don't do anything wrong June so why can't we just be happy together? Why do you keep holding back? - he spread his arms - I'm here for you so do what you want, let it go.

- This isn't right, Oliver. Please, go back to Aspen.

June turned around and started quickly walking back home to April. When she turned around again, Oliver wasn't there anymore, she was all alone.

June came back home shaking and breathing heavily.

- What's wrong June? - April sounded concerned – What's happened? What did he do?

June started walking nervously around the room.

- He kissed me.

- Oh.

- I have feelings for him April, I really do, but deep in my heart it doesn't feel right and I don't know what to do.

- I'm sorry for my reaction earlier.

- Don't worry about it, I understand.

- It's his aura. It's dark and cold and very unpleasant. When I shook his hand… It made me feel sad and scared.

- You see, I don't feel that way. I think he's cute and funny and smart and very charming and I just want him to be around, you know?

- I get that June.

- But when I'm with him, I remember that tomorrow he's going to torture someone or even kill someone and he's done it many times before. That's why I hesitate.

- He won't hurt you June. Punishing people is his full-time job, it's his life purpose and he cannot change it. He has been chosen for this and he can't just disobey.

- I know.

- June, think about it this way; If he was a police officer shooting bad guys, would you be OK with that? Or what if he was responsible for death sentences in a prison, would you still think of him as a murderer? Or what if he was a soldier at war or a spy? Do you think that James Bond was a bad guy because he had to kill?

- I don't know.

- I see no difference here, to be honest. It's not like he's walking around making people miserable, destroying their lives and killing for no reason. He gets orders that he needs to follow, that's all and he's not a bad person. He kills bad people so good people can live. But you need to get this sorted yourself June and if deep down you feel he's not good for you then break up this relationship.

June sat down, staring at the table, thinking what to say. She remembered how she felt about Jack and how bad it ended for her. She knew she was wrong about him and that was what was stopping her from being with Oliver as she didn't trust her instincts anymore. She was thinking about Jack so hard that all of a sudden, he appeared in front of her, there in April's kitchen.

- What are you doing here? - June got up quickly and took a few steps back.

April approached her immediately and took her hand. She saw Jack standing in her kitchen, looking at them. But he was not smiling like their parents, he was terrified, breathing heavily, with his eyes wide open and drops of sweat running down his temples.

- You can see me! - he shouted - Thank God! I need your help.

- You shouldn't be here. Get out!

- No! No, please hear me out… It feels like I'm in hell. There is something following me around and I am constantly trying to run away from it and hide and I'm so afraid and tired. I can't be there any longer! I shouldn't be there at all, I haven't done anything wrong.

- You killed June! - April said angrily – Thank God I was able to bring her back with my magic. You got what you deserved Jack, you killed an innocent human being and now you're paying for this. You were a vampire hunter, you were supposed to kill vampires, not people.

- I know! It was a terrible mistake and I regret it very much. But it was an accident, I only wanted to hurt June to keep her out of the way, I have never meant to kill you June. I'm sorry. Please, you need to help me, please, I'm begging you.

- Get out! Get out! Now!

Jack disappeared. They looked around to make sure he was not there anymore.

- I don't want to talk about it – June said before April managed to say anything – I don't want to think about him anymore so he doesn't show up again.

June went to take a shower and calm down. Her hands were still shaking when she was rubbing the soap and trying to focus on the pleasant warm water running down her back. April was in the kitchen, thinking about Jack who appeared again right in front of her. But without June around, April couldn't hear his desperate peals for help.

June tried hard not to think about Jack. He deserved what he got and she was not interested in helping him so she was thinking about Oliver instead. She enjoyed their short kiss and it felt wonderful to hear 'I love you' said so honestly for the first time. She couldn't stay away from him and she didn't want him out of her life but she didn't want to love him either. She decided to treat him like a friend at least for now until she has figured out her feelings for him. She would stay in touch and let him visit her in New Orleans but nothing more than that. She needed to get her emotions and feelings sorted once and for all. *'There is something seriously wrong with me'* – she thought lying in bed next to already sleeping April – *'Oliver is great and I can't imagine him hurting a fly. Maybe April was right and I should think of him as a secret agent. Bond was killing bad guys and all beautiful women were always so attracted to him and he was as charming as Oliver. But this is a real life and not a movie and there are real people getting hurt. How can I accept that? If only he could quit that job and start being just a regular witch... I can't believe that on a planet of nearly eight billion people I had to start falling in love with someone like him... Is it really so hard to come across a normal, regular guy? Why can't I love somebody without any magic involved? Maybe because I am a descendant of a witch, I am destined to be with someone magical? Maybe I couldn't escape my destiny even if I tried?* - June looked at the clock, it was nearly three in the morning - *OK, that's enough. Let's try to fall asleep before I go completely mental.'*

Chapter 7

After nearly two months in New Orleans, June finally booked her flight to Aspen. She decided she would pack all her stuff and move to New Orleans for good. She spoke with Oliver every day and their platonic relationship was working fine. She loved her job and fun she had with April and her friends. She was less lonely there than in Aspen with Hayley. She got herself a separate apartment to give April more space as she had her own life to take care of and needed some privacy. She found a nice place walking distance from April's flat and it was just perfect. Two-bedroom flat, not too big, not too small, very bright and cosy.

When June finally got to Aspen after her seven-hour journey, it was already one in the morning. She took a taxi from the airport as Liam's car was broken and Hayley sold hers months ago. Once she entered the house, she went upstairs straight to bed. She hated travelling, especially flying. She hoped Oliver could teleport her to Aspen but when she called him, he didn't pick up or call back so she decided not to bother him anymore, after all, they were nothing more but just friends.

In the morning, June called Hayley and Liam and asked them to help her with the packing, the moving van was supposed to pick it all up the next day.

After a whole day of hard work, Liam went back home and left the girls alone so they could talk. They got the rest of the ice cream out of the fridge and sat comfortably on the sofa in the living room downstairs.

- I'm glad you like New Orleans, June – Hayley started – I told you it would be a nice change for you. I hope Oliver didn't disturb you there?

- We talk every night but it's my fault, I texted him first.

- What? Why would you do that? I thought you wanted to get him out of your life.

- Yes, I wanted that… But I've met so many guys and none of them was interesting enough, there was no spark with anyone. I don't know, maybe there is something wrong with me.

- There is nothing wrong with you June, you're just young and you don't know what you want, that's normal. Do you know what? Let me meet this guy. Let me see what the whole fuss is about. Let's have a dinner, all four of us, in my place.

- Would you really invite him in?

- Sure. He seems like a nice guy and you like him so why not? April said he's OK.

- I really don't know what to do Hayley. I have some feelings for him but I'm afraid he's not good for me.

- Is it because of Jack?

- Yes, but I don't want to talk about him. - June panicked that Jack would appear again if they stayed on that topic for too long - Hayley… What was it like when you met Liam for the first time? I know it was just a dream but it was a very realistic one and all your decisions were as they would have been in real life. You've never told me the whole story, so how did you meet him? How did you find out what he was?

Hayley thought for a moment trying to decide where to start.

- I was attacked and Liam saved me. He told me straight away that he was a vampire, he was completely honest with me from the very beginning. I didn't let my guard down but the more we talked the less afraid I was.

Everything he said was so fascinating and unbelievable and I wanted to hear more. He was perfectly nice and polite… And handsome - Hayley smiled – So we just kept seeing each other. I liked the way I felt when I was with him and I enjoyed every moment we spent together.

- So you didn't care he was different.

- In contrary but I liked that about him. For some reason, somehow, despite everything… I felt safe with him and I wanted him to be a part of my life. I don't know, maybe it was magic, maybe it was Leah messing with my head. Bradley was gone, I was really depressed and Liam was keeping my mind busy with all his incredible stories. I felt good with him, he was my savoir. But I knew it was just temporary because he was not human and that thought was breaking my heart. But the bottom line was that, at the end of the day, it didn't matter what he was and what he was capable of. The only thing that mattered to me was that I felt great with him and he was a good man who wouldn't hurt anybody. You say Oliver is different, so what? He's a witch, just like April, he just has some tasks to be done, that's all.

- Witches call him a demon witch.

- I know, that's why this is your decision June and I can't tell you what to do. I know you like him very much but if he makes you feel uncomfortable and afraid then you should stay away. Don't feel sorry for him, he'll find someone eventually… Maybe there is a female version of what he is and they can pair up and torture bad guys together or something.

They both laughed.

- I will tell him we can be friends and nothing more. If he needs someone to talk to, I will listen but we can't keep seeing each other.

- If that's what you want.

- That's the problem, Hayley, I don't know what I want. I want him away because he scares me but when he's away, I miss him and want him to be close. I feel I'm falling in love with him but at the same time I don't want to love him. I wanted him out of my life but I kept thinking about him every day to the point I eventually texted him to see how he was. I blame Jack for the way I feel now about Oliver. I'm afraid to trust my heart again and with all magic involved, I am still trying to look at everything logically. I am terrible, Hayley.

- You'll figure this out, at some point. Whatever is meant to be, will be and you can't avoid what fate has prepared for you. You worry too much June, try to relax, have some fun and believe that life will sort out itself. Look at me, I'm a vampire and I met the love of my life thanks to my dead witch ancestor. And believe me I had never hoped my future would look like this, I'd never wanted this but it is what I got and I couldn't be happier any other way with anybody else by my side. Eventually, you will know what's right for you and destiny will push you in the right direction, trust me.

They talked for a few more hours and at three in the morning, they took a walk back to Hayley's. They were walking slowly as the night was unusually warm. The sky was cloudless and the full moon was showing in front of them, lightly illuminating their path as all streetlights were off.

- It's nice to have a walk in the middle of the night and not to be afraid of anyone. - June said.

- Welcome to my world, this is one of the best things about being a vampire. I used to stay home after sunset but after my transition now I go out a lot. Of course the thought of vampire hunters makes me less confident but with Liam by my side I feel safe.

- Are you afraid now?

- No, I am here with you and I know they only attack when there is nobody around. You make me feel safe too, June.

- I didn't expect I would hear this from you Hayley. Thanks, you can count on me.

They got home safely and went straight to their beds. June fell asleep a few minutes later but Hayley lied in bed awake.

- How was it? - Liam asked Hayley when she cuddled up to him.

- She is so confused about that boy so I suggested we would meet him and I invited him over for a dinner. You know what? June asked me today to tell her how we met and I have never told that story to anyone before. These are really good memories, you know? It was a terrifying evening when I was attacked but meeting you was the best thing that happened to me and I'm glad Leah put you on my path.

- I'm glad you think so. Although I wish we have met under different circumstances. She didn't have to put you through all that stress and fear.

- Maybe… But I don't think I would change a thing if I could turn back time. I think what we have is perfect as it is and we got this because of what we've been through. It was just meant to be.

The next day June asked Oliver to come over to Hayley's for a dinner. They also planned karaoke in the evening and they already put their names on the list. Hayley together with June prepared a roasted chicken with baked potatoes and a salad and the smell in the kitchen was making everyone hungry. Oliver was right on time bringing some flowers for Hayley and a bottle of red wine. It's been a while since he visited someone in their house and socialised with others so he was a bit tense and nervous.

- Hi Oliver, nice to finally meet you. Come in, I'm Hayley.

They shook their hands. There was no unpleasant feeling like it has been with April so Oliver felt a bit more confident.

- Hi, nice to meet you both and thank you for inviting me over. I must say it is a very nice and cosy house considering it's a couple of vampires living here… I'm sorry, I didn't mean anything.

- And what did you expect?

Hayley took the flowers and went for a vase while Liam and Oliver were following her to the kitchen.

- I didn't really know what to expect, I have never met any vampires before. I know a lot about them and I was really surprised to find out that you two are totally different from what I've heard so far. It's good to see that you managed to build a nice life here for yourselves.

- Thanks Oliver. I hope you're hungry there is plenty of food prepared.

- It smells very delicious. Where's June?

- She took my dog out to the garden when she heard you at the door. Lexi is very protective of me and she's not very friendly with the strangers.

Once Hayley has finished that sentence, June walked in. She was wearing just a t-shirt and jeans and looked very casual but she was still able to take Oliver's breath away.

- Hi – she said quietly and her heart skipped a beat as she was happy to see him again.

- Hi June, you look ravishing.

- Ravishing? - June laughed – Stop joking, I didn't even brush my hair.

- It doesn't matter.

June blushed and sat at the table next to Hayley. She was looking at Oliver every now and then and stayed out of the conversation. Liam and Oliver got on like house on fire having so much to talk about. They were fans of the same teams, they both liked motorcycles and surfing and they even started planning a road trip across the country on their bikes. Girls were eating and occasionally quietly laughing at the guys when they got too excited talking about what they liked. After dinner, they all went to the nearby pub for karaoke as planned.

- There were only two spots left so we'll sing in twos, me and Hayley and you two – Liam said.

- I won't sing – June said quickly.

- Why not? - Oliver asked. - I bet you can.

- I just don't feel like singing but you can go alone if you want.

They had a good time listening to others. There was no particular theme so they could sing whatever they wanted. At some point Hayley and Liam went dancing joining a few other couples. There was plenty of space between the tables and the stage.

- Would you like to dance too? - Oliver asked June.

- No.

- I thought you loved dancing, you were having so much fun during our dance classes.

- I just don't feel like dancing right now.

- What's wrong, June? You wanted to see me, you invited me over and now you act like you don't want me to be here.

June got up and started walking towards the exit and Oliver followed her out.

- June, what's going on?

- I want you to know that I can't be with you… I can be your friend and you can keep texting me and visiting but we can't be anything more than that.

Oliver looked surprised. He thought June finally decided to move back to Aspen and give their relationship a chance but clearly that was not the case.

- Why would you say that? June, I love you. And I know that you…

- Stop, it doesn't matter. My common sense is telling me that…

- Forget about common sense. If you want to be with me then…

- But I don't, OK? I don't want to be with you.

June had tears in her eyes and her voice was breaking.

- You really mean it, don't you? Very well then. Let's have fun tonight this last time and I promise you will never see me again.

Oliver went inside angry, confused and disappointed. June wiped her tears, took a deep breath trying to fight the tears and followed him back inside. They were right in time for Hayley and Liam to sing Islands In The Stream. It was easy to tell how much in love they were by seeing the way they looked into each other's eyes when they were together on that stage. June envied them they had each other. They looked perfect together and they had the whole eternity to share. They seemed to be the luckiest couple in the world and June hoped that one day she would be as happy as them. Once they finished, Oliver got on stage. The lights went off and there was now only one spotlight illuminating the stage. Oliver had an excellent voice and the crowd loved him, everyone was clapping and whistling to encourage him. June was carefully listening to the song and realised it was especially selected for tonight and the lyrics couldn't be a coincidence:

(…)And here I go again on my own.
Going down the only road I've ever known.
Like a drifter I was born to walk alone (…)

June started having tears in her eyes again and Hayley noticed that.

- June, what's wrong?

- Nothing. He's a good singer, isn't he?

- Very good!

Oliver got off the stage and walked to the table but didn't sit down.

- I'll be leaving now.

- Why? - Hayley looked surprised.

- I had a really great time with you guys and it was nice to meet you. I'll see you around.

He looked at June but didn't say anything. Then, he turned around and left. June sat there for a minute and then ran out after him.

- Oliver! Wait!

He was already at the end of the street but he stopped. She ran over as fast as she could.

- I'm sorry. - she said trying to catch her breath - I didn't mean to hurt you, I don't want you to completely disappear from my life so please, let's stay friends.

- I can't be friends with you June. You know how I feel about you and I can't watch you being with someone else.

June didn't say anything. Tears came to her eyes again.

- You know what June? Meeting you made me realise that I would always be alone. - Oliver sounded very disappointed.

- That's not true.

- Is it? Here you are, a girl who's already entangled in the world of magic with witches, vampires and the dead being a part of her reality and even you, of all people, cannot accept who I am. I'm not a monster or a bad guy and you know it so I don't understand what the problem is. Bad people are killed around the world every day by police or some other task force and nobody has any problem with that so why my job has to be an issue?

They were standing away from everyone, in the middle of an empty street. Suddenly, a group of five teenage boys emerged from around the corner.

- Phones and wallets, now! - one of the boys yelled.

- Get out of here – Oliver said. His voice was deep and serious.

Boys laughed.

- Don't try to be a knight in a shining armour, man. You are a big guy but there are five of us and only one of you. You won't impress your girl if you get your pretty face smashed. – they laughed again - Are you going to give us that money now or what?

They were getting impatient. Suddenly one of them drew June to himself and put a knife to her throat.

- Your money or your life? - he sounded very confident.

June quickly reached to her pocket and got the phone out.

- Take it! I don't have any money.

- What about you, big guy? Your money or her life?

June was terrified. She was feeling the knife on her throat and the blade was hurting her leaving a thin bloody line on her skin. Suddenly, the irises of Oliver's eyes started to glow as if they were made of fire. He got his hand forward and there was a real flame dancing on his palm. Then, he started whispering something and the flame got bigger. Boys got terrified, dropped June's phone and started running away, tripping over their own feet. Oliver got back to his usual self within a second. He picked up June's phone and handed it over to her.

- Take your phone and go back to Hayley and Liam. These guys will not bother you again.

June took the phone from Oliver but didn't say anything. She was shocked.

- Goodbye – Oliver said and disappeared.

June stood there speechless and motionless for a minute or two before she started slowly walking back to the pub.

- Hayley, how could you ignore the truth about Liam and just accept him the way he was? - June asked when they were already back home

- June, how can you accept me and Liam? - Hayley asked in return.

- I don't know. You're my sister and I love you despite anything. And Liam… You trusted him and you assured me he was good and I believed you because I trust you… But there is nobody who can assure me that Oliver is OK, nobody knows him.

- Let me make you some herbal tea, it will help you calm down.

June sat at the kitchen table, resting her chin on her palm. Her eyes were red and swollen from crying. Hayley quickly brewed some tea and sat at the table with June.

- If you want my honest opinion – Hayley started – I think that you need to compare your life with and without Oliver being a part of it. Are you happier with him or without? When he's away, do you miss him? Is he really such a bad guy? Because I had real fun with him today and I think he's great. Give it another thought, June. Give yourself some more time and when the time's right, you'll know what to do, trust me.

- I hope you're right. Hayley, I have never been so confused in my entire life. I think there have been so many magical things going on in my life for the past year that I just can't take anything new anymore. Witches, vampires, hunters, the dead… And now there is this super-secret witch agent fighting evil. I think it's just too much to take.

June was lying in bed, unable to fall asleep. Every time she closed her eyes, she saw Oliver and his glowing eyes. When she finally fell asleep at dawn, she was dreaming about him. She saw him in that street among the same boys who attacked them that evening, but in her dream, Oliver killed all those boys mercilessly tearing their bodies apart. June wanted to scream and run away but she couldn't make a sound and she was running in slow motion constantly tripping, couldn't get away from that horrifying scene.

- June, wake up!

Hayley was sitting on June's bed and shaking her gently by the shoulders. June opened her eyes and looked at Hayley scared and shocked.

- Thank God Hayley, it was so terrifying. What a nightmare.

- I heard you breathing heavily and crying. Everything's OK, you can go back to sleep now.

- No way, I am fully awake now and I don't want to see again what I have just seen.

- Cup of coffee? Or maybe you'd like to go for a walk with me and Lexi?

- What time is it?

- Nearly six.

- OK, I'll get dressed and we can go. Hopefully, fresh and cool morning air may get those terrible images out of my head for the rest of the day.

June was back in New Orleans by the end of the day and all her stuff was already in her new apartment so April stayed to help her unpack. They spent the whole night on tiding up, unpacking, decorating and talking. At eight in the morning, June was half-alive so April used her magic to keep her going for the rest of the day. After the whole day of talking to the dead and the tourists, June went back to her new apartment and went straight to bed without even taking a shower. She was so tired that she fell asleep the moment she lied down and closed her eyes. For the first time in moths she didn't have time to think about Oliver.

- So what do you think about Oliver? – Liam asked when he was searching for a movie for their usual evening marathon with Hayley.

- I think he's very nice and funny. - Hayley said sitting on the couch and already eating some popcorn - I don't know why June is so weird about him, she obviously has some feelings for him.

- This is very weird. I understand that she may feel insecure because of Jack but this guy is definitely worth giving a chance. I liked him. I never really had any friends but Oliver already knows who I am and we have so much in common. We have discussed an idea of going across the country on our bikes and I always wanted to do it but never had a good companion and going alone didn't sound like fun.

- I think it is a really great idea. You should go.

- Do you think it would be OK? Wouldn't June mind?

- Why would she? After all, she introduced him to us. Did he give you his number?

- No, but he told me where he lives. Maybe I could pop in tomorrow and see if he's still interested?

- Sure, why not? I think you two would have so much fun.

- And what about you? I may be gone for a week or two, depending on how many hours a day we would be on the road and how far we decide to go.

- I don't mind. Have some fun, Liam. I have the whole eternity to spend with you so I think I would be OK if you disappeared for a few weeks. I'll try to survive without you being around. I'll have Lexi to keep me company so I won't be completely alone. I can always go to New Orleans for a few days if I feel lonely so don't worry about me. You deserve to have some fun away from home and I think you spend far too much time around girls and you need to do some man stuff for a change even if it means that you won't be around for a while.

- Wow, you're the most understanding girl in the world.

- Maybe… Or maybe I just love you very much and I trust you and I know that you're too smart to do anything stupid to jeopardise this great relationship we have.

- As usual, you're absolutely right.

The next day in the morning, Liam went to Oliver's house. It was one of those big old houses right outside the city, with a beautiful mountain view.

- Liam – Oliver looked surprised opening the door – hi, what are you doing here?

- I wanted to talk. Is this a good time?

- Sure, come in.

Although the house looked old from the outside, it must have been recently renewed as the interior looked very modern and fresh. It looked like Liam's previous houses - a house but not a home. It felt cold, hotel-like, stylish but not cosy. There were no decorations on the walls or shelves, but there were many photographs on one of the walls in the living room. They seemed old, some of them were even black and white.

- So what brings you here? - Oliver didn't offer a drink or a seat. He obviously wasn't used to having guests.

- Are you still interested in that cross-country ride?

- Sure, I just didn't know you were serious about it.

- Of course I was serious. When would you be ready to go?

Oliver thought for a moment.

- How about tomorrow?

- Tomorrow? I thought you wanted to take care of some stuff before the trip. We may be gone for weeks.

- I can always pop in if I need to. You know I can teleport, right?

Liam looked at him shocked.

- No, June didn't mention anything. That it really cool. OK, so how about tomorrow at seven? Or is it to early?

- Seven sounds great. Don't pack too much Liam, I can always teleport back here and bring you anything you need or forgot.

- How convenient. I don't think I would ever find a better companion for this trip. So where do you want to go first?

- I think we can go to San Francisco. It would be about twenty-hour ride so we can spread this over two or three days and then we'll see where to go next.

- Let's play it by ear then, shall we?

- Sure, I don't need a plan. Wherever our bikes will carry us.

- Exactly. OK, great. So I'll see you tomorrow morning then.

- See you tomorrow.

Oliver closed the door behind Liam and looked at the photographs on the wall, smiling. It was a while since he has been out on an adventure. Those pictures presented his parents and grandparents and Oliver himself when he was still a child. These were all memories of the good times and people who were long gone. Oliver hasn't put any new pictures on that wall in years. He couldn't find anyone for longer than just a few months. He met many nice people but nobody worth remembering. There were no great moments worth capturing, nothing that he could happily go back to now. There was a life full of loneliness, bad people and fleeting acquaintances so now he really looked forward to a road trip with someone who had an aptitude for being a true friend.

Chapter 8

Liam and Oliver have been having a great time on their trip so far. The weather was perfect, no rain, no burning sun. In Utah, they made a last-minute change and instead of taking the road fifty towards San Francisco as planned, they decided to take the road fifteen and go through Las Vegas towards Los Angeles. After over ten hours on the bikes and a few twenty-minute breaks, they were checking into their motel by eight o'clock in the evening. Liam made a quick call to Hayley. Although they have seen each other that morning, they already missed each other. They have been nearly inseparable since they started living together and Hayley missed Liam very much now being home all by herself. But she didn't want to admit that out loud afraid that Liam may turn around and come back home. She wanted him to go on that trip and have some fun and she didn't want him to feel guilty that she has been left behind.

The boys ordered some dinner and a couple of beers in the pub by the road. The music was playing loud, the air was full of smoke and the place was quite crowded.

- So how are you feeling so far? Do you like the trip? – Liam started the conversation.

- Yes, I like it very much, it's fun. I've always wanted to do it but I had the same problem as you did, there was nobody to go with me.

- Yes, that's the problem, nobody has time for stuff like that. People are too busy with their jobs and families.

They sat in silence for a few minutes eating and drinking. They didn't feel uncomfortable and had no need to keep the conversation alive. They felt perfectly fine just eating together with not a single word spoken, but Liam wanted to find out more about Oliver. He already treated him like a friend so he decided it would be good to know something more about his companion.

- I like your house.

- Thanks, it's my family house. My grandparents built it and I grew up there. When my parents and grandparents died I thought about selling it but eventually, I moved back in and re-did the interior. I like that place, it's full of great memories, the best memories, to be honest.

- Do you have any siblings?

- No, it's only me.

- So how long have you been by yourself? When did your parents die?

- About thirty years ago. I was raised by my grandparents mostly, they died nearly a decade later.

- Forgive me but I don't understand. How old are you?

- I'm forty this year.

Liam took a good look at Oliver, shocked and speechless.

- How's that possible? You look twenty-ish.

- The magic I practice keeps me young and healthy. I am not immortal though, I just eliminated a few things that may kill me.

- So you have something in common with June then.

- What do you mean? - Oliver looked at Liam surprised.

- She wears a ring that protects her from illness and passing time. I'm surprised she hasn't told you.

- She mentioned the magical pendant but forgot to mention a magical ring.

- Yes, well, she's full of surprises.

- She is indeed.

- Forgive me if I'm too blunt again but why aren't you two together?

- Because June doesn't want to.

- Of course she does. She loves you, it's so easy to tell.

- Maybe she loves me but she'll never admit that and despite her feelings, she doesn't want to be with me. She told me that right to my face.

Liam didn't know how to comment on that. He didn't feel comfortable talking with Oliver about his love life.

- It's getting late so let's finish this dinner and go to sleep. There is another long trip ahead tomorrow.

- Do you want to visit Las Vegas before we hit the road again?

- I think we can just ride through it without stopping. Unless you want to.

- Fine by me. I have already seen it once.

- So have I.

Suddenly, Oliver got a piece of paper out of his pocket. He read carefully what was on it and threw it into the ashtray on the table. The paper started burning and turned into ashes within a few seconds.

- I need to go now Liam. I have a work to do.

- Is this how you get the orders?

- Yes and I need to take care of this one right away. I will be here in the morning, I won't keep you waiting, you have my word.

They both left the pub and started walking back to the motel. There were too many people around them so Oliver needed to go into his room first. Once he's locked the door, he disappeared, teleporting to the address written on the paper.

June walked out of the pub and started walking back home. It was already late at night and quite cold. She was not far from home and there were many people around her so she felt safe. She was out without April as she wanted to meet new people without her sister constantly looking over her. She had a good time but didn't meet anyone interesting enough. It didn't matter how funny or smart or cute or charming these guys were, none of them compared to Oliver. It bothered June that she couldn't find anyone. She thought about Oliver at least once a day nearly every day since that night in Aspen when she saw him last time. She wanted him to be close and away at the same time. She wanted him to call but she was also trying to forget about him. Many times, she typed a text message on her phone and then deleted it unsent. She has never felt that way about anyone else. Her feelings for Oliver were so full of contradictions that June didn't know what she should do and what really was best for her.

She was walking home, deep in thought without even realising that she was alone on the street, leaving the dancing crowd far behind. Suddenly, someone approached her from behind and put to her face a handkerchief soaked in chloroform that made her fall asleep right away.

When June finally woke up, she was tied to the chair in a place that was dark, cold and smelled like a basement. At first, she thought about screaming for help but she was afraid that it would just attract attention of the wrong person. She took a few deep breaths, trying to stay focused. She had a look around but couldn't see anything in the darkness. Her throat was completely dry and her hands and feet were numb. She began to tremble with cold and fear and tried to break free from the ropes but she couldn't as the knots were too tight. Eventually, she started to cry feeling helpless and being sure she was going to die. She was not afraid of death though, she was afraid of how much pain she would have to endure before she would eventually join her parents on the other side.

April woke up suddenly in the middle of the night, her heart was beating fast and she was short of breath. She turned the lights on and went for a glass of water to the kitchen. She couldn't understand what was happening, she didn't have a nightmare and yet she was cold and scared.

- Oh no, June!

April dialled her sister's number but there was no connection. She put a map of New Orleans on the kitchen table, cut her finger with a knife and let a few drops of blood fall on the table. She put her hands over the map and started chanting: *'omnibus propinquis locate.'* As she was repeating the spell, two drops of her blood started moving across the map. When she finished the spell, her blood was showing two spots: one was her apartment the other one was somewhere deep in the Bayou.

- June, what are you doing there?

She didn't expect her sister to be so stupid to go to the Bayou in the middle of the night all by herself or with someone she has just met. April thought for a moment trying to figure out what to do. She wanted to call Hayley but at the same time she didn't want to worry her sister. But she was sure something was not right and she had no clue what to do.

- What's wrong? - Hayley answered her phone without 'hello' knowing April wouldn't call her in the middle of the night if everything was OK.

- June is missing. I woke up feeling scared but I didn't have a nightmare. I thought that maybe it's June, you know, with the twin connection and me being a witch… So I called her but she didn't answer. I did the spell and I see she's in the Bayou. Hayley, I don't know what to do.

- Hold on. - Hayley hung up and quickly called Liam.

- Struggling to sleep without me?

- Is Oliver there with you?

- Yes, he's right here. Hayley, what's wrong?

- I need to talk to him right now.

Liam handed over his cell phone to Oliver.

- Oliver, I need your help. Liam told me you can teleport, is that right?

- Right.

- I need you to get to the Bayou in Louisiana as soon as possible. June is in trouble and she needs your help.

- I'm on my way.

Oliver disconnected and gave the cell phone back to Liam.

- We need to go.

- We? - Liam repeated surprised – Does this mean you can take me with you?

They went outside the bar and had a look around to make sure nobody saw them, at least nobody sober. Oliver took Liam by the wrist and whispered the spell. Within a blink of an eye, they were somewhere in the woods.

- Is this Bayou?

- Yes, now we need to find June.

Liam closed his eyes and started to listen carefully but there was nothing apart from typical sounds of the night. He heard an owl somewhere up in the trees, bats quietly flying over their heads and mice rustling through the leaves under their feet.

- I can't hear anything.

Suddenly, he heard a distant scream somewhere on their left and started running towards the source of the sound, leaving Oliver far behind.

June started panicking when she heard the footsteps on the stairs outside. She stopped crying and listened carefully, holding her breath. Suddenly, the door to the basement opened and a beam of light came through. Then, someone turned the lights on, hurting June's eyes which, by then, got used to the darkness.

- You're awake right on time.

It was a man in his thirties, short, clearly overweight, with long curly black hair and big rounded glasses. He was smiling and looked quite friendly despite being a monster capable of kidnapping people.

- Please – June said fighting tears – Please, don't hurt me. Have I done something to you? I don't even know you. Please, if I had done something, I'm sorry, I'm really sorry.

The man put on an apron and some thick rubber gloves. He took two glass bottles from the shelving unit in the corner and mixed their content together. There was a white smoke coming out of the dish, making a soft hissing sound.

- No, no, no, this is not happening – June said panicking even more. - This isn't real. Why are you doing this? What have I done? Talk to me, please, let's talk.

But the man just smiled, not saying anything. He approached June with the dish in his hand. June screamed and started writhing on the chair trying to break free.

- Get away from me you psychopath!

Suddenly, the door to the basement opened wide so quickly that they couldn't even say whether it was a person or just a wind as all they saw was just a blur. The guy in the apron was pushed to the corner with great force.

- Liam! - June yelled when she finally realised what was going on – Liam get me out of here!

Liam got the knife lying on the table and cut the ropes tying June's hands and legs. She got up from the chair and fell on Liam being far too dizzy to walk.

- Don't worry, I got you. - said Liam and gently picked her up.

They were about to leave when the guy started clumsily getting up from the floor. In that moment, Oliver appeared in the doorway. He looked at June, making sure she was OK, then he looked at the guy who was now standing in the corner, leaning against the wall disoriented and confused. The back of his head was bleeding and his glasses were now somewhere on the floor. Oliver reached his hand forward, holding his palm out towards the man and his fingers outstretched. He started saying the words in a language that nobody else understood. The guy looked at Oliver with fear. Then, he grabbed his head with both his hands and started to scream. He fell to his knees and the blood started pouring from his nose and ears. A few seconds later he fell on the floor dead, with his eyes still wide open, red and watery. Oliver turned around and looked at June again. He was angry but also scared and sad.

- Are you OK? Did he do something to you?

- I'm OK – she replied with her voice shaking. - Please, take me home.

Oliver held Liam's wrist again and they all appeared in Hayley's living room a second later.

- June! - she yelled – June, thank God, you're OK!

Hayley hugged June tightly, relieved her little sister was alive. She led her to the sofa, helped her sit down and covered her with the blankets as June was shivering.

- What's happened?

But June didn't say anything, staring bluntly at her cold and numb hands.

- Please, talk to me June – Hayley asked again – You're safe now.

June looked at her sister with her terrified wide eyes.

- Someone attacked me – she nearly whispered - When I was walking back home. When I woke up, I was tied up… It was dark and cold and I couldn't see or hear anything. Then… That guy showed up. He didn't say anything, just… Smiled… I can see his face so clearly even now…I'm completely awake, with my eyes open and yet… I can see him in front of me ready to hurt me…I can still see his face.

Hayley handed June a pillow.

- Try to get some sleep. You're safe here, I'll watch over you, I promise.

- I don't think I'll be able to fall asleep.

Hayley stroked June's head as she was now lying on the sofa with her eyes closed. Her face was still wet of tears.

- Thank you both – Hayley whispered looking at Oliver and Liam.

- I think you should call April, I just texted her that everything was OK but she's awaiting some explanation. We'll go back to our motel now. If you need anything just give me a call.

- Thanks again. Enjoy your trip.

Liam kissed Hayley goodbye and disappeared with Oliver. Hayley called April to tell her what June told them. They decided it would be better for June to stay in Aspen for a few days before going back to work. They thought her life was on the right track and everything was OK but obviously it wasn't. The fact that June decided to go out at night all by herself just proved how lonely she truly was, despite her twin sister living just around the corner.

A few days passed by and June came back to New Orleans. She didn't want to talk about that terrible night in the Bayou either with Hayley or April. She wanted to forget about it and live her life as if nothing has happened.

It was a warm evening and she was walking home back from work when she saw Oliver waiting for her outside the building where she rented her flat. She stopped at first when she saw him but then decided to approach him to see what he wanted.

- Hi. – he said, giving June one of those charming smiles.

- Hi. What are you doing here?

- I wanted to check up on you, see how you are. So, how are you?

- I'm fine.

- Do you want to talk or do you want me to go?

June thought for a moment before she responded. After all, Oliver saved her life.

- Would you like to come in for a cup of coffee? I bought some cake yesterday, it's quite good.

Oliver looked at her surprised. They have known each other for months and that was the first time she wanted to let him in.

- Sure, sounds good.

They went upstairs to June's flat without a word. June led Oliver to the kitchen and asked him to sit at the table. She poured the coffee and sliced some cake and then sat down not saying anything so Oliver decided to break the silence.

- I like it here, it feels very homey.

- Thank you.

It was clear June wasn't fine. She was sitting in her own kitchen terrified. Oliver could feel her overwhelming fear and sadness which completely suppressed her feelings for him.

- Talk to me, Love. – he sounded concerned.

- Why are you really here? I told you we couldn't be together and you made it clear you didn't want to be friends with me so why did you come?

- Maybe I changed my mind. Maybe I want to be your friend after all.

- But why?

- Because… I miss you. I don't have many friends so I think I should not push away those few who want to be in my life. So once again, how are you? Your sisters worry about you.

- How do you know that?

- Because I spoke with Hayley, she is one of those few friends I have. Her and Liam.

- You're friends with them?

- Sure, they are a very nice couple, very entertaining and fun. I've been on my trip across the country with Liam for over a week now. Technically, I'm in my motel room right now somewhere in Austin, Texas. I'm surprised Hayley hasn't mentioned that to you.

June took a sip of her coffee clearly thinking intensively what to say.

- I'm glad you're having fun.

She kept drinking her coffee but Oliver kept staring at her clearly waiting for her to answer the question which he has already asked a few times that evening.

- You want to know how I am? OK, let's see… I have nearly died last week. In fact, this was the second time this year when someone tried to kill me and I don't even know why, it's not like I'm a bad person or something. I have done nothing wrong to anybody but for some reason, people want me dead. I go to work every day and act as if nothing has happened but the truth is that I'm afraid of my own shadow. I don't go out after sunset anymore, even with April. The only place I feel safe is my home and it's because April has put so many different spells on it that there is no way anyone or anything could get through. I don't even have a spider here or a fly, the place is completely empty and the only living thing in here is me. I have nightmares that I run through the Bayou in the middle of the night or that I wake up tided to the chair in a cold and dark basement, so I barely sleep. I started to think that every stranger is a psychopath and there are no more normal people out there anymore. I can see that man with his horrible smile whenever I close my eyes… I truly hate my life… I don't know how much longer I can take.

June started to cry. She got up from the chair and turned her face towards the window so Oliver couldn't see her tears. He got up too and approached her putting his arms around her to console her.

- You're safe with me. I'll always be there for you, to protect you and take care of you. Whenever you need me I will be there within a second, you can always count on me.

June turned around and cuddled up to Oliver, pressing her covered in tears cheek against his t-shirt.

- I'm an idiot, Oliver. If I had kept seeing you, nothing would've happened. I would've spent my free time with you and you would've kept me safe. But I'm stupid and I thought you were not good for me and I pushed you away looking for God knows who. That's why I got into trouble, because I was so tired of not having anyone that I started being reckless and irresponsible. I'm sorry Oliver. I'm sorry for the things I said and…

- You don't have to apologise, Love. You did what you felt was right.

June took a step back and wiped tears from her face.

- I haven't really thanked you for being there for me that night so thank you, Oliver. You saved my life.

- I'm glad I could help.

- Your coffee is cold, let me make you another one.

June poured the cold coffee down the sink and prepared a fresh one. She felt better now after she confessed to Oliver. She admitted out loud what bothered her and she felt as if some weight was lifted off her shoulders. She came back to the table and sat down.

- Enough about me, – she said – tell me, how have you been?

But Oliver didn't say anything and just kept looking at June truly concerned.

- Please, talk to me about something, anything, just keep my mind busy.

- The trip has been real fun. - he said trying to sound cheerful - Liam's a very nice guy and Hayley's great too. I'm glad you introduced them to me.

- I'm glad you got on.

There were a few seconds of silence as they were drinking their coffees.

- Come b…

- Stay h…

They started talking at the same time and that made them smile.

- Sorry – Oliver said – You go first.

- No, you go.

- OK… Come back to Aspen, you loved it there. New Orleans is not for you, it's for April and you don't have to follow her everywhere she goes. Let her have her own life here, among other witches. She doesn't need you.

- But I like it here. I like those witches and I like my job. I helped so many people say goodbyes to the ones they've lost and if I can't be a medium in the French Quarter, where else then? I feel I fit in. But maybe… Maybe you could move here?

- And live among witches? Have you seen the way they look at me? No way. Besides, Aspen is my home. I have my only two friends there, how could I leave them?

They sat in silence for a couple of minutes, thinking what to say next.

- It's getting late – Oliver said when June turned the tap on to do the dishes - I should go now.

- Stay with me. - June said unexpectedly.

Oliver looked at her surprised.

- Sure, I can stay. I will watch over you so you can have a proper sleep.

- That's not what I meant, I don't need you to watch over me.

June passed Oliver by and started walking slowly towards her bedroom. Once she passed the door, she looked back at Oliver over her shoulder.

- Are you coming or what?

June woke up the next day in the morning. She slept through the whole night, first time since the Bayou incident. She didn't wake up in the middle of the night covered in sweat and she didn't have any nightmares. She saw Oliver sitting in the armchair by the bed, drinking tea and looking at her, smiling. His blond hair was even more messy than usual.

- Good morning Love, did you sleep well?
- Very well. It was a great night.
- Yes, it was… Marry me.
- What?
- Marry me, June.
- I don't think it's a good idea.
- Why not? We are perfect together. You already tried living without me and it wasn't fun. I tried living without you and I didn't know how. I thought about you every day and I want to be with you forever.

June got up and approached Oliver, sitting on his lap and putting her arms around his neck.

- Can we talk about this later? We are together now and it feels right so let's focus on today and don't think about tomorrow.

Oliver didn't respond and just smiled.

- I hate those smiles. - June said - You have no idea how charming you are.

- Let me call Liam first. I don't want him to wait for me, he doesn't know I'm here.

- Right, I forgot you are on your road trip. Where is he?
- Austin.

- I have never been in Texas… Maybe you can take me with you and we can see the city? You can stop for one day, you don't run against time, right?

- I guess it would be OK… All right then, get dressed and let's go.

June checked online the current weather forecast in Austin, put some clothes on and laced up her trainers. Oliver took her into his arms, whispered the spell and suddenly, they were in the middle of the motel room.

- That was cool – June said smiling.

Oliver put June down and they left the room seeing Liam waiting by his motorbike.

- What a nice surprise! - he said when he saw June and Oliver walking out of the motel - Now I understand why Oliver was not answering his phone.

- That's my fault – June said - He just popped in to check up on me and I asked him to stay.

- That's fine, June. I'm glad to see you two finally together. So what's the plan?

- I thought you could take a short break from the road and we can see the city? The weather is lovely and I don't have to work today.

- Do you know what? I think I'll leave you two and pop back home to see Hayley. Oliver, can you arrange that for me?

- Absolutely. June, wait here, I'll be back in a minute.

He was back in twenty-two seconds to be exact. They left the motorbikes at the motel and teleported to the city centre. They were walking around the city, holding hands and enjoying each other's company. June saw how all girls passing them by were looking at Oliver.

- That's not good, – June said – We need to do something to make you less attractive. I'm afraid someone is going to try to steal you from me.

Oliver laughed.

- No need to worry Love, I am not going anywhere. You can put a big red tattoo on my forehead saying 'taken' if it makes you feel any better.

- Do you know what? I think it's a great idea! I think I may actually do that.

- So where do you want to go? What do you want to see?

- I don't know… Let's take the bus.

They took the Double Decker and had a tour around the city, sitting away from the crowds and their hungry eyes. In the afternoon, they paddled on the Lady Bird Lake. They had a few laughs when one of them ended up in the lake every now and then. They had a perfect weather for an afternoon at the lake. It was nearly thirty degrees Celsius, the sun was not burning as the sky was cloudy but there was no rain in the forecast. The wind was quite strong but warm and pleasant. They could watch the busy city life from the middle of the lake, away from the noise and chaos of busy Austin streets.

- Tell me, how your witch business started – June asked when they drifted away from the other boats.

- I was born a witch.

- I know but… Your work… How did it start?

- Oh… That… - Oliver put the paddles away - I was sixteen years old and a demon showed up in our house. I was alone and frightened although he looked friendly and wasn't scary at all, it was just an idea of a spirit of a stranger being there that scared me. He told me exactly who he was and what he wanted from me. Obviously, it was a decision I couldn't possibly make, I was too young so I said I needed to discuss that with my grandparents but he insisted it needed to be my choice and no others… So I said 'no' and he disappeared. I told my grandparents all about it and they were terrified. They assured me I've made the right choice. But a few months later I got sick… really sick. Doctors couldn't help me, there was something wrong with my lungs, I had problems with breathing and I was in pain. The doctors said I would die. My grandparents tried to save me with their magic but they were not powerful enough and I was just getting worse. I remember the dream I had when I was lying in bed with high fever. I saw myself in different places around the world, I tasted delicious food, I experienced amazing things, I was truly happy. Then, I woke up. I was still in bed, my real life was a nightmare and I wanted it to end. I didn't want to die tough but I wanted the pain to disappear and I wanted to feel well again. That's when the demon showed up again. He said that all I've seen in my dream could be real, I could be happy, I could stay young and healthy, there would be no pain, no illness, no suffering ever again... The vision he presented to me was very tempting and all I wanted in that moment was to live. So I made a deal with him. Five minutes later there was no pain, no fever, I was perfectly fine.

- Do you think that demon was responsible for your illness? That he brought that upon you to make you work for him?

- I think so, I mean, it would've been too much of a coincidence that I was about to die so shortly after I rejected his offer and he appeared right in time to make his offer again. But I asked him about it one day and he denied everything. He's a demon though so I don't expect him to tell me the truth.

- Have you ever met the devil?

Oliver smiled.

- No, June, I don't think it's that easy. You were in heaven once, did you meet God?

- No.

- Exactly. Anyway, I have never told my grandparents the truth, they believed it was their magic and help of the ancestors that saved me that day. They both died before they noticed I was not growing old but I think they knew… Or at least suspected something. My aura was not as dark and cold as it is now but I'm sure they could feel the difference, nonetheless. They have never said anything about it though, never asked a single question and never made me feel any less loved. After they died, I was all alone. I didn't have any real friends, the ones I knew when I was a kid – the other witches – they turned their backs on me when they realised who I became. I had a few human colleagues, someone I could go to a bar with or spend New Year's Eve with, but I could've never been truly honest with them so I couldn't call them my friends. I travelled around the world alone and at some point, eventually, I got used to it. I enjoyed the company of strangers and I had fun with different people every day. I was never alone… But always lonely… And then I met you. - Oliver smiled and gazed at June – You were so beautiful and nice and funny and I loved spending time with you. I started to believe that I could build my life in Aspen with you and maybe even tell you the truth one day. But you found out on your own and destroyed everything.

- Hey, don't say it like that – June got upset – I had some issues of my own and you scared me.

- I know Love, I'm not angry with you I just think that things could've been better if it had been done my way. But it doesn't really matter now, I don't care about the past, I only care about now and my amazing future with you.

June blushed.

- I love you, June and I have never been happier. This day is the best day of my life and I could stay in this boat with you forever.

June looked at Oliver with a gentle smile.

- I love you too.

- Wow, this is the first time you said it.

- I know it took me a while to…

- … I don't care, I'm just happy you finally admitted it.

He leaned forward and kissed her.

- I know you said something about staying here forever, but I'm getting a bit hungry and the sun is already coming down so let's grab something to eat and go back home.

- Your wish is my command – Oliver said with a smile, took the paddle and started rowing towards the shore.

- Are you staying with me tonight? - June asked with a note of hope in her voice when there were sitting at the kitchen table in her place, eating a takeaway they grabbed in Austin, before teleporting back to New Orleans.

- Sure, but I need to pick up Liam first thing in the morning so we can hit the road by seven. So did you have a good time today?

- Yes, it was very lovely. I have never paddled before so it was fun and very challenging I must say. And Austin is a very lovely city.

- So where else do you want to go? You know I can take you anywhere. No travelling, no packing… You can be wherever you want within seconds.

- How convenient. So are you my personal travel agent now? - she smiled.

- I can be.

- I have never really thought about travelling. I don't like spending long hours on the bus or plane and I get tired easily but with this new travelling way that you offer I may consider visiting some places.

- Make a list, I'm happy to go anywhere with you.

They took a few more bites before Oliver finally decided to ask June a question that has been nagging him since morning.

- What made you change your mind? Don't get me wrong, I am very happy we are together and I want it to last… But I want to know what's changed.

June waited for a moment as she didn't want to talk with her full mouth.

- I nearly died. When I was sitting in that basement I thought it was the end and then when I was back here and safe again, I realised that I don't have the whole time in the world after all, that every day may be my last and I have been just wasting my time on being lonely. I wanted someone normal but then I realised how could I bring someone normal into this crazy, magical world? How could I live with someone without being completely honest with him? Or how could I tell someone the whole truth about my family and myself without sounding completely insane? I was so shocked and confused and scared when Hayley introduced Liam and then again when she decided to become a vampire. Then, April stopped that storm and that really freaked me out…

- What storm?

- I'll tell you later… So anyway… I realised that looking for 'mister right' is just such a waste of time as I would never find anyone perfect. And there you were, my prince charming. I loved so much about you and I liked myself when I was with you and how I felt when you're close. And it's not only because you're handsome, I enjoy being with you because you're funny and clever and you know how to make me laugh and I feel safe with you and that's what I was truly after. So… I decided I would just ignore what you do. April made me realise that this is just your job, that you're like a police officer or a spy and you hurt people because you must and not because you want to.

- Wow, I think this was your longest monologue ever.
June smiled.

- I'm glad you see it that way – Oliver continued - Although I can't believe how much you took into consideration to finally decide to be with me… I mean… All I thought of was 'I like her and she likes me and we have a great time together' and that was it. I didn't have to make a list and consider all the pros and cons.

- I don't believe you. I think if I was ugly or really stupid you wouldn't want to be with me.

- You're probably right. But luckily for me, you are smart and very beautiful.

Oliver was about kiss June when suddenly he got all serious and started unfolding a small piece of paper which appeared in his pocket.

- What is it?

- I need to go.

- What? Where?

- I have a job to do.

Without saying anything more, he quickly kissed June goodnight and disappeared.

June didn't fall asleep, waiting for Oliver who eventually showed up right after three in the morning.

- Why aren't you sleeping yet?

- I've been waiting for you. Tell me, what did you do?

- I don't want to talk about it.

- But I want to know. I want to understand how it works.

Oliver sat on the edge of the bed.

- Have you ever seen any of those weird videos on the internet showing some random stuff like… For example a wheel detached from the car rolling across the street and hitting someone in the head? Or a lighting striking someone before the storm even started? Or some weird stuff falling on people out of nowhere?

June nodded.

- So this is what I do… I create accidents like that. But it's not always about taking someone's life, you know? Sometimes there is someone who's on the wrong track but can still be saved, all I need to do is to open their eyes, make them realise that life is worth living the good way. Some people change their perspective when they think they're about to die or…

- Was I kidnapped because of you?! - June said angrily.

- What?! No! Of course not! I would never do anything like that. How could you even think that?

- I'm sorry. It's just what you said and what has recently happened to me and… I'm sorry…

- I hope you believe me?

- I do. I don't know why I said that, I shouldn't have, I'm sorry. So… if you don't have to kill people, why did you kill that guy in the Bayou?

- Because he was a hopeless case. I looked at him and I knew there was no good in him, that no matter what happened next, he would find a way back to hurting people and I couldn't let that happen. He wouldn't change, he couldn't be fixed, he was damaged beyond repair.

- What if someone finds him in that hut?

- Nobody will as I have burnt that hut to the ground. If the police ever find any remaining, they will think it was an accident, nobody would investigate.

June sat quietly, deep in thought staring at the wall across the room.

- June, don't think about it anymore. - Oliver sounded concerned - That guy was a beast, don't feel sorry for him. He got what he deserved and I don't regret what I've done. I would do anything for you.

Oliver took his shoes off and lied down next to June, holding her tightly in his arms.

- Now, tell me about that storm that April stopped. I want to know all about it.

Chapter 9

Lily was sitting in her room, looking at the photos of Jack and crying. She still didn't know what has really happened to her best friend. He visited her in Boston back in April and stayed in her place for a month. The last time she saw him was in Aspen. He entered that house he's told her about and never came out. Lily spent nearly four weeks watching that house day and night before she finally decided to come back to Boston. Now, with the help of a witch friend, she sent a message to every vampire hunter being nearby to come over to Boston. She had a large piece of land just outside the city so they could meet there undisturbed.

On the tenth of September at twilight, nearly twenty vampire hunters arrived at the big plantation house just outside of Boston. Although they showed up in the form of different birds and insects, they all entered the house in their human form. When Lily entered the living room, she saw people sitting everywhere, on the chairs, sofas, floor, stairs and even windowsills.

- Good evening everyone, thank you for coming. A friend of mine Jack Watson has been missing. He was hunting a group of vampires in Aspen when he disappeared. He told me he came across an unusual type of vampires. Apparently, they were still bound by family ties and…

- That's nonsense! - someone yelled from the crowd.

- I've seen them and it's true. Everything that Jack told me and what I am about to tell you now is true.

Everyone was looking at Lily, listening carefully, not meaning to interrupt again. She told them everything she knew; About Hayley, Liam and April and their jobs and pets and how they led seemingly normal lives.

- A few weeks later, Jack and I went to Aspen as he had a plan how to kill those vampires. I was sitting across the street, watching Jack getting into the house. I waited there for weeks but he has never come out. I've seen those vampires, the witch and a human coming in and out but not Jack.

- When was that?

- In May.

- In May?! And you waited four months to tell us about it?! Why didn't you call this meeting in May?

- I didn't know what to do.

- So what's the plan now? Are we going to Aspen?

- That's the thing, I still don't have a plan. We can't attack them inside the house and we can't kill them on the street either.

- How come witches let this particular group to be protected with magic? We need them to do something with the spell so we can get inside that house.

- I can talk to my witch friend but I would need a few of you to go with me. I can't deal with these vampires myself.

A few raised their hands and volunteered.

- Great, thank you. Those few, could you please stay to discuss the plan? The rest may go now.

The crowd started slowly leaving the house and only five hunters stayed. It was less than Lily hoped for but still a good number. She called her witch friend and ask her to come over. The girl showed up an hour later.

- Vivian – Lily greeted her friend with a smile - Thank you for coming. Let me cut to the chase, we'd like to ask you for a favour. We need you to come to Aspen with us and remove a protection spell from one house.

- Whose house?

- There is a couple of vampires living there.

- I have never heard of vampires being protected by the spell so if these really are, there must be a reason for it. I think you should investigate this before…

- One of the vampires has a witch sister who put the spell.

- I see… I think I know what's going on, I heard of cases like that. Sometimes a witch can cast a spell to prevent the vampire nature from taking over after transition.

- What does it mean? - Lily furrowed her brow.

- It means that the vampires living in that house are not like any other vampire you've seen before. They are more human, capable of loving and caring.

- That's impossible.

- I'm telling you the truth. Observe them and see for yourself, I bet you won't see them attacking people.

- They killed my friend! - Lily yelled with unhidden anger.

- Did you witness that?

- No, but he got into that house and never came out. It's been months and I haven't heard from him and I'm sure he's dead.

- Do you have his toothbrush or a hairbrush? I could verify for you whether he's alive or not.

Lily quickly went upstairs to one of the rooms and searched through Jack's bag. Everything was as he left it before they went to Aspen. She got the toothbrush out of his bag and came downstairs to hand it to Vivian. The witch squeezed the item in her hands, closed her eyes and started repeating the spell. After a minute, she opened her eyes and gave the toothbrush back to Lily.

- You're right, he's dead. I'm sorry.

Although Lily suspected Jack was dead, it was still shocking when the witch confirmed that information. Tears came to her eyes.

- You see?! - Lily said angrily - They killed Jack and we need to do something about it.

Vivian thought for a moment.

- I want no part of it so I won't let you into that house. I'm sorry but we don't know what really happened and I can't let you kill these vampires without any proof they really killed your friend. Witches don't get involved in vampire business.

- I can't believe you won't help me. You've picked the wrong side, Vivian.

- I am not picking any sides Lily, I just don't want to be involved and if I were you I would let it go. I'm sorry Jack is gone, I really am, but the road you want to take is very dangerous.

- I can take care of myself. - she looked at the witch with a look full of anger - I think it's time for you to leave.

Vivian got up from the couch and left the house in a hurry, not looking back. She drove back home fast to pack her bag and leave for New Orleans with the first available flight. She's heard of a real medium among the witches of the French Quarter and she needed that medium to talk to Jack to find out what has really happened. She was worried about Lily and didn't want her to end up dead and although she didn't want to get involved, she needed to know what has really happened before her friend decided to stand up against a family of vampires and a powerful witch.

June was at work as every other day, sitting in a dark room with only a few candles lit. She got up to open the window and listen to jazz when a new client came in.

- Hi, come on in, please sit down.

- Hi, my name is Vivian and I am a witch from Boston. Before we start the session, could you please be honest with me and tell me if you really can talk to the dead or is it just a performance for the tourists?

- I can really talk to the dead, yes. I promise, you won't waste your time here.

- Good, because I really need to talk to someone. His name is Jack Watson.

June looked at Vivian with her eyes wide open.

- Who is he to you?

- Nobody, I didn't even know him but apparently he was killed and I wanted to clarify that for my friend who cared deeply for him.

June got nervous, her hands started to shake.

- I can't help you, I'm sorry.

- What? Why?

- Because I knew Jack and I don't want to talk to him. I don't want to see him again.

- You knew him? Do you know what's happened to him? Was he really killed? We suspect a pair of vampires killed him in their house in Aspen.

- Tell your friend that it didn't work and you couldn't talk to Jack.

- She doesn't know I'm here. Why won't you tell me what you know? Why won't you let me talk to Jack?

- Because he killed me! He came to my house and stabbed me to death. I was brought back to life by magic but if it hadn't been for my witch sister, I would've stayed dead, that's why I don't want to see him ever again.

- Why would he want to kill you? - Vivian looked confused - Did you know he was a vampire hunter?

- Yes, I knew. It's… Complicated.

- Listen, June, something is happening and innocent people may die. I can stop that but I need to talk to Jack, I need your help, please.

- I said no, I'm sorry.

Vivian looked disappointed but she decided not to put any more pressure on June as she clearly didn't want to help.

- Possibly, a war is coming. Vampire hunters are appalled that witches protect some vampires who allegedly killed one of theirs. If I'm right, I don't want to be involved and if I were you, I would figure out how to stay out of it too.

Vivian got up and started walking away.

- Wait, let me gather the witches of the French Quarter and you will tell them all you know. Maybe someone else can help you.

- Thank you. I know how hard it must be for you and I appreciate you are still willing to do something to help.

June called April and asked her to organise the meeting although she didn't know what to expect. She was afraid of witches' reaction, after all, her family killed someone. When April magically got rid of Jack's body, they thought all their problems disappeared as well. Nobody thought that the events of that terrible day would come back one day haunting.

All witches from New Orleans gathered on the cemetery shortly after midnight and Vivian told them everything she knew about Jack and his disappearance. She also warned the witches about vampire hunters who may possibly come after a witch living in Aspen. The more she said, the more witches were sure which vampires Vivian had in mind. All French Quarter witches knew Hayley and Liam.

- April, June, is there anything you'd like to add?

The question was asked by Iris, the most powerful witch. Although she was only in her late forties, she was considered an elder in witch community and that made her a leader. Everyone was now looking at the twins, expecting some explanation.

- We knew Jack – April started. - He wanted to kill Hayley and Liam and used June as a bait. He followed her home and once she's invited him in... He stabbed her. Hayley saw her sister seriously wounded lying on the floor writhing in pain and she... Acted without much thinking.

- What does it mean?

- She attacked Jack and killed him. But the truth is, I wanted to kill him too for what he did to June. He was a vampire hunter and we didn't blame him for coming after Hayley and Liam but he came after June and killed her, an innocent human. Yes, June died that day but thankfully, I was able to bring her back. So don't look at this the wrong way, it is not as simple as saying that a vampire killed a hunter. A caring sister killed her sister's murderer and that is what has really happened.

Witches didn't say anything. They were all processing what April has just said, trying to come up with a proper solution.

- I think we need to hear it from Jack. - Iris decided - June, summon him now.

Having hesitated for a few seconds, June finally took April's hand and all witches joined hands. Unwillingly, June tried to bring Jack with her thoughts. Suddenly, his spirit showed up right in front of her. She took a step back and looked at Jack with anger and disgust.

- What's going on? - Jack asked, having looked around the cemetery and all witches looking back at him. - Why am I here?

- We need you to tell us how you died – Iris asked.

- No, – June interrupted - We need you to confirm our version. A simple yes or no will do. Jack, did you follow me home and stabbed me to death while you tried to kill my vampire sister?

Jack looked at June. He was sad and scared and his voice was shaking.

- Yes – he replied quietly staring at his feet with shame.

- Did my sister kill you when she saw you standing with a knife over my body?

- Yes – he admitted again. It was easy to tell he was full of remorse and deeply regretted what he's done - I'm sorry.

- Isn't it enough? - April asked. - He admitted this is what happened. He's a murderer and he's paying for his sins in afterlife.

- I didn't mean to kill June. - Jack said looking around at the witches - I knew she would try to stop me from killing the vampires so I wanted her out of the way. I didn't know she would die. My plan failed and I'm sorry but it was an accident.

- That accident ended fatally to an innocent human. – Iris said - And now the hunters are angry with the witches and we are on the brink of war. You will have to explain yourself again in front of those who wish to avenge you.

Jack thought for a moment before he responded.

- I want something in return, I want you to bring me back. I can't stay in this hell forever, I don't deserve it.

- Of course you deserve it – April said angrily – We owe you nothing and you are in no position to make any demands.

- It's time for you to leave. - June said.

- No! - Jack yelled terrified. - No, please don't make me come back there, please, June, I'm begging you.

- Leave, now! - June commanded and Jack disappeared.

Everyone was standing still, looking at the spot where Jack's spirit was present just a second before.

- I will tell Lily what's happened – said Vivian - I will explain what Jack did and hopefully she won't do anything stupid.

- Yes, please do that – said Iris - And if it doesn't work, if she still plans on coming after April, please let us know and we will come up with a right plan.

June came back home shortly after one in the morning. She was tired, hungry and cold. She didn't know what to do first: take a nice hot shower, prepare something to eat or just simply go to bed. When she opened the door to her apartment and turned on the lights, she saw Oliver sitting on the couch in her living room. He looked angry.

- What are you doing here?

She took her shoes off and went straight to the kitchen. She decided to eat a sandwich with a chocolate spread – the quickest and easiest meal right after the milk with cereals. Oliver followed her immediately.

- What am I doing here?! I think it's more surprising you were not here. I worried about you.

- I'm sorry Oliver, so much has happened today that I didn't even have time to call you.

June took a big bite and made a gesture asking Oliver to wait a minute as she couldn't talk. Oliver took the milk out of the fridge, poured a glass and handed it to June. She took a sip.

- I think my sisters may be in danger.

- Because of Jack?

June looked at Oliver shocked.

- How do you know that?

Oliver sat down at the kitchen table while June was still standing by the counter devouring her sandwich.

- I came over here right after eleven but you were not here. I called you a few times but you didn't answer.

June took a cell phone out of her back pocket and noticed five missed calls.

- I'm sorry.

- I called April – Oliver continued – and she said that you're busy and would call me later. I decided to track your phone and I found you on the cemetery with all the other witches. I didn't listen from the beginning but I know it's about some Jack.. So tell me, what am I missing here? Why was it so important to have this spiritual seance in the middle of the night?

June put an empty glass aside and sat down in front of Oliver. She looked serious and even sad. Her voice was quiet and shaking.

- Jack killed me, so Hayley killed him in return. Now, some hunters want to find Hayley to avenge Jack and they want to punish April too.

Oliver looked at June without a word so June continued.

- We needed Jack to admit to all this so the witches knew what has really happened the night he died. We don't want anyone to come to Aspen looking for revenge.

- You were killed? Why haven't you told me? - Oliver couldn't sound any more surprised – I knew you died and went to heaven but I thought it was an accident. You've never mentioned you were murdered.

- You didn't need to know that and I didn't want to talk about that with anyone.

- Can we talk about this now?

- Oliver, it was a really long day and I am very tired. Can we talk about this some other time?

- Of course, I'm glad you're OK June. Do you want me to stay?

- Not tonight, you can go back home. I need a good night sleep.

June got up and started walking to her bedroom. She leaned on the door when she reached the room and looked at Oliver. Her eyes were red and her face was pale from the lack of sleep.

- Thank you for caring, Oliver. It means a lot.

Oliver smiled, winked and disappeared living June all alone.

He teleported straight to Hayley's front door, the light in the bedroom was still on. He didn't consider showing up in the middle of the night inappropriate as he knew Hayley and Liam usually didn't sleep much. He texted Hayley instead of knocking as he didn't want Lexi to bark. Hayley went downstairs and let Oliver in and Liam followed with Lexi, calming her down and petting to make sure she wouldn't bark.

- Is everything OK? - Hayley asked. She was surprised to see Oliver visiting them so late at night. He's never done it before.

- Sorry to bother you but I saw the lights on and figured you're not asleep... I wanted to talk to you about Jack Watson.

- Why won't you talk to June?

- Because she doesn't want to talk about what's happened to her but I need to know.

Hayley asked Oliver to sit in the living room. Lexi was following him sniffing his feet and jeans. She knew him and didn't treat him as a stranger anymore but she didn't like to be petted by him for some reason so Oliver never paid much attention to her and just let her be.

- Jack was June's boyfriend, she met him during one of her guitar lessons earlier this year. It turned out he was a vampire hunter who wanted to kill me and Liam.

And so Hayley told Oliver everything about April's predictions and their plan to catch Jack. Even though June was alive and fine, it was still painful for Hayley to go back to that terrible day and talk about her death. She also admitted to killing Jack although she didn't remember any details of doing it. Liam said a few words every now and then to add a few more details that Hayley overlooked. Oliver was sitting and listening carefully. He was angry with Jack and felt sorry for June, she suffered so much that day and he understood why she didn't want to talk about it. He thanked Hayley and Liam for their time and came back straight to June's apartment but she was already asleep. He sat on her bed and gently touched her cheek. She furrowed her brow but didn't wake up. He teleported back to his house in Aspen and went straight to bed. Although it was nearly three in the morning, he couldn't fall asleep. He was thinking about June and how difficult it must have been for her to see Jack again and even talk to him. He felt sorry for her and decided he would do anything he could to protect her from more pain. He didn't know how he could get involved in that conflict with the vampire hunters but he would find out if there was anything he could do to help.

Vivian went to Lily the next day she came back from New Orleans. The other five hunters were still in her house, trying to figure out how to deal with the vampires from Aspen without witches' help. They didn't want to let that go so they were happy to see Vivian back, thinking she has changed her mind and wanted to help them after all.

- I'm glad you're back – Lily welcomed Vivian with a big smile - Come on in. So what made you change your mind?

- I didn't change my mind, I came here to make you change yours.

The smiles disappeared from their faces immediately. They didn't look sad or disappointed but angry.

- What's wrong with you witches? - One of the hunters said - You side with vampires now?!

The hunters didn't scare Vivian. Although there were six of them, she could take them all down with a simple spell within a second. Despite being quite young, Vivian came from a very powerful bloodline.

- Listen to me – she said keeping her voice calm but firm - I spoke to Jack Watson, he died because he killed a human that day. An innocent young girl died because of his poorly prepared plan.

- Did you really talk to Jack or was it some trick?

- I really talked to him. I saw him and heard him speak, it wasn't a trick or illusion, it was real.

- So he wasn't killed by the vampires then, was he?

- Well… He was but Lily this is not just about a vampire killing a hunter, it is about a devastated, heartbroken and terrified sister killing her sister's murderer when he was still there with a knife in his hand. I know it's terrible and I'm sorry it ended this way but be honest with me and tell me which one of you wouldn't do the same if you saw your sibling's murderer standing defenceless right in front of you?

The hunters didn't say anything for a minute. They were looking at one another confused, waiting for someone else to speak first.

- I don't believe this – Lily finally broke the silence – I will not believe this! This was a trick! Jack wouldn't hurt anyone and that human you mentioned, I saw her a few times after that day and she was very much alive.

- That witch sister, the same one who put the protection spell on the house, she brought that girl back to life with her magic. She's very powerful, her ancestor was a very powerful witch too and if you make your move against her or her family, she'll kill you all.

- Is that a threat?! - Lily was livid, her brows were furrowed and her face was red with anger – I am done with witches siding with vampires! You better stay away from this, I really don't want you to get hurt, Vivian. If you don't want to help, at least don't get in my way.

- Be careful Lily and choose your words wisely, you don't want to start a war against witches. That witch from Aspen is now in New Orleans and she has the whole community supporting her. There is six of you on one side and a very powerful army of French Quarter witches on the other. And it's not about vampires anymore, is it? You're angry with the witches because they won't let you kill those vampires. If you want to go after the vampires, that's fine, but if you try to hurt the witch or her human sister, you may regret this.

- Is that supposed to scare us?

- Yes, and if you're not scared yet, you are a fool, Lily.

- I think it's time for you to leave before we do or say anything we may regret.

Vivian looked at the hunters one last time and left the house without saying anything else. Once she was back in her flat, she cast a spell preventing the magical creatures from entering as she was afraid the hunters may do something stupid to scare her. Then she texted Iris: '*be prepared*'.

Oliver was lying in bed with June, with her head on his bare chest. He was stroking her hand, staring at the ring.

- I think there are still a few more secrets between us, don't you think?

June got up and sat on the bed looking at Oliver, puzzled.

- What do you mean? I don't have any secrets.

- What about that ring? I've heard it's magical like your pendant.

- Oh this! - June looked at her ring - It's not a secret, I've just forgotten to tell you about it. How do you know anyway? Who told you about the ring?

- Liam did.

- So you know already so what's the problem?

- I thought there was a reason you haven't told me yet. Very well then, good we had that clarified but there is something I need to tell you. Although I don't have a ring like you, I am still protected by the same spells. I can't get ill or grow old, just like you.

- That's great! How come? Wait! I know! It's the part of the deal you've made with the demons, isn't it?

- You're absolutely right. But you got your ring only recently so it doesn't change much for you... I have been practising my magic for years.

- What are you trying to tell me?

- I'm trying to tell you that I'm forty this year.

- So? Who cares? - June said without hesitation - It doesn't matter how old you are, we get along and we love each other. We're both adults so the age difference is not that important, Liam is nearly two hundred and it doesn't seem to bother Hayley.

- I'm happy you see it that way. - Oliver drew June closer and kissed her - Where else would I find that much understanding? We are a perfect match, don't you think?

- Maybe... Or maybe I'm just young and in love and that makes me stupid and naive.

- Maybe you're right, but it works great for me so I won't complain.

- So you've just admitted I'm stupid and naive?

- No, this is what you said and I just choose not to argue with you.

- Very funny! Go away old man, it's time to go to sleep.

- Old man?!

- Well, if I'm stupid and naive, I'll throw two more adjectives: indecisive and inconstant. How about that? Do you still want to marry me?

- You can throw as many adjectives as you want, I still know you are the only one for me and I will love you forever.

- Be careful with your words, Oliver. Forever is a very long time.

- Not for someone who doesn't count down the time.

Later that day, when June was already asleep, Oliver gently took the ring off her finger and teleported straight to April's apartment.

- You can't just show up like this out of the blue! - she yelled - You'll give me a heart attack!
- I'm sorry April, but don't talk about any heart attacks I know you can't have them.
- What do you want? - She asked still shaking.
Oliver showed April the ring.
- I want you to add something extra to this ring, I need to be sure that as long as June wears this ring she cannot die.
- I can't do that Oliver. I want my sister to be safe just as much as you do but I cannot perform that spell.
- Why not?
- Because there are consequences and you can't make someone immortal without a catch.
- Catch? Like what?
- I don't know… I assume as in this case the spell would be put on an object and not a human, the consequences would be borne by the witch casting the spell and I don't know what may happen to me. I can't risk dying, my family needs me alive.
- Then teach me, show me how to do it. I am a witch after all I can do it, I just need to know the spell.
- Are you really ready for it? Oliver, I don't know what would happen to you… You may die.
- I'm not afraid to die, besides, I don't think it would get that far so I can take the risk.
- Wow, that's very honourable. It looks like you're not all bad after all.
- Thanks. - Oliver replied sarcastically.
April took a piece of paper and wrote a few words down.
- Can you read Latin?
- Of course.
- Good. Here, this is the spell. Try to memorise it, then take the ring into your hands and repeat these words three times. Do you want to do this now here? You know… In case something happened to you.
Oliver sat down and looked at the words.

- Take my ring too. - April said – Let's kill two birds with one stone.

She took her ring off her finger and handed it to Oliver. He squeezed both rings in his hand and said the spell out loud three times like April said: *'Anulum latorem a morte et vulneribus defende.'* He opened his hand and looked at the rings but nothing changed.

- Do you think it's done? - he asked looking at April.

- I don't know. Can't you tell?

- How can I tell?

- Did you feel something? Anything?

- I don't think so… I mean… All my spells always have immediate visual effects.

- Right… And how are you feeling? Everything's OK?

Oliver nodded. April put the ring on her finger then she went to the kitchen and came back with the knife.

- There is only one way to find out.

She cut her palm with the knife. The wound was deep and started to bleed immediately but then, it started to heal and it was completely gone within a few seconds, leaving only a few blood drops on the floor.

- I think it worked. - April said with a smile.

They stared at April's hand which was covered in blood only a moment ago.

- Great, thank you April for your help. I've cast a spell to help someone for a change. I think I could get used to it.

April got her notebook out and handed it to Oliver.

- Take it, these are all the spells I considered useful and wanted to keep handy.

- Won't you need it?

- I know them all by heart now so it's all yours. Maybe you'll find something for yourself in there.

Oliver thanked April for her help and teleported back to June's bedroom. She was awake, sitting in her bed and texting.

- Where have you been? - she asked. - I woke up and you were not here so I wanted to text you to see if you're coming back.

- I went to see April, she helped me upgrade your ring. We have put some extra spell on it.

- Really? What is it?

June took her ring back and put it on her finger.

- As long as you wear it, you won't die.

- What do you mean I won't die? Am I immortal now?

- As long as you wear the ring yes, nobody can kill you.

- I thought April couldn't cast spells like that.

- I did it.

- You cast that spell? I thought you could only do black magic.

- I can do magic in general I just don't know any spells, but April gave me her spell book so soon enough I should be able to do something more.

- That's great, thank you Oliver, it was very thoughtful. I think now I can accept the fact you're a witch, it came in handy.

- You see? And you wanted a regular human. How stupid of you.

When June woke up in the morning, she sat in her bed for five minutes and just stared at Oliver as she couldn't believe her own eyes. It was him but he looked different, older. There were a few grey hairs on his head and a few wrinkles in the corners of his eyes. He was clearly not twenty anymore.

- Good morning Love.

Oliver woke up feeling June's gaze.

- There's something wrong with you.

- What do you mean?

June got up and handed a small pocket mirror to Oliver. He looked at his reflection and stormed out of the bed straight to the hall to look into a much bigger mirror hanging on the wall.

- How's that possible? - he asked himself out loud.

He looked at his reflection for one more minute, touching his face and hair. He couldn't believe it was truly him and he wasn't just dreaming.

- April was right – he said, slowly walking back to the bedroom – Those spells do have consequences.

- So you aged so much over night because you cast that spell yesterday?

- I think so. There is no other explanation, it seems that all this power that kept me young and healthy all these years has disappeared.

- Does it mean you will grow old from now on?

- No, I think it was a one-time quid pro quo.

- Don't worry Oliver – June said with a gentle smile – You still have that boyish and charming James Dean look that I love so much.

Oliver smiled and lied down next to June.

- I'm glad you think that. I thought I would always look young so I don't think I will accept this new look so easily. I think I should go to the hospital and do some blood tests to make sure I'm not sick or something. Hard to say what to expect.

- I'm sorry it happened to you, Oliver.

- Don't worry, I did this for you and I would do it again if needed. As long as you're safe nothing else matters. By the way, April is safe too, I put the spell on both rings.

- That's great! Although I can't believe she asked you to do it knowing there might be some catastrophic consequences. But I'm glad she's safe, I appreciate your sacrifice, Oliver. I think you must really love me then.

- You have no idea.

Chapter 10

Hayley and Liam got up at six as usual and went out for their morning walk with Lexi. It was a part of their daily routine. Hayley made that promise to herself when she decided to have a dog that no matter what the weather would be or how busy she would be, she would take her dog for a long walk every morning and every evening. When she was human, the morning walks were between eight and nine, but since she's been a vampire, she moved that to six o'clock. She liked the fact that the streets were still quite empty so early in the morning and there were not that many sounds and smells to distract her, especially on a cold and foggy early October morning.

They left the house and noticed six ravens sitting on the tree across the street. It seemed unusual as they have never seen so many ravens around here. In fact, they couldn't recall seeing any ravens at all. Hayley took Liam's hand and started to walk, nervously looking back over her shoulder every few steps.

- Don't worry Hayley – Liam whispered – It's just birds.

But when they came back an hour later, the birds were still there, they haven't moved an inch. Hayley quickly locked the door and drew the curtains.

- This isn't normal, Liam – she said walking nervously around the kitchen - It's them, it's the hunters, they came after us.

Liam pulled back the curtains and looked at the tree. The birds were still there, sitting and waiting without a single sound.

- You might be right Hayley, it doesn't look normal. I don't remember seeing ravens around here before… And yet… If these really are the hunters, why wouldn't they pick up something less obvious and less noticeable? Why not a fly or a sparrow? Why ravens?

- I think they want us to know. Maybe they want us to be scared. I'll call April and let her know.

- Don't worry Hayley, we're safe here, they can't come in even if you left the door wide open, your sister made sure of that.

April flew to Aspen later that day. After her brief conversation with Hayley over the phone, she decided to come over and see for herself. She got off the taxi in front of Hayley's house and looked at the tree. The birds were still there, watching the house. April reached both her hands out and took a deep breath but before she even said the first word of the spell, all birds started flying away in panic. Hayley opened the door.

- What have you done? - she asked looking at an empty tree.

April got inside the house and locked the door.

- Nothing, I was about to do the spell to check if these birds were in any way magical when they all started to fly away. I think it was enough to prove they were real hunters.

- They saw a powerful witch and freaked out – Liam joined the girls in the kitchen. - Hi April, good to see you again.

- We need to start seeing each other under different circumstances. Every time I'm here, something is wrong and someone's in danger.

Hayley brewed some tea and handed the cup to April.

- Are you hungry?

- No, I'm fine. I ate when I waited for my connecting fight in Houston. I wish I could teleport like Oliver. Travelling would be so much easier that way.

April took a sip of her Earl Grey and looked at Hayley and Liam who impatiently waited for her to say what she thought.

- I don't know what these hunters have planned but there is something going on that I haven't told you about. Apparently, some hunters from Boston want to avenge Jack. They are sure one of you killed him and they want revenge. However, they need a witch to get inside your house, but instead of helping them, that witch came to New Orleans with a warning. Although the French Quarter witches don't like vampires and never truly sided with any before, they don't want to see you get hurt. After all, you are my family. Moreover, they know what happened to June and they are angry with Jack for killing a human. Now, the hunters have a bone to pick with the witches as they accuse them of siding with vampires against them. I don't know what direction it would go and how it's going to end. Obviously, the hunters came here but I don't know whether they are here only to watch you to make sure you really are different… Or they are here waiting for a good moment to attack. You need to be careful now more than ever. Do your shopping online, let Lexi into the garden instead of taking her for a walk, don't leave this house. You are safe here.

- For how long? And what if they found a witch willing to help them? - Hayley asked with a note of concern in her voice - Would they be able to get inside?

April looked at them both without a word. Her face was serious.

- Yes. - she eventually said.

Hayley got up panicking, her hands were shaking.

- We can't stay here.

- Don't worry Hayley, they won't find a witch…

- How can you be so sure, April? Do you know all the witches? Maybe there is one who hates vampires so much that she would be willing to help those hunters? It's not about one Jack anymore, you saw for yourself, there are six of them out there! We won't stand a chance.

Hayley started to cry feeling helpless.

- Come to New Orleans with me, we can protect you there, the streets are filled with magic, there are witches on every corner.

- Will they welcome us with their open arms? I know they let the vampires come and go through their city but would they be OK if we stuck around for a few days or weeks?

- I have a better idea – Liam interrupted - Let's go to Europe, far away from here. They won't find us there.

- They can easily follow you to the airport and get on the plane unnoticed. You can't run from them like that, you need to hide.

- But we can teleport and they don't know about it. How could they possibly know where we were if we just disappeared?

- That may work, actually. It's a very good plan, Liam. Pack your bags, I'll call Oliver.

Thirty minutes later Hayley and Liam had their suitcases ready. As there would be no official border-crossing, they could take a few bags of blood in their baggage.

- So, have you decided where you want to go? - Oliver asked.

They were so focused on getting out of there that they didn't even notice Oliver's new look. Liam looked at Hayley clearly happy for her to decide. Hayley thought for a moment and then replied with a smile:

- Rome.

Although it was nearly ten o'clock in the evening in Aspen, Hayley and Liam showed up in front of Palazzo Dama at six o'clock in the morning the next day. It was nine degrees Celsius and the sun wouldn't be up for at least another hour. It was a nice and classy two-storey five-star hotel. A lady in the reception was exceptionally polite and booked a room with no check-out date. Liam left his credit card, giving the receptionist one of his charming smiles and the girl blushed, gazing at Hayley with embarrassment. They climbed the set of dark brown stairs to get to their room on the first floor. Although the walls and the floor were painted in dark colours like the stairs, the lobby was full of light. Chandeliers above their heads looked as if made of crystals. The walls were covered in paintings, mostly portraits. The hotel had its spirit and looked like no other. Liam opened the door to their room. It was bright and specious, having all different shades of beige and brown. A warm yellow light from the lamps gave that room a homely look. They unpacked their bags and ordered some breakfast. Hayley went to the bathroom which was also white and beige. There was a large walk-in shower that caught her attention.

- Liam…
- Yes?
- Would you like to take a shower?
- Why? Do you think I should?
Liam showed up in the open doors.
- Look at that shower, I thought we could save some water and get in there together.
- Sounds like an excellent plan, Hayley. Let's save the planet. - He said with a smile and locked the door.

As Hayley and Liam had fun in Italy, April and Oliver stayed in their house in Aspen, trying to figure out what to do next.

- I will lock all the windows and doors and make sure the curtains are drawn everywhere. - April said - Not quite sure what to do with Lexi… Can you teleport a dog?

- Sure. Although she doesn't like me very much so I think you would be the one to take her.

- That's fine, I will take her. The hunters are probably still watching us. Although they flew away, they probably came back as something less noticeable. If we could just all disappear without walking out that door, they would stay there and watch the house for a while before realising nobody's home.

- Let's do that then. Take care of these curtains now and I will turn the water and the heating off.

April and Oliver did as they said and they were at April's ten minutes later. Lexi was extremely confused, not knowing what has happened. One second April was holding her closely in her home in Aspen and the next second she's in an unknown place that she has never seen before and yet it carried a familiar scent of her 'auntie April'. She started walking around the apartment with her nose down to the floor and her tail wagging intensively.

- Thanks Oliver, much better than a flight.

- I will go now, but please let me know if you need anything. I want to help you with these hunters and if there is anything I can do…

- Of course, I will let you know. You are helping already, you know? Hayley and Liam wouldn't have gotten out of that house without you so thank you. And I'm sorry for what has happened to you. It's easy to tell what the consequences were of that spell you've done the other day. I'm glad you're still alive though. It could've been much worse than just a few grey hairs.

Oliver smiled and disappeared without a trace. April took a deep breath and looked around the room.

- OK Lexi, you can sleep with me if you want. Tomorrow, I will buy you some dog food. I hope you'll like it here but please behave. I don't want anything damaged, understood? You are a smart dog so I'm sure you know what I'm talking about.

April went straight to bed without even taking a shower or having anything to eat. She was tired and decided that going to sleep would be better than any spell she knew. She squeezed between the wall and Lexi which decided to take the bigger half of April's double bed. She put her arm around the dog, cuddling her face into the soft warm fur and drifted away.

Lily flew around Hayley's house trying to see inside but all curtains were drawn and she saw nothing. Her friends were trying to penetrate the house as the smallest spider or midge but there was no way in.

They observed the house for two days non-stop and saw nobody coming out and yet, the house seemed empty. Finally, the hunters flew away in different shapes and forms and turned into their human form when they were outside the city, deep in the forest.

- I don't know how they did it but they are not inside – Lily said to the others - It's impossible they are still in there sitting quietly, not using any light. And what about the dog? They didn't let it out for hours, it didn't bark even once.

- Maybe that witch can teleport? - said someone from the crowd - Or make people invisible?

- Maybe… But if she can teleport, why did she arrive in taxi the other day? It doesn't make sense. Nothing makes sense!

Lily sat on the fallen tree confused and angry. One of the hunters sat right next to her.

- Maybe we should give up? Maybe these vampires really are different and we could just let them be? They don't hunt people, they seem to have a normal life with jobs and that dog…

- Are you insane? - Lily got up nervously - They are vampires and you are designed to hunt them down and kill. All of them, with no exceptions! I don't care what they eat. They killed my friend, one of our own, and we can't let them get away with it.

- But you clearly see it's impossible to fight them. They have a witch on their side, a whole coven of witches, as a matter of fact. We saw them coming in and they have never come out and yet somehow they are not there. They can be anywhere! How do you plan on finding them? In order to defeat them, you need magic but even your friend Vivian doesn't want to help. We are on our own and we can't win. I'm sorry Lily but I don't think there is anything we can do. I don't want to start a war that we cannot possibly win.

Lily didn't say anything. Nobody did.

- I'll go home now – the girl continued - there is no point to linger here.

She turned into a wild goose and flew away. Hunters looked at one another and slowly started leaving one by one until Lily was all alone. She sat down again and cried, feeling more helpless than ever before.

- What have you done, Jack? - she said out loud - You got me into this mess so please help me finish it.

Jack sat next to Lily but she couldn't see him. He wanted to console her but there was nothing he could do and seeing her covered in tears was breaking his heart. Now, he regretted asking Lily for help. He should've never asked her to go with him to Aspen. He should've never gone after those vampires. He should've listened to Hayley and left the city when he still had a chance. He regretted every decision he has made that led him to his death.

- I'm sorry Lily. - he said although she couldn't hear him – I'm sorry for everything I've done.

June got to the place where she worked, locked the door behind her and made sure the sign 'closed' was still hanging on the door. Having spoken to April earlier that morning she decided to talk to Jack although she didn't want to, but they needed his help. She took a deep breath to calm down.

- OK, Jack – she said out loud – We need to talk.

Jack appeared a few seconds later.

- June…

- Don't talk to me! - she interrupted aggressively – I will be the one talking and you listen.

Jack nodded without a word.

- We have a problem. Because of you, there is a group of hunters who want to hurt my sister for killing you. You know why you died and you know it was your fault. We never planned on killing you, we just wanted to trap you inside my house so April could put a spell on you preventing you from turning into an animal, that's all that we have planned, nobody wanted you to die… So, I need you to talk to Lily who clearly seems to be the leader of this rebellion and convince her to drop it, to stop hunting Hayley. She needs to accept the fact that you're gone and move on with her life, away from Aspen.

Jack was just looking at June not saying a word.

- You can say something now.

- June, I'm sorry for what I've done. If I could turn back time I would but how can I ask Lily not to avenge me? Hayley avenged you a few seconds after I hurt you. If I had killed you and managed to escape that day, do you really think she would have given up? No, she would've searched the whole world inch by inch trying to get me. I didn't have to die that night, you have no idea what I am going through, I have no moment of peace…

- Stop it! I don't want to hear it. Are you going to help or not?

- Bring me back.

- What?! Are you insane?

- Bring me back and I promise these hunters will leave your sister alone. She'll be safe.

- No, I can't do it.

- Then you're on your own. I won't help you otherwise.

June thought for a moment, getting angrier with Jack.

- You stood against my family once and you see how it ended for you and it was only a few of us. Now, there is a whole coven of New Orleans' witches ready to protect my sister and they will not back down. If you don't do anything and Lily makes her move against us, she will die along with all the other hunters supporting her. We will kill every single one of them. Mark my words.

Jack looked at June with his eyes wide open. He knew she was serious. She didn't just try to scare him, it was a real threat and she would stop at nothing until she's sure her family was safe again.

- I need to think about it.

- There is no time for that! Lily and a few other hunters have been watching Hayley's house for hours now. They have already started whatever they'd planned and we cannot let them go any further.

- Why can't you just bring me back, June? You said yourself you didn't want me dead.

- Because I hate you! You killed me Jack! How can I forgive you something like this?!

Jack didn't respond to that. He couldn't find any right words that would change June's feelings.

- Never mind – she said - I'll figure something out – she took a step closer and looked Jack right in the eye - And I can promise you that all your friends will die. I will stop at nothing and you will regret not helping me… Now go!

Jack disappeared. June unlocked the door and changed the sign to 'open'. She made herself a cup of camomile tea to soothe her troubled mind and waited patiently for her clients to show up.

Hayley and Liam left the hotel shortly after nine o'clock in the morning. They had a very nice breakfast and now was time for sightseeing. It was cloudy and quite cold and the forecast predicted rain so they decided to take a hop-on bus and reduce walking to minimum. They went to Passeggiata del Pincio which was a walking distance from the hotel. The square was completely empty as obviously October morning was not the most desired time for sightseeing Rome. Their first bus stop was at Ludovisi so they needed extra fifteen-minute walk to get there. Once they've got to the bus stop, they were immediately surrounded by the salesmen yelling *'umbrellas'*, *'ponchos'* and *'selfie sticks'* from all directions. They thought it would be rude not to buy anything so they spent a few euros on an umbrella which they would need sooner or later anyway.

The weather was terrible throughout the whole day. Once it's started to rain around noon, it kept raining till the evening with only a few short breaks. Hayley and Liam spent the whole day on the bus trying to avoid walking as much as possible. They went to Pizza in Trevi – one of the best pizzerias in Rome, situated only twenty-five-minute walk from the hotel. It was open till midnight which was very convenient. Having eaten one of the best pizzas ever, they decided to take a walk back to the hotel. It was even colder now but at least it wasn't raining anymore. The streets were quiet and empty which was a huge relief to their vampire ears. Suddenly, someone behind them said 'hi' and they turned around. It was a man in his late thirties, not particularly attractive, though well-dressed and smiling from ear to ear. Liam quickly realised it was a vampire but Hayley had no clue.

- I watched you for a while – he continued – Back there in the restaurant and I thought maybe you'd like to join me tonight. It's always more fun with a good company.

- Join for what? - Hayley asked.

- I'm on my way to the night club. It's always very crowded and loud and there is plenty of food around. People are so drunk that they don't even know what's going on and who sits next to them. You can do whatever you want and nobody will know or care. Apart from a few flashing lights, it's quite dark inside. So, what do you say? Interested in a little adventure?

Liam knew exactly what that man had in mind - he wanted to hunt but Hayley still had no idea.

- Sounds good, what do you think, Liam? We checked Cuban night out, let's see what the Italian one looks like.

- I think we will pass – Liam said – Maybe some other time.

- Why? - Hayley continued – I want to go.

- Come on – the guy said smiling – She wants to go.

Very unwillingly but Liam agreed to go. There was no way he would let Hayley go alone and he didn't feel like arguing in front of a stranger right in the middle of the street.

- What's your name? - asked Hayley as they started walking along the street.

- Romeo.

- This can't be your real name.

- But it is. - he added smiling.

The night club was near so they didn't need to walk for too long. There was no name showing anywhere on the building. The door was large, heavy and black and there was no security outside. They went downstairs to a large room full of people. The music was extremely loud and the lights were flashing aggressively. Romeo led them to a table where five girls were sitting with their heads either on the table or at the back of the seat. Their eyes were only half-closed but they seemed completely unconscious. Romeo sat next to a young girl wearing a paper crown and a t-shirt saying '*bride-to-be*' and he put his arm around her.

- This one is mine.

Romeo winked to Hayley and smiled. In that moment, she noticed his black eyes and teeth. He turned his head towards the bride-to-be and bit her neck. The girl didn't even react, she was far too drunk and disconnected from reality. Hayley looked at Liam shocked but he didn't look surprised.

- You knew! - Hayley whispered to Liam – Why didn't you tell me?

- How and when was I supposed to do it? He was listening.

Hayley was looking at Romeo embracing his new 'Juliet' and slowly taking her life. She was sad and felt sorry for the girl but at the same time she envied him that he could enjoy his vampire life and not care. She could smell the blood from where she was standing and she wanted it. Liam noticed Hayley was looking at the girl as if she was hypnotised, she didn't even blink. He pulled her by the hand and got her out of the club.

- Hayley, what the hell are you doing?

She looked at him confused.

- I… I was thinking… Maybe I could try it?

- You can't be serious!

- I don't mean to kill anyone, I just want to try it.

- I can't let you do this.

- Why not? Did you see those girls? They won't feel a thing.

- But you will and it will haunt you. You have no idea what the fresh warm blood tastes like, but once you knew it, you would never be happy with the cold blood bags you store in your fridge. Trust me, Hayley.

- But what if...

- Let me put it this way, it's like... All your life you've had old dry bread and now you have a fresh warm bread roll, straight from the oven and it's delicious. How eager would you be to go back to the old bread? It took me decades to get used to this way of living but even after so many years, I can still remember the taste. If you had bitten one of those girls, it would've made you very happy for those few minutes but then you'd be miserable. It's like a drug, you always want more. You would regret it, I'm sure of it.

Hayley was looking at the closed black door. She could still clearly hear all those people inside, she could even smell blood somewhere among the smoke, alcohol, perfumes and sweat. But how could she tell Liam he was wrong? How could she know that? He's been a vampire for nearly two hundred years and he had an enormous baggage of experience and knowledge. She sighed loudly, turned around and started walking away from the club.

- Let's go back to the hotel, this is not the right place for us.

Liam took her by the hand and smiled.

- You did the right thing today, Hayley. I'm proud of you, I know it must have been hard.

- I trust you Liam and if you say it would have been a mistake I know you're right. I feel sorry for that girl back there. She was getting ready for a new chapter of her life and now she's dying in some cheap night club, surrounded by strangers. That's very sad.

- I know. You can only make sure you are not a monster like Romeo and you don't bring suffering and death to anyone.

They kept walking slowly back to the hotel in silence. The streets were still empty and quiet. A few taxis passed them by but apart from that, there was nobody around.

- Completely different from New Orleans – Liam said. - I didn't expect Rome to sleep at night.

- Me neither but I like it this way.

- So do I.

- Liam, I was thinking… Maybe we should send some vampire hunters here so they can cleanse this beautiful city of all the Romeos.

- Don't worry Hayley, I bet they are already here. They will find him sooner or later.

- I hope you're right.

The next day in Rome was completely different to the previous one. The sun was shining on the perfectly blue sky and the temperature was pleasantly higher. Hayley and Liam decided to have a nice walk around the city, enjoying Italian food and ice creams. They walked through the alleys, away from the crowds, exploring more peaceful parts of Rome. They spent the whole day out, visiting different cafes, restaurants, pubs, bars and night clubs. It was already after midnight when they were walking back to their hotel. The streets were empty just like the night before and the city was quiet. Suddenly, a pair of large black wolves appeared out of thin air a few meters in front of them. Their gaze was cold and empty and they were clearly ready to attack having their heads low and their teeth bare. Hayley was staring into their yellow hollow eyes knowing it was the end.

- Run – Liam whispered - I'll stall them.

- I won't leave you.

Before any of them made their first move, Oliver and June appeared right between the couple and the wolves. Seeing what was going on, Oliver put his hand in front of him and a circle of fire appeared around them separating them from the wolves. The hunters looked at them confused but didn't come any closer as the flames were too high. Oliver reached his other hand out towards the others and they all teleported back to the hotel, leaving the hunters disoriented and shocked. Hayley breathed a sigh of relief and threw her arms around Liam's neck, bursting into tears.

- I'm sorry to interrupt you guys – said Oliver - But it's time for you to leave the city. Those wolves will be looking for you.

- Come on Oliver – said June – nobody will find them here any time soon. We'll come back later. Let's give them a moment alone.

Oliver and June disappeared, leaving Hayley and Liam alone in their hotel room. Hayley took a step back, letting Liam go and wiped the tears from her face.

- I really thought we were going to die there.

- Me too – Liam said brushing Hayley's hair off her face - But I didn't worry about me, I lived more than enough and I am not afraid to die. But I couldn't stand a thought of you getting hurt.

Hayley sat on the bed and hid her head in her hands in despair.

- I can't do this anymore, Liam. - her voice was shaking and her heartbeat was incredibly fast - I fear death even more now than I did when I was still human. I can't sit at home and wait for some witch to let those hunters inside my house but I can't keep running and hiding for the rest of my life either. I don't want to live like this. There must be something that can be done to protect us, I won't believe that all those powerful witches are so powerless in this matter. There must me some spell, something, anything...

- Let's go to New Orleans. April was right, we will be safe there. The city is filled with magic and the French Quarter witches are eager to help.

Hayley looked at Liam feeling completely hopeless. Her eyes were red and full of tears.

- Look at me Liam. Do I look like a powerful fearless and invincible magical creature to you? I start to believe that becoming a vampire was the worst thing that has happened to me. I wish I could just wake up and realise it was all just a dream, just like last time.

- I'm sorry Hayley. I promised you a limitless life full of adventures and instead…

- It's not your fault Liam, don't blame yourself. I'm glad I have you and I have never regretted being with you. Meeting you was the best thing that happened to me and whatever happens next won't change the way I feel about you. I love you, very much.

She got up and cuddled up to him again.

- I love you too.

Oliver and June appeared again in their room.

- Thank you for saving us – Hayley said – How did you know where we were?

- We located your phones when we realised you were not in your room. It looked like we showed up right in time. Pack your bags, you can't stay here much longer.

- Oliver, could you take us to New Orleans? We'll stay there for a while.

- Sure. It's just six o'clock in the afternoon there so there is still time to find you a nice room before the nightfall.

Hayley and Liam packed their bags quickly and checked out. Ten seconds later, they were standing in June's apartment in New Orleans.

- Call April – Hayley said to June – We need to discuss what to do next.

Hayley and Liam reserved their room in Omni Hotel, walking distance from June's and April's apartments. Once they've received the keys, April cast the protection spell to make sure nobody could get inside uninvited. When Liam went out with Oliver to enjoy jazz and bourbon, the girls stayed in the hotel. Neither June nor Hayley wanted to be out after sunset so they decided to have their girls night in the hotel. They were sitting in one of the luxury suits on the top floor. It was not just a room but the whole apartment with the balcony, very elegant and expensive. Liam wanted Hayley to enjoy her stay in New Orleans and hoped she would feel better surrounded by wealth and splendour, able to forget about the terrible world outside. The girls sat comfortably on large sofas, drinking their tequilas. The coffee table was covered with snacks and sweets. Vanilla ice creams were slowly melting down, completely forgotten. Girls wanted to enjoy being together again but the circumstances were making them sad and uneasy.

- So – Hayley broke the silence – We don't have a plan, do we?

- Nope – June sounded completely hopeless.

- There must be something – April was not giving up – I'm a witch! I brought my dead sister back to life, I am very powerful and I bet there are even more powerful witches out there and I won't believe that there is nothing that can be done.

- OK… Let's say everything is possible. - Hayley started thinking out loud - What would you do, April? What spell would you cast?

- I would get rid of all vampire hunters, I would dis-activate the spell.

- We can't do that, these hunters are needed to protect people. I met a vampire in Rome and he was a beast. I hope these two wolves found him just like they found us. I think witches are right saying that vampires would be completely out of control without hunters around. This is not an option then so what else would you do?

- I would make you resistant to the bite, stronger.

- OK… But I am already a vampire so how much stronger can I really get? You know better than anyone that there are consequences to spells like that so I don't think anyone would like to give it a go and cast the spell, afraid of what may happen to them.

- What if you were invisible? - June asked – Maybe you could wear a ring or something?

- Maybe… April, what do you think? Is it possible?

- Probably, I just need to find a proper spell.

- Great, I'll leave it with you then and now cheers!

The girls clinked their glasses and drank another round of shots.

- What would you do if you were truly invisible? - June asked.

- I would finally feel safe.

- Yeah, I know… But what would you do? I mean… How would you use it?

- I don't know… Maybe I would mess with people by moving their stuff around, making them believe that their houses are haunted or something.

- That's cool. What about you April?

- Hm… Interesting question… I don't know, nothing comes to my head… What would you do June?

- I would rob a bank.

- What?!

- Oh come on, like you didn't think about it. Imagine you can go wherever you want unnoticed and you can get out of there and not get caught. Of course I would go for the money. I would bring back home whatever I want and no one would know… I really hope you'll find that spell April, I could really use some money.

- If I do, I won't cast it for you, June. I don't want you to become some criminal.

- Would you take my dreams away just like that? - June made a sad face that made April laugh.

- Dear sister, you are worse than I thought. I'm afraid to think what you're truly capable of under right circumstances.

- Dear sister, I'm a devil in disguise

When Liam and Oliver came back to the hotel in the morning, they found June and April sleeping on one sofa and Hayley sitting on the floor with her head against the same sofa, also asleep. That night the girls discovered that despite being a vampire or a witch, the alcohol had exactly the same impact on them as on humans.

- I'm not sure I even want to know what has happened here last night – Oliver said looking around the room.

Tequila bottles were lying on the floor empty, the ice creams were completely melted, the crisps were here and there on the carpet and the coffee table was covered with empty candy wrappers.

- Definitely too much alcohol and far too much sugar – Liam said with a smile.

He approached Hayley and crouched down in front of her. He touched her hand and she woke up.

- Good morning.

Hayley looked at Liam and Oliver and got up off the floor. She had a look around the room with her eyes half-open.

- Did you have a good time? - Oliver asked smiling. It was amusing to see Hayley in that condition.

- To be honest, I don't even remember much. - She looked at her sisters huddled together on the sofa. - Are they alive?

- I hope so – Oliver replied and approached the girls. - Wakey wakey!

They woke up and tried to get into a sitting position but they were blocking one another so it took them longer than expected to finally sit.

- What time is it? - April said rubbing her eyes and yawning.

- It's seven in the morning. How are you feeling?

June looked at Oliver with just one eye as the other one was still closed.

- I feel as if something ate me and then spat back up.

- Me too – April said.

- What have you done last night?

- That's a very good question, Liam. I wish I knew…

He looked at Hayley looking for some answers.

- Don't look at me – she said – I don't remember much. I thought I could hold my drink but I clearly can't… I need to take a shower.

- I need some water – June got up and slowly walked to the kitchen.

- I think I'm going to be sick – April got up and ran to the toilet.

Oliver and Liam were standing in the middle of the living room looking at each other completely puzzled.

- Looks like a hell of a party to me – Oliver said laughing.

- Yeah, I wish I've been here.

- Yeah, me too. I think we should never leave them alone again.

- Definitely. We can't miss another party like that. - Liam said smiling and called the hotel reception asking for a room service.

Chapter 11

Someone has knocked on the door. Lily was surprised as she didn't expect any guests, especially so close to midnight. She put her robe on and opened the door. It was a teenage girl, dressed all in black, wearing heavy make-up and having her lower lip pierced. Her black fringe was slightly covering her even darker eyes. Lily knew the girl was a witch, she could sense it.

- What do you want? - Lily said angrily, assuming the witch came over looking for a fight.

- I heard you needed a witch so I'm here to help you.

Lily didn't look angry anymore but genuinely surprised.

- OK… Come in. I'm Lily.

- Emma.

The girls shook their hands and Lily led her guest to the kitchen. She put the kettle on and brewed some tea, gazing at her guest interested and intrigued.

- Why do you want to help? - Lily asked and although she tried to sound friendly, there was still a hint of suspicion in her voice.

Emma was staring at her hands and nervously rotating the mug on the table surface.

- My father died two years ago. He was killed by a vampire when he was going back from work in the middle of the night. He was three minutes away from home, when that happened. - Emma's voice was shaking but she didn't cry - He wasn't a witch so he was completely defenceless. Since then, I have been trying to kill as many vampires as possible. I wander around at night, waiting for someone to attack me. Vampires don't scare me, I have enough power

181

to protect myself. You can imagine my surprise when I found out you asked witches for help and they refused. - she snorted – So I decided I will step forward and help you out. I won't stand a thought of some vampires walking around completely untouchable. I can't believe the witches are actually protecting them with the spells. It's outrageous!

- Apparently, these vampires are different.

- There is no such thing as a good vampire! - Emma was looking Lily right in the eye livid – They should die! All of them! They shouldn't have been created in the first place.

- This is exactly what I think but the witches didn't want to listen to me. I can't believe that they protect these vampires knowing that they killed my friend. I wanted to do something but nobody's on my side. I was on my own.

- Not anymore, I'll help you. With your teeth and claws and my magic we can defeat them. If we take them by surprise, one by one, they won't stand a chance.

- I like that – Lily smiled. - So what's the plan my little witch?

Next day in the morning Emma and Lily packed lightly and boarded their plane to Aspen. They decided to act quickly. The plan was simple, Emma would break the protection spell and Lily would attack. They needed to move fast and without hesitation. They could easily protect each other and no vampire would stand a chance against their duo so they had nothing to worry about.

As the house in Aspen appeared to be abandoned, they decided to look for vampires in New Orleans. It was easy for Emma to locate vampires in the city. They killed three random ones before they eventually located Hayley in June's apartment. It was nearly thee in the morning but the lights were still on. Emma put her palms against the door.

- This is a very strong spell – she whispered - A combination of four different spells to be exact so it may take me a bit of time to break it.

- Take your time, I've waited long for this and a few more minutes or hours won't matter at this point. I just want this done.

Lily sat on the stairs resting her chin on her left hand and watched Emma doing magic. The witch was standing quietly with her palms against the door. She didn't say the spell out loud afraid that Hayley may hear her whisper. They could clearly hear both sisters inside, the music was playing quietly in the background and the girls were laughing a lot.

An hour later, Emma took a step back and looked at Lily.

- It's done, we can come inside.

Lily turned into a lioness and Emma opened the door for her. They saw Hayley and June sitting in the living room. Their smiles disappeared from their faces the moment they noticed the door was opening. Without hesitation, the hunter jumped towards Hayley, leaving her no time to defend herself. The lioness threw Hayley on the floor with a great force and dove her teeth into her neck, turning the body into ashes nearly instantly.

- No! - June yelled with horror.

She looked at the ashes on the floor and the tears came to her eyes. She directed her gaze full of anger at Emma.

- You will pay for this – she said through clenched teeth.

Emma smiled, snapped her fingers and made June slump to the floor. The hunter turned into her human form and approached June.

- What have you done to her? - she asked Emma, surprised and anxious.

- She was helping vampires so she was just as bad as them.

- Is she dead?!

Lily crouched on the floor and put her fingers on June's neck looking for pulse but felt nothing.

- You didn't have to kill her – she said angrily– She was human! And I'm not here to kill people!

- I plan on killing every member of that devilish family and April is next on my list.

- We can't go after the witch. Vivian was very clear about it, she gave us a green light to kill the vampires but if we go after the witch, the whole community will go after us. Are you strong enough to protect us?

- No, but I don't care. You're either with me or against me Lily so make your choice now.

Lily looked at June. She didn't want her dead, the girl was not a threat and she didn't deserve to die, but there were three more vampires to kill and Lily knew she wouldn't be able to continue that quest on her own. She took a deep breath and looked at the witch.

- Come on, we need to finish what we've started. There is one more vampire in this town.

- April, what are you doing here? It's late. - asked Liam when April showed up in his hotel room in the middle of the night.

- I wanted to talk to Hayley, I called a few times but she didn't answer. Something's wrong – April sounded genuinely concerned.

- She's with June, don't worry, they probably had a few drinks and fell asleep.

Suddenly, April turned around and started to stare at the door. She put her palm gently against it and looked at Liam with panic.

- Someone is trying to get in.

- What are you talking about? Who?

- A witch. But the spell is strong so they won't be able to break it just yet.

- Why would they want to get in? April, what's going on?

- I don't know… I will open the door and check who it is.

- Is it safe?

- I don't know but it's worth trying.

Liam took a few steps back and stood a few meters behind April. Against witches, April's magic would be more useful they Liam's physical strength. When she opened the door, they saw Emma standing right outside with her hands reached out. Lily was standing behind her, leaning against the wall. They both looked at April shocked as they didn't expect to see her there.

- Run! - Emma yelled to Lily.

The hunter ran away as quickly as she could and hid behind the corner where April's magic couldn't reach her. At the same time, April said aloud a single word and Emma immediately passed out. Lily leaned out from around the corner and watched Liam dragging unconscious Emma into the room. The hunter wanted to kill Liam right there on the corridor but she knew April would kill her first if she tried anything. She sighed feeling completely helpless and started to walk towards the elevators. There was nothing she could do in that moment so she decided to leave the hotel, wait and think.

Liam and April waited impatiently for Emma to wake up. She has been unconscious for nearly five minutes now but for them it felt like ages.

- Oh for God's sake! Wake up! - April yelled with frustration.

The witch woke up completely disoriented.

- Who are you?! - April asked with unhidden anger.

Emma didn't say a word. She was tied up to a chair with strings soaked in magic so she couldn't get out. It was clear that she wouldn't talk so April put her hands on Emma's head and cast a spell: '*Ostende mihi quid accidit.*' Ten seconds later, she took a few steps back and sat on the sofa looking completely devastated.

- April what is it? What did you see? - Liam asked panicking.

April didn't answer. She was sitting hunched over with her jaw down and her eyes full of tears. She looked at Liam and burst into tears completely.

- April, talk to me, what happened?

- Your wife is dead – Emma responded with a hint of triumph in her voice.

Liam looked at April again waiting for her to deny it but she didn't say anything and just kept crying. Liam stood there, in the middle of the living room completely paralysed. When he looked at Emma, his eyes turned black and he was livid. April quickly jumped between him and the witch before he made his move.

- Wait! You can't just kill her, at least not yet.

Liam took a deep breath to calm down. April snapped her fingers and Emma lost her consciousness again before she said anything that could make Liam lose control.

- So what's happened April, what exactly did you see? I need to know.

With her voice breaking, April told Liam about Emma's plan and how she broke into June's apartment with Lily.

- Why are you crying April? You can bring them back right?

- Let's go to June's, the witch can wait for us here.

When Liam and April opened the door to June's apartment, they saw Oliver sitting on the floor with June's head on his lap. He was stroking her hair, looking not sad but nervous.

- I don't understand what's happened. She was wearing the ring so how can she be dead?

- The ring! I've completely forgotten about it.

April ran up to June, put her hand or June's forehead and repeated the spell for a few seconds. Suddenly, June woke up struggling to catch her breath. Oliver picked her up and helped her sit on the sofa.

- I died again, didn't I?

- How are you feeling? - Oliver asked holding her hand.

- Why does it keep happening to me?! - She looked at the ashes scattered on the floor and then at April - What are you waiting for? Bring her back!

- I... I don't know how.

- What?!

- I don't even know where she is now. She's a vampire and I don't know where to look for her.

- So... She's dead for real?!

- For now yes, but I will do anything to fix this. I will find her and I will bring her back, I promise you.

- Whatever it takes?

- Whatever it takes.

April brought a clean glass jar from the kitchen, put it on the coffee table and started chanting. Suddenly, the ashes started lifting off the floor and gathering inside the jar.

- Keep an eye on her. - April handed the jar to Liam – She will rise from these ashes like a phoenix.

- Can someone tell me what's happened here? - Oliver asked but nobody wanted to give him any explanation, thinking what to do next.

- That witch! - June yelled – That damn witch! We need to find her!

- She's in my hotel room – Liam said – Unconscious and tied up to a chair with magic.

- I'm going to kill her.

- Get in line.

- Why is she still alive anyway?

- Nobody touches the witch – April said – We may still need her. Plus, if the witches decide to step in, they may want to talk to her. We also need to find the hunter and that witch can help us with that, willingly or not. I will gather the coven.

- And what are we supposed to do in the meantime? - June was frustrated.

- Stay here and wait. I will put another protection spell on this flat so you can be safe here from the hunter. That witch is in Liam's hotel room and I don't want any of you anywhere near her. I need to go now, nobody leaves this place. I have already too much on my plate and I can't worry about you too.

April left the apartment but before she went downstairs, she cast a spell preventing the others from leaving the room. Shortly after she left, June opened the door only to discover that she was unable to step outside.

- I knew it! We're trapped, she doesn't trust us. - June shut the door with anger.

- And she's right to do so – Liam said staring at the jar he was holding gently in his hands. – First thing I wanted to do once she's left was to go to the hotel and see the witch.

- What for? It wouldn't change anything. She'll suffer for what she's done when the time is right but for now, we need her alive.

- Why, exactly? What is it that she can do for us?

- I don't know, but this is what April says and I trust her. Don't worry Liam, we'll get Hayley back.

- How can you be so sure? What if she's really gone?

- Don't say that. I've seen so many magical and unbelievable things that made me think that nothing is impossible anymore. April will find a way to bring her back. I've died twice but somehow I'm still here. Have some faith, Liam, everything is going to be OK.

Liam wanted to believe June but the truth was that the love of his life was gone and his world shuttered into pieces. He looked at the glass jar now standing safely on the shelf and sighed. There was so much he wanted to tell Hayley, so many questions he wanted to ask. Although they haven't been together for very long, he couldn't remember what his vampire life was like without her. There was his happy childhood spent on games and adventures with Isabella. There were his teenage years spent on hunting and training with his father. There were his twenties and early thirties where he had to work hard to provide for his family as father was gone. Then, there was nothing but decades spent in darkness that he successfully erased from his memory. And then, there was Hayley, his bright light, his best friend, his savoir. How could he now come back into the abyss where Hayley was not a part of his life? How could he come back to living an empty meaningless life? It was more than just a broken heart, it was a loss beyond estimation and he didn't know what to do.

- Don't worry Liam – said June seeing Liam deep in thought and clearly concerned - We'll bring her back.

- She became a vampire so she could be stronger and safer, but most of her short vampire existence she spent on worrying and being afraid of death. Yes, we had a few moments of joy but they were brief. This is not what I wanted for her, this is not what I promised her when she decided to turn. I have created a colourful and promising image of her new life by my side but all she got was fear and death. Maybe if she hadn't turned, she would still be alive.

- Don't think it's your fault, Liam. It was her decision and she has never regretted it. She wanted to be with you, live her life with you as equals, she loved you and wanted to be with you at any cost. You can't keep thinking 'what if' Yes, she died but so did I and now I'm back and so will she. April just needs more time to figure this out but I am sure she'll bring Hayley back to life, we just need to be patient. Don't worry Liam, everything will be OK we just have to wait.

April planned the meeting with French Quarter witches for   five in the morning. In the meantime, she went to her apartment and prepared the spell. Once all ingredients have been ready, she lied down on the floor, in the circle she made with the soil and cast the spell to see Leah. They met in the wooden hut as usual.

- I know why you're here, I know what's happened to Hayley, I can feel my connection with her has faded. I'm sorry, April.

- How can I bring her back?

- Nobody has ever resurrected any vampires before.

- Because they had no reason. Vampires are vicious monsters and everyone wants them dead, but it doesn't mean that resurrecting them is impossible, right? Witches will help me, despite their aversion to vampires, they liked Hayley.

- Truth be told, I am not quite sure how to do it. We don't know where she is and whether her spirit really is anywhere. All witches are here, humans are in heaven or hell…

- Jack was a vampire hunter and he was in hell with humans.

- But Jack was more of a human than Hayley. I really don't know where to look for her, April. I don't know if vampires have a spirit that continues its existence in the afterlife.

- I won't accept the fact that she's gone. I brought June back I can bring Hayley back too. I won't leave my sister somewhere all alone. There must be a way!

- I will ask around and do whatever I can, I promise. I'm sorry for your loss, April.

- Don't give up on her, Leah, I know she can be saved, I can feel it. She is somewhere and we'll find a way to bring her back. There must be someone who knows what to do and we'll find them among the living or dead.

The coven gathered at the cemetery five o'clock sharp. All New Orleans witches were present. With her breaking voice and tears running down her cheeks, April told them what's happened. Witches were shocked that Emma sided with the hunters against her own kind and humans. Hayley's death didn't shock them too much but the fact that Emma killed June too and came after April moved them to the bone. She committed treason and needed to be punished.

- We cannot kill her – said Iris – We are more civil than the witches hundreds of years ago, we have rules that we need to follow and we will not punish anyone with death. She will be shunned and her powers will be taken away. After death, she will not join our ancestors in afterlife.

- That's it?! - April was appalled – Is that all you're going to do? She killed my sister!

- But you brought her back to life.

- I'm talking about Hayley!

- Hayley was a vampire and we cannot punish a witch for killing a vampire.

- How can you say that Iris?! She was my sister! You knew her! You all knew her! You talked to her, laughed with her, sang… - April burst into tears - I can't believe I left Aspen and both of my sisters for you. I thought New Orleans was my home but clearly I was wrong. You built a community where I don't belong. You are not my family. But my real family needs my help now and I will not let them down.

She started marching away but before she left the cemetery, she turned around giving Iris a look full of hatred, anger and sorrow.

- You can all go to hell.

April went to the hotel to make sure Emma was still unconscious and tied to the chair. She called Oliver and asked him to teleport everyone to his house outside Aspen. Conveniently, he had a large basement, perfect for their prisoner. April cast the protection spell on the house and another spell to prevent the witches from finding them there. Oliver prepared the guest rooms for his friends and lit a fire in the living room to heat the house. Typical November weather in Aspen was a bit of a shock when they teleported in their clothes proper for Louisiana temperatures.

- I assume your little gathering didn't go so well? - June said, sitting on the couch under a large fluffy blanket, drinking hot ginger tea with honey and cuddling up to Oliver who was emanating warmth.

- We cannot count on the coven. I was wrong about them, I thought they were my family… My friends… But I was mistaken. In a witch community only witches matter and the rest of the world doesn't exist outside their perfect, magical reality… Forget about the witches. You have me and you have Leah and we have each other.

- What did Leah say? Is she going to help?

- She doesn't know what to do yet but she will help.

- So what do we do now?

- I… I don't know.

After a few hours of intensive thinking and going through different books and journals, they still couldn't find anything that would help them bring Hayley back. June went outside for a short walk hoping that cold fresh air would clear her mind. She wanted to be alone, to unleash her emotions - her suppressed anger, sorrow and fear. She went to the woods behind Oliver's house. She was walking ahead for a few more minutes as tears were blurring her path. Then, she fell down to her knees in a soft layer of snow and started to scream. She lived through the death of her parents, her own death – twice and the kidnapping but Hayley's death was above it all. She has never felt such pain before. After Hayley's transition, June was sure her sister would never die, especially with April's incredible powers. She truly wanted to believe that Hayley still could be saved but seeing both April and Liam so scared made her hope cling on by a thread. She thought about the hunter and the witch and that hatred was what she was holding on to now. The witch was untouchable for now, but the hunter was still somewhere out there and she needed to be taken care of, she needed to be punished.

After thirty minutes June came back and joined the others in the living room where they were sitting on the floor surrounded by pages.

- How about killing the hunter? - June said unexpectedly and everyone looked at her surprised - I have an idea.

They decided to use Emma's phone and try to lure Lily to Aspen. They sent a text message 'I escaped and followed them to Aspen. They are in a house outside the city. I'm waiting for you so track my phone and get in here ASAP'

April took the protection spell down and put a different one so Lily could get in but couldn't stay in her animal form inside the house.

- Do you really think it will work? - April said looking at June.

- Definitely, the hunter is quite motivated to get us killed so any chance we can give her, she'll take it. That's what I would do.

Lily was unsure whether the message from Emma was genuine or not but she decided to go to Aspen, nonetheless. She didn't have anything better to do and she had no other plan and going to Aspen sounded like the best option.

She has been outside Oliver's house by the dusk. She couldn't see Emma anywhere and was worried because the witch was not answering her phone. The hunter looked through the windows creeping low on her feet and saw April and Oliver in the living room, feverishly going through some old journals. Then, she saw Liam in the kitchen, sitting at the table all alone, staring at the cup of coffee. He was clearly miles away, totally off guard. *'This is my only shot'* Lily thought. *'I could kill him quickly and leave the house before anyone gets into the kitchen, I can do it without Emma. I don't care about the others, I'm here only for the vampire and he looks like a simple target sitting all alone. Emma will be fine, she can take care of herself. If she wants to kill them all that's not my problem, I don't care.'* Lily had a look around one more time to make sure her plan would work. There were no neighbours, nobody wandering around. She turned into a mosquito and quietly flew through a slightly opened window. Suddenly, unwillingly, she turned back into her human form right in front of Liam. Now, she was standing in the kitchen completely defenceless and powerless, paralysed by shock and fear. Before she managed to make a move, Liam got to her within a blink of an eye and pushed her against the wall. He was standing close, holding her by the neck and looking her deeply in the eye with his black, horrifying, vampire eyes.

- You could've left us alone but you chose to stand against us. The actions you've taken can only lead you to death. You came here looking for a ruthless merciless beast and so here I am, right in front of you. I will never forgive you for what you've done to Hayley. You have taken everything from me and now I will have my revenge.

Liam bit Lily's neck, leaving a terrible wound. Within a few moments, she bled to death in his arms. When her dead body loudly dropped on the floor, April and Oliver ran to the kitchen to see what's happened. They saw Lily lying on the floor by the fridge, with her full of tears eyes still open and her jacket soaked in her blood. Liam was standing over her with his face covered in her blood.

- Get rid of her – he said not even looking at April or Oliver.

He passed them by and went to clean up. His face was full of anger and sorrow and his eyes were still black. He went to the bathroom upstairs, locked the door and looked at his reflection in the mirror. Black eyes, dark veins underneath, lips and chin covered in blood. A few drops fell into the sink.

- What have I done? - he said quietly looking into his own dark eyes staring back at him - Hayley would be so disappointed to see mi like this.

The anger faded away and turned into sorrow. His eyes were blue again, full of tears. He started nervously cleaning his face and hands looking at the red water pouring down the sink. He took a step back, leaned his back against the door and slumped to the floor. He covered his face with his wet hands, resting his elbows on his knees and started to cry.

By midnight, everyone was in their beds. It was a long and tiring day and the events of that day left them all exhausted and broken. Liam was lying on the sofa in the living room, the fire from the fireplace was gently illuminating the room. In silence, the clock on the wall sadly reminded Liam about the time he didn't want anymore. He was looking at the glass jar standing alone on the shelf. Thoughts were running through his head leaving him wide awake and restless.

- If there is anything you need just let me know – said Oliver who appeared suddenly out of nowhere – I want you to feel comfortable here, you may need to stay her for a while.

- Thanks Oliver, I appreciate your help.

- No problem. How are you feeling?

Liam didn't answer so Oliver came closer and sat on another sofa opposite to Liam.

- Go on – he insisted – Talk to me.

Liam sat down and looked at Oliver.

- I feel worse than I felt this morning. I thought about killing that hunter all day and now that she's gone I don't feel any better. I wanted revenge but it didn't release me from the pain. That hunter came after me because she saw a monster in me, a beast, and have I proven her wrong with my act? Maybe all vampires are truly the same, maybe she was right about me. Maybe deep down I am a monster.

- Don't say that, Liam. You killed her because she killed Hayley.

- And she killed Hayley who killed Jack who killed June… There is an endless chain of actions and reactions and if we follow that road we'll get into conclusion that we all are guilty of something and one way or another we all deserve to die. Maybe Iris was right saying that there was a better way to punish someone than death. I shouldn't have killed her. It didn't change anything for me, it didn't change the way I feel… The way I've felt all day. She was a vampire hunter, it was her job to kill vampires, just like yours is to kill bad people and I punished her for it. Who am I now, Oliver? I led a decent life despite what I am and now I killed a young girl although I didn't have to. I am following a path into darkness and I am afraid of who I will be at the end of it. I could have such an amazing future with Hayley by my side, we could live forever but now… Now my future is crumbling before me and I see no happiness, no hope…

Oliver was trying to find right words but nothing he wanted to say would make Liam feel any better.

- I think I am not the best person to advise you here. I know losing Hayley left you broken and you can't think positive right now but the pain will subside eventually and you will find peace. But now is time to grieve and you are not alone, you have April and June who are as heartbroken as you are and they share and understand your pain. I'm not telling you to give up hope and stop trying to bring Hayley back, but I think she deserves a proper funeral and memorial. We're back in Aspen now and this is her home. Talk to April and June and try to organise something tomorrow. Let Hayley be at peace until you've figured out how to bring her back.

Liam nodded without saying anything.

- Now, try to get some sleep, you look tired.

Oliver went back to his bedroom and cuddled up to June.

- How is he? - she whispered.

- Devastated. He needs time to heal just like you and April.

June let a few teardrops sink into the pillow. She missed Hayley very much.

- June… We were all so busy thinking about Hayley and that witch and the hunter that nobody really asked you how you were. So when you died, did you go to heaven like last time? How was it?

June didn't say anything so Oliver sat on the bed and looked at her covered in tears face.

- Talk to me Love.

June sat on the bed as well and wiped the tears. She was looking somewhere far away, trying to put together all things she remembered.

- I don't remember dying. That witch must have done it very quick because one moment I was standing in the living room and the next thing I know I'm in darkness. Then, I saw the meadow like last time and my parents. I managed to talk to them this time as I was dead for longer. Then, like last time, some unseen force pulled me back and I was alive again.

- So it was not such a bad experience after all.

- No, it was not… But I don't want to keep doing this, it makes me feel weird and… - June paused.

- What? What is it?

- I can't talk to my parents anymore, I lost that connection.

- I'm so sorry June. Did you come back with some other gift?

- I don't know. If I had, it's nothing obvious as I haven't discovered anything unusual. I'll miss talking to my parents. I got used to the fact that I could see them whenever I wanted… But I made my peace with their death once so I can do it again. I know now that they are in a happy beautiful place enjoying each other's company and that makes me happy.

- I'm glad you're OK June. When I saw you lying on that floor, for a second I thought you were dead and I panicked. But then I saw the ring on your finger and I knew you would wake up at some point. I can't imagine what Liam is going through. I don't know what I would do without you… June when you were in heaven with your

parents, did you see Hayley too? She died before you so
she should have gotten there first.

- No, she was not there, I didn't see her anywhere. I
don't know where Hayley is and if I hadn't lost my gift I
could try to summon her so we could talk. I thought about
her intensively all day hoping that maybe I would see her
or feel something... Anything... But there's nothing.
Same with my parents, I can't reach anyone on the other
side. Why that bloody witch needed to kill me! I could
help in brining Hayley back and now I can't do anything,
I'm completely useless.

- Don't say that June, we'll figure something out. Now
try to get some sleep, you won't come up with anything if
you're too tired to think.

The next day in the morning, Liam got up at six after a
sleepless night and decided to take Lexi for a walk. It was
still dark outside but it was not snowing anymore. Liam
didn't have any winter jacket so he left the house wearing
only jeans and a t-shirt and although it was freezing
outside, he didn't pay any attention to the weather. He was
walking slowly, pulled ahead by Lexi. He stopped when
she stopped and he walked wherever she wanted to go. He
was not thinking about anything and yet, he was
disconnected from reality, completely unaware of the
surrounding, numb.

After thirty minutes when Lexi stopped again, Liam
realised she led him home. He hesitated for a moment and
then opened the door and walked inside. It was dark and
cold as the heating was off for a while. All windows were
covered and the house was as they left it before their trip
to Rome. Liam unleashed Lexi and turned the lights on.
He put the heating on and looked around. Despite the
biting cold, the house looked cosy and homely and was
full of happy memories. He started walking up the stairs

looking at the photographs hanging on the wall all the way up. The wedding day, Hawaii, Cuba, some Christmas days, some birthdays. He touched each photograph with nostalgia, taking deep slow breaths. He could still hear Hayley's laughter echoing off the walls.

He walked into the bedroom, the bedding was still in a mess. He crawled into the bed and cuddled up to Hayley's pillow as it still smelled like her. In spite of being devastated and heartbroken, he couldn't share any more tears. Lexi jumped on the bed and licked Liam's face. When he moved away wiping his cheek, she lied down with her head on Hayley's pillow.

- You miss her too, don't you? I know you know she's gone, I know you can feel it, you are a smart dog. It looks like it's only you and me now but don't worry, I'll take care of you.

Liam put his arm around the dog and with his face on Hayley's pillow he instantly fell asleep.

His future was now like a broken glass - it used to make sense and mean something but now all he could see was shards, chaotic, meaningless and useless. All he could do now was to leave the shards scattered in front of him as trying to put them back together would only bring more pain, just like trying to pick up pieces of the broken glass would cut his fingers. If he was a human, he would just watch time as it passed by and wait for the death to come. But time meant nothing for an immortal. And although he considered dying once or twice, he still hoped that Hayley could be saved and he didn't want to lose a chance for a happy life by her side only because he was not strong enough to get through the hardest part. He needed to wait, regardless how painful it could be, he needed to stay alive.

When the girls and Oliver woke up later that morning and discovered Liam was not there, they assumed he went home. They teleported there and found him in the bedroom still asleep, completely unaware of their presence. They went downstairs and turn off all the lights that Liam left on earlier. They made themselves some tea and waited patiently for Liam to wake up.

- Yesterday – Oliver started – I suggested Liam that you should take care of Hayley's funeral.

- Hayley's what?! - June yelled – We are still trying to figure out how to bring her back and you want us to give up?!

- I'm not telling you to give up but…

- Oliver's right. - April interrupted - June… I'm sorry to admit this out loud but Hayley is gone. I talked to Leah last night and we consulted other ancestors too and nobody knows what we can do. Nobody has ever brought a vampire back from the dead and nobody knows how to do it. Nobody knows where her spirit can be or if she even has one. I feel terrible saying this but… It's impossible, June.

Suddenly, they saw Liam standing in the doorway. He didn't look angry or sad but completely emotionless as if he waited for a passport photo to be taken.

- There will be no funeral – he said quietly – Putting Hayley in rest would mean that we are letting her go but we clearly are not. I understand, at this moment, there is no way to bring her back but I will not stop hoping. Her ashes will wait here in her home for April to come back with the right spell. I will not accept the fact that she's gone. She's somewhere out there and we will find her and bring her back.

With nothing more to say, Liam turned around and started walking back to the bedroom with Lexi walking right behind him. He lied down in bed like before and fell asleep again, keeping his head on Hayley's pillow and his hand on a cold sheet in a spot where Hayley should be lying.

Chapter 12

Hayley woke up lying on the cold ground, in the middle of a maze. She got up and had a look around. She couldn't remember how she got there and the place looked completely unfamiliar. The sky above her head was dark and cloudy and the visibility was significantly reduced by the dense fog. At first, she couldn't comprehend what was going on but then it started slowly coming back to her.

- Oh my God – she said aloud to herself – I'm dead.

Tears came to her eyes as fear was gradually taking hold of her. She fell to her knees and started to cry feeling hopeless and terrified. She knew where she was. It was hell, it must have been. The enormity of the emotions was unbearable.

- Look at you.

Hayley heard a familiar voice and opened her eyes. Bradley was standing in front of her. He looked so real, exactly how she remembered him but his gaze was full of disgust and anger.

- Brad? What are you doing here?

Hayley got up and wanted to embrace her husband but he took a step back.

- You're not Hayley I once loved, you're a monster.

- No, Brad, you don't understand. I am a vampire but I'm a good one.

- Do you really think so? Why are you here then? By mistake? God makes no mistakes. You're evil, that's why you're here.

- Why are you like this? Why would you say that? - Hayley looked at Brad suspiciously - You're not him, are you? Who are you? What do you want?

Suddenly, April, June and her parents appeared out of thin air. They all looked disappointed and angry.

- You were such a good girl – said mum – a psychologist, helping people… Now, you're a murderer.

And then came the fear. Overwhelming and unbearable. Hayley started to run knowing that if she stopped, something terrible would happen.

After a time that seemed an eternity, the fear subsided and she stopped running. She wiped the sweat from her forehead and tried to catch her breath. Then, she fell to her knees once again, overwhelmed by guilt and despair.

- What have I done? I destroyed my life by letting Liam change me into a monster. I shouldn't have killed that boy. If I had been human, I wouldn't have done it. I've made a mistake… I shouldn't have done it… I've made a mistake.

The sadness, guilt, remorse and fear were eating her alive even though she was no longer among the living. She knew why she was in hell and she regretted what she's done but that wouldn't change anything for her now. There was no turning back, no other way but through hell. She was damned and there was nobody who could save her now. She got up and started to run again, constantly looking over her shoulder. Tears blurred her vision so she kept tripping over, hurting her palms and knees. In her mind she could see herself killing Jack. She could see her reflection as if she was looking into a mirror. Her terrifying monstrous black eyes devoid of humanity. She could see herself as a monster and that image would now haunt her for eternity.

Chapter 13

Liam was dead inside. He didn't want to talk to the twins, Oliver or even Isabella. He was hardly leaving his house, spending most of his days and nights staring at the ceiling completely motionless and fully awake. The only thing keeping him alive was Lexi, he felt responsible for that dog and wanted to make sure she's well taken care of. She reminded him of Hayley and was his only connection to her.

Unwillingly, he got up from the bed and went slowly to the kitchen downstairs. He opened the fridge and reached for one of the blood bags. He was about to pour its content to an empty glass but then he hesitated. He looked at Lexi that was watching his every move hoping he was preparing something delicious for her.

- I'm so pathetic – he said aloud looking at the dog – I am one of the strongest creatures walking this earth, invincible and unstoppable, I can do whatever I want but instead I sit here all miserable, drink some old and cold blood which is disgusting by the way, and I waste my life. I tried to remain as human as possible and look at me! All I got is pain. My life made sense only with her but she's gone now so what's the point? I'm a vampire… And so I should start behaving like one.

Liam threw the blood bag back into the fridge and changed his clothes. He put his elegant shirt on and used the perfumes he got from Hayley. It was an early Friday night. November after sunset was even more freezing that year than usual. Liam walked quickly to the first open bar he came across. Although it was only nine o'clock the place was already pretty crowded. He found a free spot by the bar, sat down and ordered martini. Having looked around, he noticed two young girls looking at him and giggling. He was perfectly aware of how handsome he was. Today, a decade ago or even a century earlier, he always attracted a lot of attention - that one thing hasn't changed as the years passed by. Shortly before eleven, when the girls were now quite drunk, Liam finished his last martini and approached the happy table.

- Good evening ladies – he said with the most charming smile – What are you celebrating?

- She is getting married – said the brunette pointing at her blond friend – But she's now completely passed out! – she added laughing

- I'm not! - said the blond girl but her forehead was still leaning on the table.

The waitress approached the table with a tray full of shots.

- We didn't order anything – said the brunette looking at the waitress confused.

- I did – said Liam – These are on me.

He took one shot and sat down next to the semi-conscious blond girl.

- To the bride-to-be! - he said and raised his glass.

The brunette raised her glass too and drank along with Liam.

After a few more shots, the brunette started drifting away.

- I shouldn't have done that – she said holding her head in her hands – I'm so dizzy.

A few seconds later, she was sitting with her head thrown back, quickly falling asleep. Liam sat next to her and put his arm around her, she didn't react. He had a quick look around but nobody was observing him so he bit the girl's neck as gently as he could, afraid she could still wake up. He fed on the girl making sure not to kill her and then left the bar in a hurry, leaving both girls sleeping with their heads on the table. He walked quickly thinking about what he's done and not paying any attention to other people he was passing by. When he got home, he went straight to the bedroom and laid across the bed with his feet still on the floor. He was staring at the ceiling with a smile. For the first time since Hayley has died, he felt happy. He didn't think about his pathetic empty life or his dead wife. He still felt that girl's blood pulsing in his veins and it felt great. It was a like a drug, making him feel carefree and joyful. Liam closed his eyes and fell asleep instantly. That night, for a change, he was not tormented with any nightmares and he slept the whole night until Lexi woke him up shortly after six in the morning as it was time for her long walk.

- Ok ok, stop barking, I'm up. - said Liam sitting up on the bed.

He put on his shoes and a jacket and let Lexi drag him ahead. It was freezing outside and snowing. The streets were empty on Saturday morning as the shops were still closed and nobody was rushing to work. Liam took a deep breath and watched the warm air forming a quickly disappearing vapor. *'She would love it today, morning walk with Lexi right before sunrise, empty streets and the snow. She would probably have her Christmas tree already decorated.'* Liam started feeling sad again, thinking about Hayley. But he knew what would make him feel better – a trip to Chicago. After Emma has been banished from New Orleans, that was where she moved. She has been left defenceless and disconnected from her ancestors. Her powers have been taken away by the coven so she was nothing more but human now. Tormenting the person who helped kill Hayley sounded like a perfect way to spend that day so Liam prepared food for Lexi and took her to the twins who have moved back to their old house after Hayley died. They were still welcome in New

Orleans but they didn't want to be there anymore, still angry with the witches.

- Liam, hi. - said April surprised to see Liam knocking on her door so early on a Saturday morning. - Come on in.

- I won't stay. Could you please look after Lexi this weekend? I thought I could visit Isabella, I haven't spoken to her in a while.

- Of course, no problem, it sounds like a great idea. Is Oliver taking you to your sister?

- No, I feel like having a proper trip, you know… I want to get out.

- Sure, I understand… It's good to see you Liam.

- You too – he said with a vague smile and walked away, handing April the leash.

Liam was in Chicago at five in the afternoon. During his three-hour flight he was thinking what he would do to Emma. He remembered how bad he felt after killing Lily and revenge didn't bring him any joy or relief so he decided not to kill Emma. All he wanted was to see fear in her eyes, he wanted her to be afraid for the rest of her life.

He rented a car and drove outside the city to a small old house that Emma inherited from her grandparents. It was a bungalow with a typical small white fence. He parked around the corner and made sure nobody saw him outside the house. Through the window, he saw the witch sitting in the living room and watching TV. Although she didn't look happy, it still made Liam angry that she was still alive and Hayley was not. His eyes turned black and his heart began to beat faster as his anger grew. He thought about breaking the front door and storming into the house but he needed to stay in control. Last time he lost control he ended up with a dead body and his face and hands covered in blood. He walked around the house and checked the back door – it was unlocked. Liam opened it slowly and walked into the house as quietly as possible. He walked slowly through the kitchen into the living room. Emma was sitting with her back turned to him so he crept through the room and stood behind the sofa. The TV screen turned black for a second between the scenes and Emma noticed Liam's reflection. She got off the sofa briskly and turned around.

- Oh God – she whispered in horror.

- In contrary, little witch. Tonight, I'm the devil.

Emma took a few steps back and tripped, falling on the floor.

- No, no, no, please, don't do this.

- Why? - Liam approached her slowly and crouched beside her – You showed no mercy to Hayley so why should I show mercy to you?

- I'm sorry – she whispered through tears.

- No, you're not sorry that Hayley is dead. You're sorry because I'm still alive. You're sorry that your stupid actions brought this upon you.

Emma didn't say anything and just burst into tears. She knew that nothing and nobody could save her now.

Liam lifted her off the floor and grabbed her by the throat, being careful not to kill her. She was staring at him with her eyes wide open and although her heart was beating rapidly, her breath was shallow and slow. Liam looked her in the eye and found exactly what he was hoping for – the fear. Emma was terrified, staring back into his black horrifying eyes thinking he was death. Liam smiled satisfied with what he achieved that evening.

- I won't kill you, it would be too easy. I killed the hunter and it didn't bring me any joy but this… - he smiled again – This is exactly what I wanted. I want you to know that you cannot run and you cannot hide. There is no place on earth that would shelter you from me. You will spend the rest of your life looking over your shoulder, wondering which day would be your last. You will see my face every time you close your eyes and you will find no peace as long as you shall live. You're alive only by my will and I will claim your life when I feel like doing so. You helped kill a good person only to revive a true monster instead.

Liam let go off Emma and she fell to her knees struggling to catch her breath. He looked at her one last time and left.

He was sitting in his car, taking deep breaths and trying to calm down. The anger subsided and he smiled, it was a good day. He looked at his happy face reflecting in the mirror then he started the car and drove to Rockford.

- Liam, what are you doing here? - said Isabella letting her brother into her house.

- I'm visiting. Is that bad?

- No! Of course not, I'm just surprised to see you. You didn't even want to talk to me and now you're here so you can't blame me for being a bit shocked.

- I'm sorry, sister. I just needed some space, I needed to deal with everything alone.

- I'm sorry Liam.

- Me too… Anyway, how have you been?

Liam sat down at the table while Isabella was brewing some tea.

- I'm OK, same old. I work a lot. Who knew there were so many criminals on the loose.

She handed Liam a mug and sat opposite to him.

- How are you Liam?

- I'm…stable.

- Did you make your peace with Hayley being gone?

- No, I can't just accept the fact that she's truly gone. I will never stop hoping that she'll come back home one day. April is an amazing witch and although she doesn't know what to do now, I'm sure she'll find a way to bring Hayley back one day. She just needs some time.

- There is something different about you though and I can't figure out what it is – Isabella looked pensive.

- I've… Changed my lifestyle recently.

- But you haven't killed anyone, have you?

- No… But I had a bite or two.

- Yes, that may be the reason you seem different. So how was it?

- Amazing. It's like a drug with no side effects.

- There might be some side effects if you're not careful.

- I am careful, don't worry, I won't become one your bounties.

- I hope so. So who are you after? Homeless people?

- Drunk young and stupid.

- Yes, they are an easy target. Well, I'm glad you're feeling better and it's really good to see you. I worried about you.

- Where's Ethan?

- Away. He flew to Mexico for some work project and will be back next weekend.

- Don't you feel lonely all by yourself?

- I do but I'm away a lot too. Besides, we talk to each other every day.

- Will you go out with me tonight? We can have a little drink together.

- I can't, I have very poor self-control and that makes me very dangerous. Besides, it was difficult for me to switch to blood bags and I don't want to go through that process again.

- That's understandable… I have a confession to make… I came to see that witch in Chicago.

- And what did you do?

- Just scared her, made her aware that I'll be watching her. It felt good to see her so terrified, thinking it were her last moments. The witches were right, there were better ways to punish someone than death.

- I'm glad you got this out of your system. Now, enough about the witch, she is exactly where you wanted her so we can forget about her now. Let's go for a walk. It's quite lovely outside and tonight is a supermoon and I really want to see it. You know how much I love a full moon and seeing it as it is the closest to the Earth is something that I just simply cannot miss.

Liam was preparing for his next night out, 'a night of the hunter' as he started to call it. Every week, there was someone he could join for a quick drink, it was incredible how many young people got drunk to the point they couldn't quite comprehend what was going on. Sometimes there was a group of three, sometimes it was just a couple of friends. Girls in their twenties or thirties, reckless and stupid.

That night, Liam headed to the Sterling Aspen bar. He liked that place for it's dark and purple interior. He could always find someone interesting sitting in the corner under a large photograph of a zebra – a symbol of a perfect and easy prey. Sometimes, when he was there early on a Friday night, he was taking a seat under the lion, waiting for someone interesting to join him. He was like a lion himself, waiting patiently for a perfect moment to attack. That night, he joined three ladies sitting at the zebra spot. The night was still young but high volume of tequila shots was doing a great job fast.

- We should go home now – said one of the girls - Before we pass out.

- True – said the other one – I've had more than enough. Let's go.

- Come on, it's still early – said the third one – Let's stay a bit longer, I don't want to go back yet.

- Why won't you two go back now – said Liam – And I'll stay with Charlotte? I'll walk her home later, you have my word.

The girls thought for a moment and then decided to go on with Liam's plan.

- OK, why not? You're too charming for a serial killer.

They laughed and left their friend alone with Liam.

Charlotte was quite interesting and funny. She made Liam laugh talking about her silly adventures. She drank far too much and should change her lifestyle before she'd get hurt. She couldn't be more than twenty-three and although she was not very pretty, she looked friendly and nice. Maybe with a little bit less make-up and a bit longer hair she would be more attractive.

At eleven o'clock, Charlotte was half-alive, talking complete nonsense, barely aware of where she was and what was going on. Liam embraced her gently and bit her neck. She furrowed her brow but didn't fight back. He let her go when she completely passed out and put her head gently on the table.

- Liam?!

It was April, standing right in front of him, shocked and angry.

Liam wiped his mouth, got up, took April by the elbow gently leading her outside.

- Something's wrong? - he asked when they were already outside, away from the crowd.

- Are you serious?! What the hell?!

- I don't understand what your problem is, April. I didn't kill her.

- But you fed on her.

- I'm a vampire and this is what vampires do, they feed on people.

- This isn't you, Liam. I thought you're better than this. Hayley would be disappointed at you.

- Would she really? This is exactly what she wanted and I was the one to dissuade her from that idea. I think she would understand, I even think that she'd join me.

- You disgust me. - she said through clenched teeth.

- I don't care what you think April. I have fun, I feel happy and I won't stop so if you don't like it, kill me. You're powerful enough to end my life within a split second so do it!

April didn't say anything. She was looking Liam in the eye and she saw his pain. Although he claimed he was having fun, deep down he was still the same man shattered into pieces and hurt and what he did that night was his way of dealing with his grief.

- I won't stop you Liam but I want you to know that I don't approve what you do and I will never be OK with it.

- Fine.

Liam turned around and went back inside. He woke Charlotte up and asked her for the address. He helped her get up and they left the bar. She had her arm around his neck and he held her around the waist. He caught taxi and made sure the girl got back home safely. She was so stupid to stay there with him – a total stranger. If he was someone else, probably she would've already been dead.

Chapter 14

The end of the year was approaching fast. On Christmas Eve, everyone gathered at Oliver's house. There was no joyful music, no laughter. June and Isabella were preparing food in the kitchen and Oliver was setting the table. Christmas tree was up, standing alone and forgotten in the corner. Nobody even turned the lights on. Liam was sitting on the sofa petting Lexi lying with her head on his lap. He looked miserable, thinking how much Hayley always loved that time of the year and what that day would be like if she was still alive.

- Liam, let's go to your place. - April said unexpectedly pulling Liam out of his deep thought - I want to see Hayley's ashes.

- Why?

- I have a theory that I wanted to test.

They put their jackets on and left the house promising everyone they would be back in time for dinner.

- So what's the plan?

- You see… I thought that all witches could bring people back to life with a proper spell but apparently I was wrong. That day when Jack killed June, I brought her back to life with my magic and apparently this is my unique gift. Some witches can heal people, some can see the future and I can do this. Last week, I took a stray cat home and… Well… I killed it with magic. But then I cast the same spell I used on June and it worked, the cat is alive. So I was thinking that maybe it's not so much about knowing where the spirit is but about knowing where the body is. When I was doing magic over June's body, I was not looking for her spirit anywhere, I was focusing on her body as it was right in front of me and it was tangible. Same with the cat, I was not looking for its soul. So if I had managed to bring back a creature that probably doesn't even have a spirit, maybe I can bring Hayley too.

- But how can you do the same spell with the ashes?

- I can't. But I finally mastered a spell that would help me turn the ashes back into the whole body. We have nothing to lose, Liam. It's worth trying.

- Of course, I'm up for anything.

- I'm still angry with you though.

- But you're not doing this for me, you're doing this for your sister.

Once they've entered the house, April poured an entire bathtub of warm water. Then, she added a few drops of her blood along with a handful of soil and lit some candles. Liam brought the glass jar and carefully poured the ashes into the water. April took a step back and started chanting with her eyes closed and her hands gently lifted with her palms up. She repeated the same sentence over and over again: '*Aquam, ignem, terram et aerem, hos cineres iterum integros fac*' Suddenly, the candles lit up even more and the water got uneasy spilling on the bathroom floor. Within a minute, Hayley's body showed up in the bathtub. Liam covered her with towels and sheets and carried to the bedroom. He gently dried her face and covered her with a warm blanket as if she was already alive. April kneeled on the bed, put her hands over the body and started chanting again. She was repeating the spell until her nose started bleeding.

- April, stop.

- I can do this.

- You're going to hurt yourself, stop.

April wiped the blood from her face.

- Give me your hand, I need more power. If I channel you, it will work, trust me. I'm close, I can feel it.

Liam gave April his hand and she started chanting again: *'Ad corpus redeat spiritus.'* With every word, he could feel he's strength was fading away and he was getting more and more tired, sleepy and dizzy. April's nose was still bleeding, she was shaking as if she was cold and her voice was breaking. Suddenly, she stopped chanting and they both fell on the floor as if some unseen force pushed them away. In that moment, Hayley woke up breathing heavily. She sat on the bed and looked around shocked and frightened.

- Hayley! - April yelled – Thank God, it worked!

Hayley looked at her without a word.

April got off the floor and hugged her sister tightly laughing through tears.

- Hayley, how are you feeling?

Hayley was staring at April with her jaw down and her eyes wide open. She looked at Liam and herself rapped in sheets and towels.

- What's wrong? Hayley please say something - April got anxious.

- I… - she started – I don't remember anything.

- What is the last thing you remember?

- Nothing… I don't remember anything… I don't know who you are, I don't know who I am. What's happened to me?

April looked at Hayley shocked, thinking what to say.

- Let me bring you some clothes, you must be cold.

She made a gesture at Liam asking him to follow her. They closed the door so Hayley couldn't hear them.

- Why did she lose her memory? - Liam asked – Why is she human again?

- I think that amnesia is some side effect. She has been dead for weeks and we don't even know where she was and what's happened to her. I don't know why she's human again, she died as a vampire so she should have come back as a vampire… Let's give her some time to adjust. I will try to help her get her memory back but it won't happen overnight, she needs time. Don't put too much pressure on her, OK? Be patient. The most important thing is that she's alive again. Now go to Oliver's and let them know what's going on, I will be there shortly with Hayley.

Liam hesitated. He didn't want to leave Hayley, he wanted to go back to that room and put his arms around her and never let go. But eventually he put his trust in April and decided to do as told.

April came back to the bedroom with some warm clothes. Hayley was still sitting on the bed looking worried and scared. She was shivering with cold as her wet hair was covering her bare back.

- Here's your clothes – April said with a gentle smile putting some jeans and sweater on the bed – Your name is Hayley Anderson and I am your sister April. Don't worry…

- 'Don't worry'?! I don't know who I am or who you are and what's happened to me! How can you expect me not to worry?!

April put her hand on Hayley's shoulder and did a spell to calm her down.

- I know it's scary and you have many questions that I cannot answer right now but I promise you, everything will be OK. Now try to relax and enjoy the rest of the day.

Hayley was breathing slowly, looking April right in the eye as if she was hypnotised. The spell worked.

- Are you hungry?

Hayley nodded without a word.

- Good. We have a delicious dinner ready not too far away from here and we would love you to join us. It's Christmas Eve today and we don't want you to spend it alone, although we seem to be total strangers, we are your family. Let's make this evening perfect and stress-free and tomorrow we'll start working on getting your memory back. I will do everything I can to help you.

- Are you a doctor?

April smiled.

- Something like that. Come on, get dressed and let's go. There is a bunch of hungry people getting very impatient.

Hayley got dressed and started walking down the stairs. She looked at the photographs hanging on the wall and although she was still a bit sad and scared, she didn't cry. She went out with April and kept walking without saying anything for a couple of minutes. She was looking around as if she tried to guess where she was. When it started snowing, she stopped and looked up at the sky with a smile.

- I love Aspen this time of year. It looks so magical when it's snowing .

- So you know you're in Aspen, that's good.

- I recognise this place, I know I've been here before but that's the only familiar thing so far. April… That man that was in the house today with you… Who is he?

- That's Liam, your husband. Don't worry, you will remember everything just give yourself some time. Step by step, slowly. Don't put too much pressure on yourself.

- You seem to be a very good sister.

- Thanks. I assume you'll be delighted then to know you have two of me. Soon enough you'll meet my twin sister June.

- Twins April and June? That's cool.

They stopped in front of Oliver's house.

- You're ready?

Hayley took a deep breath and nodded.

April opened the door and they both walked inside. Everyone was gathered in the living room looking at Hayley and smiling. Lexi broke free from June's grasp and ran towards Hayley barking, jumping and trying to lick her face.

- Hi darling!

Hayley started cuddling Lexi and petting her. For a moment everyone was hoping that the dog jogged her memory but then Hayley asked about the dog's name.

- This is Lexi and she's your dog.

- What a sweetheart. I love dogs!

Hayley took off her jacket and boots and looked at everyone.

- Hi – she said quietly and shyly.

Oliver approached her with his charming smile.

- Hi Hayley, I'm Oliver. Welcome to my humble abode.

- I like your house, it's very lovely.

- Thank you. Find yourself a sit at the table and make yourself comfortable. Dinner will be shortly.

Hayley approached the table where everyone else was already sitting. Nobody knew how to start the conversation so they were sitting quietly looking at one another.

- I know you don't want to overwhelm me – Hayley started – But I think it would be nice to know your names. Can you tell me one thing about yourself so I can memorize it better? For example I'm Hayley and I have a German Shepherd called Lexi.

- You already know that we are your twin sisters April and June – April said pointing at June.

- I don't think you need to point at me – June said – It's obvious who you had in mind.

- I'm Isabella and I'm a bounty hunter.

- I'm Ethan and my girlfriend is a bounty hunter. Sorry, I don't really think there is anything interesting about me that is worth mentioning.

- This can't be true, I bet you are a very interesting person.

Liam looked at Hayley thinking what to say.

- I'm Liam and… I'm a writer.

Hayley smiled at him shyly. April has already told her he was her husband and she appreciated he was giving her space, respecting the fact she didn't remember him.

Oliver came over carrying food.

- I'm Oliver and I… Have a turkey.

Everyone laughed. They all started eating and talking casually about weather and their hobbies and plans for the next year. Hayley was listening to them all carefully trying to memorize as much detail as possible. Although they seemed to be complete strangers, soon enough, they made her feel home.

The dinner turned out to be the most joyful event of the year. Despite having dozens of questions and no answers, Hayley still had fun. April's magic helped her enjoy that evening in spite of everything else going on. It was nice to see so many happy faces even though they didn't look familiar at all.

- I'm sorry, but I think it's time for me to go home. I'm really tired. - Hayley said yawning.

- You can stay here with us if you want – April said – there is plenty of room.

- Thank you but I'd rather go back home, I hope you don't mind.

- No problem, whatever you want.

Hayley got off the table and started putting her boots on.

- Can I take the dog?

- Of course, she's yours.

Hayley put Lexi on a leash.

- Liam – she said with unhidden hesitation – Could you walk me home, please?

Liam looked at her surprised as her request was very unexpected. He started putting his jacket on when he heard April's barely heard whisper *'don't tell her anything.'* He slightly nodded to let her know that he heard her request.

- Thank you all for this evening, it was very pleasant. I appreciate your effort .

- It's good to have you back, Hayley – said June - Have a good night and see we'll you tomorrow.

Liam opened the door for Hayley and they both left. They didn't say anything at first, walking in silence, enjoying a quiet night. The only sound was the snow crackling under their feet and a lonely owl somewhere over their heads. As they didn't know what to talk about and the silence was becoming unbearable, Hayley picked up some snow and threw a snowball at Liam.

- What are you doing? - he asked laughing.

- I'm starting a war. Come on, play with me – said Hayley with encouraging smile.

Liam made a snowball and threw it gently at Hayley. It landed on her jacket leaving a white snowy dust. They played for a couple of minutes and even Lexi got involved, trying to fetch the balls. Two grown-ups behaving like kids, goofing around and playing in the snow. It completely removed all the tension between them and put them in a better mood.

- I can't feel my fingers! - Hayley said laughing when they entered the house - Look! - she showed her red wet hands to Liam.

He really wanted to grab her and kiss her as he missed her so much but he didn't want to make her feel all tense and uncomfortable again.

- Let me make you a cup of tea, you need to warm up.

They sat on the sofas in the living room, covered in blankets with cups of ginger tea with lemon and honey. The fire heated the room very fast and was crackling pleasantly' in the fireplace, illuminating the room with a warm yellow light. Hayley was staring at Liam who was not taking his eyes off his mug. He looked concerned, even sad.

- Liam… - Hayley managed to attract his attention - I really wish I remembered you, you seem like a nice guy and the photos on the wall clearly show we were a good couple. Tell me about us.

Liam stared at his mug again thinking intensively what to say. He couldn't tell her how they met, he couldn't point out how special and unique their relationship truly was.

- Tell me about me, what was I like? - Hayley asked a different question seeing that Liam was struggling to find right words for the first one.

- You are very lovely and nice and smart and funny. You care about your family and friends. You are open-minded and understanding…

- And what did you love about me the most?

- That you cared about me and loved me the way I was.

- I don't think it was very difficult, I mean, you seem pretty likeable.

- Thank you.

They took a sip of their tea and set in silence for a moment.

- Listen… - Hayley started again breaking uncomfortable silence - I know you miss old me and I know it's difficult for you but it's difficult for me too, you know? And I am trying really hard not to freak out but the truth is that I don't know what's happening to me and what caused this memory loss and I'm scared. I don't know what to do and how to come back to living my life when I don't know who I really am.

- I know you're struggling and I'm very sorry for you. Don't worry about me, I'm just happy to have you back.

- Do you know what's happened to me? Please, tell me I need to know.

- We'll talk about this tomorrow. I think today was pretty overwhelming as it was. Try to get some sleep, you look tired.

Liam got up and went upstairs for a duvet and a pillow planning on sleeping in the living room, leaving the bedroom for Hayley. She didn't ask any more questions seeing that Liam clearly didn't want to give her any answers. Besides, going to sleep sounded like a good plan as she was extremely exhausted.

Liam was lying on the sofa in the living room, thinking about all that happened that day. He couldn't fall asleep having thoughts running through his head. He loved Hayley and was happy to see her again but he couldn't stop blaming himself for what's happened to her. She died because she was a vampire and she turned because she met him. He was sure nothing bad would have happened to her if they had never met. Maybe he was her greatest joy but in the same time he brought so much pain and suffering into her life. Maybe she would be better off without him, especially now, when she didn't even know who he was and their relationship meant nothing to her.

At three in the morning he got up and started getting dressed and packing the money and the documents. Hayley went quietly downstairs seeing the light on.

- What are you doing? - she said looking at Liam confused.

- I need to go.

- In the middle of the night? Where?

- Go back to bed, Hayley.

- Tell me what's going on. - she started to panic.

- I need to leave.

- Where? When will you be back?

Liam looked away without a word.

- You're leaving for good, aren't you? - her voice started breaking – You can't accept the fact that I don't remember anything, that I'm different now…
- It's not like that, I'm not leaving because of this.
- Then what is it?
Liam just continued packing.
- Tell me what's going on!
- You're better off without me.
- What does it mean? Why would you say that?
- You were supposed to live a happy, safe and long life by my side but instead… All you got was disappointment.
- I don't believe you! Look at these pictures, Liam – she said pointing at the wall by the stairs - I was clearly happy with you. It's so obvious that you meant something to me.
- I don't want you to suffer any more. You can be happier without me, you can be safer without me.
- That is not true.
Liam took his backpack and put his hand on the door handle. Hayley took him by his other hand and pulled him slightly away from the door. He looked into her full of tears and terrified eyes.
- Please don't go. Please don't leave me. Whatever I felt for you I will feel again one day and when it happens I don't want you to be away. I need you, please, stay.
- I don't want to see you get hurt, Hayley.
- Then stay and protect me. Please. Don't leave me alone.
Tears were now running down her cheeks and her lower lip was shaking, she looked like a powerless and defenceless child. Liam put his backpack down and took off his jacket and boots.
- Promise me you'll be here when I wake up. - Hayley said with her voice still breaking.
- I promise.
- Come upstairs with me, I want to keep an eye on you.

Hayley laid down in bed, cuddling up to Lexi and Liam sat in the armchair by the bed observing Hayley slowly drifting away. Every now and then, she slightly opened one eye just to make sure Liam was still there.

He wanted to believe it was truly Hayley but the love he used to see in her eyes was now gone. He thought that leaving her would be best for her, that if they had never met, maybe she wouldn't have died. But despite her memory loss, Hayley cared about him more than he thought. He wanted to be honest with her and tell her the truth and all details that she was missing. She accepted him when they first met so why wouldn't she accept him again now? She was still the same person, she was still his Hayley and it was difficult for him to accept the fact that she didn't remember him. But he would never be OK if she ever rejected him knowing the whole truth. He couldn't lose her that way. He would be perfectly honest with her and tell her the whole truth eventually but today was not that day.

Hayley woke up shortly after six, Lexi was already awake waiting for her breakfast and Liam was sitting in the armchair with his head thrown back and his eyes closed. Hayley watched him for a few minutes. It was killing her that she didn't remember him and their life together, that all those beautiful and precious moments were possibly irrecoverably lost now. She really wanted to know what they have been through together and what amazing memories Liam had. She started slowly getting up, trying to stay as quiet as possible but the moment she moved, Liam woke up.

- You have an exceptional hearing, sorry, I didn't want to wake you up.

- That's OK, I don't want to sleep when you're awake. What do you fancy for breakfast?

- Surprise me, I'm not fussy.

Hayley went to freshen up and get dressed. When she went downstairs, Liam was already sitting at the table, the coffee was done and the scrambled eggs with bacon smelled delicious.

- Well done, thanks Liam.

Hayley sat at the table and watched Liam eating. He felt like in their dream, when they had their breakfast the day after the attack. He could feel her piercing gaze now like he did that day.

- Stop staring at me.

- Sorry! I didn't know you knew.

- What are you thinking about?

- I am wondering how we met.

- Long story short, you've been attacked and I saved you.

- So you're my very own hero then? Now I understand why I fell in love with you.

- Now you understand? - Liam said laughing – So until now you couldn't possibly come up with any good reason? Am I really that awful?

- No! I'm sorry, it didn't sound right. I was just wondering what it was. Whether it was your charm or your intelligence or your sense of humour. There are many reasons why I would fall in love with you, you are very loveable.

- Thank you. So are you.

Hayley blushed.

- Am I embarrassing you? – he asked amused – You know we're married, right? By the way, I have something for you.

Liam reached to his pocket and handed Hayley her wedding rings. They were destroyed along with Hayley's body the moment she died but Liam had them redone, hoping he would put them back on Hayley's finger one day.

- These belong to you, but you don't have to wear them.

Hayley put the rings on without hesitation. She looked sad though as she couldn't remember her wedding day. She always hoped it would be the best day of her life but here she was, married to a man she didn't even know, after a ceremony that she didn't remember.

They ate in silence for a couple of minutes, gazing at each other from time to time with a gentle smile.

- I think you should take me out on a date – Hayley said.

- Do you think I have a chance?

- I think you're on the right track. You need to show me some photos and videos of our wedding day. As a matter of fact, I want to see all photos we have. Maybe they will jog my memory.

- It's definitely worth trying, you have nothing to lose.

- So what do you think? – June asked April when they were on their way to see Hayley.

It was a cold morning and the sun was painfully reflecting on a thick layer or perfectly white snow.

- I am so confused. I'm happy to see Hayley back whether she remembers me or not but… I don't understand why she's human again. She died as a vampire so her body should be a body of a vampire.

- Maybe it's better that way, she didn't like being a vampire that much anyway. Besides, how would we explain to her all that magical staff now that she doesn't remember anything?

- You're right. But… Something doesn't seem right.

- What do you mean?

- I don't know, it's hard to explain… It's just a feeling.

- So, do you know how to bring her memory back?

- I have a few ideas but I can't promise any of these spells would work. Worst case scenario – we have to accept the fact her memory is gone.

- Are we going to tell her the whole truth?

- Eventually yes, but not all at once. I don't know how she may react. I know it's still our Hayley but the circumstances are different, she doesn't love us, she doesn't care about us so her reaction may differ.

- Right. At least I have nothing to worry about, I am the only normal person around here.

- Please, don't be ridiculous! You died twice, you were in heaven and came back also twice, you talked to the dead for a while and you have a ring that makes you immortal. How can you still call yourself 'normal'?

- Fine, you made your point… OK… Here's the moment of truth. - June said and knocked on Hayley's door.

- How are you feeling? - April asked when her sister opened the door.

- Still don't remember anything. I've been waiting for you, you said you could help me. So what kind of a doctor are you?

- Doctor?! - June said laughing – Very unconventional one I would say.

- Shut up June – April said giving her twin sister a look full of disapproval – I would try to put you into a short sleep if that's OK.

- You mean hypnosis?

- Kind of, yes. Would that be OK?

- Sure. I'm up for anything.

April led Hayley to the living room and asked her to lay down on the couch.

- Good luck with your magic! - June yelled – A doctor – she whispered to Liam – Can you believe this? And she was the one telling us not to fill Hayley's head with anything weird.

The moment Hayley lied down and closed her eyes, April snapped her fingers and made her unconscious. She sat by Hayley and put her hands on her head. She has been whispering different spells for over an hour. Liam and June were sitting quietly in the kitchen listening how April was getting more and more annoyed.

- I can't do it – she said to Liam and June who impatiently waited for her feedback.

- So what's the plan now?

- I have no foggiest idea. Maybe her memory will come back at some point, maybe something will trigger it someday but I don't know what to do.

- Do we tell her the truth? She keeps asking me about what's happened to her. - said Liam.

- We can start telling her some bits and pieces, gradually but not everything at once. I don't want to overwhelm her with too much information. Liam, I know you want her to know everything but I think you should wait. I'm not quite sure how she would take it.

- But she's still the same person so I assume her reaction would be the same.

- Probably you're right but we don't know that for sure. I am happy to keep it all as a secret for now but she's your wife Liam and I won't tell you what to do. It's your choice.

- I think it's time for her to wake up now – June said looking at Hayley still lying unconscious on the couch.

April snapped her fingers again and Hayley woke up. She sat down and stared at the floor not saying anything.

- It didn't work – she finally said looking at April with unhidden disappointment – I still don't remember anything.

- I'm sorry Hayley. Hopefully something will trigger your memory one day.

- Right, thanks April for trying. I wish there was some magical wand that you could just wave and fix me.

They all smiled but didn't comment on that.

- So what's the plan for today? – April asked.

- Well, as I don't have my own memories, we will use Liam's and go through some photos.

- That's a really good idea.

- I think maybe we could go to Hawaii or Cuba any time soon ?– Hayley said gazing at Liam with a smile.

- Why not? - June said – Oliver can help you with that – she added without thinking and quickly regretted it.

- What do you mean?

- Never mind. Good luck with walking down the memory lane. I hope you two will have fun.

When April and June left, Hayley approached Liam looking confused.

- Do you know what June meant when she said that Oliver could help us? Is he a travel agent or something?

Liam thought for a moment. He didn't want to overwhelm Hayley but he didn't want to lie to her either. Besides, he wanted to know what her reaction would be to something so bizarre.

- Oliver… Can teleport.

- What? - Hayley said laughing – You mean literally?

- Yes.

He looked at her smiling gently, awaiting her response.

- So what do you think about that? - he asked.

- I think you're joking.

- I'm not. As a matter of fact, I am very serious.

- So if you're not joking then I'm shocked. How's that possible?

- Don't you believe in magic?

- I do, I always have, I've just never witnessed anything magical before. So is he gifted or is he a witch or an alien? Meteor rocks? Spider bite?

- He's a witch.

- Wow. - Hayley sat down shocked and confused - Maybe Oliver can help me with his magic? Maybe there is some spell that would bring my memory back?

- Unfortunately no. We've already tried that.

- Oh, that's unfortunate.

- So how do you feel about Oliver now? What do you think about him? - Liam asked and sat next to Hayley.

- I'm interested and fascinated. It must be so cool to be something more than just an ordinary human being, to be powerful like that... Did I know that before? The truth about Oliver I mean.

- Yes, you did.

- And how did I take it?

- Same as now.

- Interesting.

- So, should I get the photo album or is there anything else you'd like to do today?

Hayley thought for a second and then looked at Liam smiling.

- I want to teleport.

They spent the whole day in Hawaii, enjoying an amazing weather, swimming in the ocean and riding ski jets but none of these jogged Hayley's memory. She had a time of her life and yet, it was not enough. After sunset, they went to the nearby bar for karaoke.

- Do you want to put your name on the list? - Liam asked.

- No way! I can't sing.

- Hayley I knew would go on that stage without hesitation. She loved singing and she loved karaoke and she had an amazing voice.

- Are you serious? Did I really sing?

- Of course you did! Many times. Go on! Maybe it will bring back some memories.

Hayley thought intensively.

- And? - Liam insisted on an answer.

- I can't do it, I'm sorry.

- Come on, Hayley. You are a great singer and I know you'll have fun. Sing with me in a duet, it will be less scary.

- I'm sorry Liam… I can't do it.

- Right… - There was no point in putting any more pressure on Heyley, it was clear she wouldn't sing that night. - Maybe some other time.

They listened to others singing and Hayley had a few laughs but Liam remained serious. He spent the whole day in Hawaii doing all those things he's done before with Hayley and yet it didn't feel the same. He saw her clearly having fun and he saw happiness reflecting in her gaze but there was no love. They used to be connected in a magical kind of way but there was no connection now, as if she was a stranger and nothing more.

They called Oliver and asked him to take them back home as Hayley didn't want to stay on the island for the night.

- I must say it's very convenient to teleport like this – Hayley said when they were back home – No packing, no planning, you just go and come back the same day without wasting any time on travelling. If I were Oliver I would go around the world and see everything.

- We can do that if you want, with or without Oliver. We can pack whatever's necessary and just go.

- Maybe… We'll come back to this but now, I want to see the photos. Unless you're tired and want to go to sleep.

- I'd rather spend that time with you.

Liam brought a box full of photographs.

- A box? - Hayley said surprised. - Why not an album?

- Because you had many photos and every time you thought about categorising them, you ended up going through them and reminiscing and after that, you didn't feel like organising them anymore.

- Sounds like me. OK, let's do this. What's the first photo you've got?

- It's you skydiving in Cuba.

- I can't believe I've done that! I'm afraid of skydiving.

- I know, but you had a phase of being a daredevil and you did a few pretty crazy stuff.

- Oh really? What else have I done?

- You swam with dolphins and sharks and jumped off the cliffs… Look at this one! It's you on stage in Hawaiian bar.

- I really sang… I can't believe this… I've done so many amazing things and I don't remember any of them. And the worst part is that it all sounds like not me… Was I really that different before the accident?

- Accident?

- Well, nobody wants to tell me what caused my memory loss so I assume I must have been in some accident. Am I wrong? What else could that be?

But Liam didn't answer.

- Never mind, I don't need to know this right now and I don't want to ruin this night with any sad stories. Give me the next photo, I want to see what other crazy stuff I've done.

They stayed up all night going through the photos and talking about the past. Hayley was listening to Liam's amazing and incredible stories about herself. She loved that cool and fun Hayley he talked about. The photographs showed a person she always wanted to be, a do-or-die type who would not say 'no' to an adventure.

- This is unbelievable – Hayley said when the box on Liam's lap was finally empty - I can't believe I've done all this. Did I change into that person when I met you? Did you have anything to do with it?

Liam smiled.

- I'm not so sure… I think your curiosity was pushing you into a lot of things. Also, you wanted to just grab a bull by its horns and live your life to the fullest with no regrets.

- I am still like that I just have some limits. I would never skydive as it's too dangerous, same with swimming with sharks.

- I believe at some point in your life you just stopped being afraid of death as much and were keener to take some bigger risk. I think you can still be that person, you just have to start saying 'yes'. Let's start with something less dangerous and scary, let's get you on the stage.

- Good luck with that. I think you'd have to drag me there.

- Maybe I will. If that could help get your old self back, I'd be happy to oblige.

Hayley looked through the window. The sun rose up high in the blue and cloudless sky and the sun rays pleasantly illuminated her face.

- I know it's already morning but I'd like to get some sleep if you don't mind. It was a very intensive day and I'm really tired now.

- Of course. I'll take Lexi for a walk and you can have some rest. I would say good night but I think it's a bit late for that so I'll say sweet dreams instead.

When Hayley went to bed, despite being tired, she was lying awake thinking about her old self. She couldn't believe how different she was. She couldn't believe all those crazy things she has done. *'How can memory loss change a person to such an extent? I was braver and crazier and funnier… I was someone else… I was a completely different person… What's happened to me? Why nobody wants to tell me? I woke up all wet and wrapped in sheets… Did I drown? Did I die? What are they all protecting me from? Why can I not know the truth? And Liam… He's such a great guy but will I ever love him again? How can I keep living my old life when I'm not the same person anymore? How can I be that amazing Hayley Anderson when clearly... I'm not...'*

- Wake up Hayley! We need to go.

Liam pulled the duvet off Hayley and drew back the curtains.

- What's going on? - she asked rubbing her eyes.

- I have a surprise for you but we need to leave now.

Without any more questions, Hayley shot out of the bed and got dressed as quickly as she could.

- Could you tell me now where we're going? - Hayley asked when they were already in the car.

- I have a surprise for you in Denver.

- Denver? But it's like four-hour drive. Why can't we ask Oliver to teleport us there?

- Because it would be a great opportunity for us to talk. A road trip, four hours stuck together in one car.

- Very well then. But remember that I didn't have any breakfast so you need to pull over somewhere.

- I will, don't worry.

- What about Lexi?

- Twins will take care of her.

- OK... Will you tell me what the surprise is?

- No, you need to see it.

First half of the day they spent in the car talking about what they liked and disliked and what they always wanted to do. Hayley was listening to Liam's many stories with unhidden interest and fascination. They reached Denver Zoo nearly five hours later. The traffic was heavy and they made a few stops to stretch and eat.

- So you brought me to a zoo – Hayley sounded a bit disappointed - When you said about saying 'yes' to adventures I hoped for something more than this.

Liam smiled without saying a single word, took Hayley's hand and started leading her towards staff entry. He made a quick phone call and someone opened the door. It was a man in his late thirties, tall and very muscular. He looked very friendly though his clothes were dirty and he smelled terribly.

- Liam, hi, you're right on time. Long time no see and you haven't changed a bit. Who's your friend?

- This is my wife Hayley. Hayley this is my friend Trevor. We used to be neighbours.

- A wife – Trevor said looking at Hayley – Congrats Liam you got yourself a very good-looking lady. Follow me, we need to hurry.

They followed Travor inside the building where only staff was allowed. In that moment, Hayley got really interested and curious. It looked like it was not going to be a typical trip to the zoo after all. Trevor took two large bottles of milk and handed them over to Liam and Hayley.

- What is it for? - Hayley asked surprised – What are we going to feed?

Trevor smiled and opened the door. Hayley saw a large cage with three small tiger cubs. They were walking around impatiently waiting for someone to get them out.

- They are four-week-old. We have a little problem with them and need to get them some medicine. Bottle of milk is better than a syringe or a pill so we decided to do it this way. Their mother is being looked after as we speak, she needs some meds too. But don't worry, they all will be just fine. OK, so everyone take one cub. They are harmless and I know they are still babies but they're quite big already so they can be difficult to manage. Hayley, let me know if you struggle.

Trevor opened the cage and the cubs went out immediately. He sat on the floor with the bottle of milk and started feeding one of the cats. Hayley did the same.

Once she's sat on the floor two cubs approached her and started fighting over the bottle.

- Let me take one – Liam said sitting next to Hayley.

He looked at her amazed and happy face. She tried to pet the cub but she needed to keep the bottle with her both hands as the cub was pushing it hard. Liam held Hayley's bottle for her so she could pet the cat. She had tears of joy in her eyes as she was petting the tiger cub. Its face was now covered in milk and looked even more adorable than before. It was making noises similar to the purrs of a domestic cat and its paws were already bigger than Hayley's hands.

Once the feeding was done, Trevor put all three cubs back into the cage so other members of staff could take them back.

- That was amazing! - Hayley said excited – I wish I could take one home, they are so cute!

- I know but unfortunately, they won't be so cute in just a few weeks – Trevor said – those cubs grow really fast and before you even know it, they weight over two hundred pounds, like this one.

Trevor went across the hall and opened another door. Hayley saw a tigress lying on the surgical table. She was unconscious although her eyes were half-open.

- Can I pet her? - Hayley asked with a note of hope in her voice.

- Sure. She's asleep.

Hayley approached the table and reached her hand out. The tigress growled quietly but didn't move. She was restless and although deep in sleep, she still looked scary. Liam took a picture when Heyley was looking at the animal amazed and excited. It was an incredible experience and she didn't want that moment to end. The fur felt so soft under her fingers. It was thick, glossy and smooth with a fluffier type underneath. Hayley looked at tigress' long whiskers that were moving rapidly as if the animal was sniffing. Some of them seemed broken. The paws were enormous and the tail was nearly three-feet-long and was hanging loosely from the table.

- I'm sorry to interrupt – said Trevor - But she'll be waking up shortly and we need to get her back. You can stick around if you want, have a walk around the zoo.

- I think we'll start driving back home. It will take us a few hours to get to Aspen.

- OK then, well, I hope to see you again some time. Take care Liam and let me know when you're in town next time. It was really nice to see you again.

The journey back took them over six hours but it was fun. There was so much to talk about and there was no single minute of silence.

- We need to print the photos from today and the ones from Hawaii – Hayley said – I need some photos on the wall that I actually remember taking.

- Don't worry Hayley, there will be more.

- Thank you for today Liam, it was real fun. Not only the zoo but the road trip too. I thought I've done some crazy stuff in my life but your life is truly insane! When did you have time to go around the world and do all these things you've done? Is there anything that you haven't done yet? From what I heard today it looks like you've been everywhere and you've done everything.

- That's an overstatement Hayley, there is still much left for me to do and see.

- Today you can tick off feeding a tiger cub and petting a fully-grown tiger.

- So can you. Another crazy thing added to your list.

- At least this one I remember.

Chapter 15

Winter was gradually changing into spring and although Liam was doing everything he could to jag Hayley's memory, she still couldn't remember anything. They've had so much fun together and Liam kept telling himself it was really Hayley but deep down he knew something was not right.

- Her memory is not coming back – he said to the twins one day - Her feelings for me are not coming back – he added with unhidden disappointment - I understand a person cannot remember what they've done or who they've met but it's impossible that someone can be different to such degree as a result of an amnesia. Don't get me wrong, she's perfectly nice and I have so much fun with her but... It's not Hayley.

- Liam, I know it's hard for you to accept her the way she is now but...

- It's not like that April, I can make my peace with her memory loss and I can start building our life together from scratch... But this is not Hayley. The things she likes and dislikes differ. She doesn't laugh anymore seeing same movies that made her laugh before, she doesn't even remember studying psychology.

- Liam, there is no way to verify whether it is really Hayley or not and whoever this person is, we can't just get rid of her, so what do you suggest? What can we do?

- April, is it even possible? – said June – That you brought to life someone else?

- I honestly don't know... Magic is not flowless, sometimes something may go wrong. But the question is if this really isn't Hayley… Then… Who is it? And where is real Hayley?

Hayley made herself a cup of coffee and sat in the living room watching the fire burning and petting Lexi lying with her head on Hayley's lap. She waited for Liam to come back from his meeting with the twins. He looked upset when he was leaving and she knew he was growing impatient as her memory was not coming back. He tried to encourage her to go back to work as apparently she loved it but she didn't know anything about psychology. The only thing she was sure of was that she loved to draw and she was really good at it but apparently this was not something she has done in the past.

She finished her coffee and went upstairs to clear her wardrobe. There were lots of outfits that she would never wear and there was no point in keeping them any longer. As she was going through her stuff she found some journal lying at the bottom of the wardrobe. Having sat comfortably on the floor, she leaned her back against the bed, opened the journal and started to read.

After his meeting with the twins, Liam spent a couple of hours wandering around the city thinking what to do. He was so happy at first when he saw Hayley alive but now he was sure it was not really her. He was worried about his real Hayley still being somewhere out there alone and scared. It was nice to see Hayley's happy face around the house and hear her laughter but he couldn't keep living a lie, he couldn't keep living with a stranger knowing she was not truly the woman he loved.

He came back home later that afternoon. It was surprisingly cold inside and the fire seemed to be out for a couple of hours.

- Hayley!

Liam worried that something has happened to her and maybe she's lying somewhere unconscious. He found her in the bedroom, sitting on the floor, leaning her back against bed, holding her diary open but not reading it anymore. She looked at him with tears in her eyes looking sad and frightened.

- Is this true? - she said quietly – Has all of this really happened?

Liam took the journal from her hands and had a quick look through.

- I think it's your diary – he said – But I've never seen it before.

She got up off the floor and looked at Liam. Her eyes were full of tears and her voice was shaking.

- Are you really... A vampire?

He looked at her without a word. She was very upset and scared and he didn't know whether telling her the truth would be the best option.

- Please, answer me – she insisted – Are you?

He nodded without a word. She looked away even more shocked.

- It is impossible, it cannot be true, it's... This diary – she continued with her shaky voice - Ends with me deciding to be a vampire too. I planned a trip to New Orleans where you were supposed to turn me. So what happened?

- I did what you asked of me.

- You turned me?!

- Yes.

- Am I a vampire?!

- Not anymore.

- What does it mean 'not anymore'?

- Hayley, you need to slow down. I will answer all of your questions later but now you need to take some rest.

- I want to know what's happened to me, Liam. I want to know everything. Nobody wants to tell me what's happened to me and I've asked like million times already. I can't believe this journal is real. I can't believe it's all really happened. It's insane!

She was walking nervously around the room, Lexi was lying on the bed observing her every move.

- So that's why I changed so much, because I nearly died… I can't believe I tried to kill myself.

- Hayley, please, calm down. I will explain everything and answer all your questions…

- I need a proof.

- Of what?

- If you're really a vampire, prove it to me because I don't believe it.

- Hayley, I don't think it's a good idea…

- Why? Because it's unreal? Or because you are afraid of something? What are you afraid of Liam? That I will reject you? That I will be scared and freak out? Clearly, I knew it once and I was fine with it so go ahead, show me something, make me believe!

Liam hesitated, but he wanted to see her reaction, he needed to know what she thought about him. Slowly, Liam's eyes started turning black and the dark veins covered his pale handsome human face. Hayley was staring back at him without a word paralysed with fear.

- Oh my God – she said quietly a few seconds later.

She approached the bed and sat down so as not to faint on the floor. Lexi moved closer but Hayley didn't pet her so she pushed her elbow with her cold nose but Hayley didn't react. She was breathing heavily, staring at the floor, with her eyes wide open and tears slowly running down her cheeks.

- Please, say something – Liam asked quietly.

But Hayley didn't say anything. She was just staring at the floor now breathing silently, trying to stay as quiet and motionless as possible as if she was observed by a predator. Liam sensed her growing fear and it was overwhelming, making even his own heart beat faster. He left the bedroom living Hayley alone with Lexi. Without much thinking he put his shoes on and went straight to Oliver who thankfully was home.

- Liam what's happened? - Oliver was worried seeing Liam so upset.

- Can I sleep here tonight?

- Of course. Come in.

Liam sat on the sofa in the living room not saying anything. It was obvious that he left the house in a hurry. Although it was cold outside, he didn't have a jacket and his hands and face were red from being freezing cold.

- Can you tell me what's happened?

- Hayley knows everything… About me and April and her transition…

- Is her memory back then?

- No, she found her old diary. There were a few pages about me and other magical stuff going on in her life at that time.

- I'm guessing she didn't take it well and threw you out?

- She didn't throw me out, I left. She was just sitting there... Terrified. She couldn't even look at me and I couldn't stand that tension.

- So what are you going to do now?

- I'll give her some time to calm down and I'll try to talk to her tomorrow morning.

- I'm surprised she reacted that way. She was OK with all this before so why now it's such a problem?

- Because it's not Hayley. Oliver, I've lived with that person for weeks and I can feel there is no connection. There aren't any feelings between us… There's… Nothing. Whoever this is, she doesn't love me and I don't love her. And the scariest part is that my Hayley is still somewhere out there and I don't know how to find her.

Liam's eyes were red and shiny but he was not crying. Once again, he felt hopeless and powerless and although he was heartbroken again, he couldn't share a single tear.

It took Hayley twenty minutes to realise Liam was not there anymore. She was sitting a few more seconds just listening, trying to figure out whether he just left the bedroom or left the house. She got up slowly and quietly went downstairs. The lights were on but nobody was there. She locked the front and back door and took a deep breath trying to calm down.

- I can't believe this – she said out loud looking at Lexi – All this time I was living with a monster. He's a real vampire! A murderer! How could I ever love him? How could I ever want to be like him? Why would I ever want to die and become something so evil? This is so unreal, I must be dreaming, this is just a nightmare and I need to wake up.

But despite pinching herself, Hayley was not waking up.

After a sleepless night, Liam left Oliver's house at nine o'clock considering that time as appropriate to see Hayley. At first he wanted to open the front door with his key but he knocked instead. He didn't want to scare Hayley and thought it would be better if she let him in, it had to be her decision. Even though she has never been so terrified before, Hayley slowly opened the door. Her face was serious and it was easy to tell that her night was as sleepless as Liam's.

- Can we talk?

Hayley nodded and moved from the door so he could come inside. He stood by the door and she leaned against the wall a few meters away.

- I believe it's quite clear how you're feeling about me right now but I need to hear it from you, nonetheless.

Hayley hesitated, her voice was caught in her throat.

- I'm scared – she whispered a few seconds later.

- You've lived with me under one roof for weeks and I haven't hurt you. You are perfectly safe with me, I can promise you that. As a matter of fact, you are safer with me than without. I would never hurt you, can you trust me?

- I… I'm sorry.

- Right… So what do you propose? What do you want to do?

- I don't know. I have nowhere to go, I don't have any money, I don't know this city that well.

- Would you like to move in with April and June? I'm sorry Hayley but this is my home and I won't move out. This is the only place where I feel I belong and I'll stay here. But obviously you can't live with me anymore… You can't even look at me.

- I'm sorry Liam. I wish I could feel differently but… I don't.

- I will give you some time to pack. How much do you need? An hour? Two?

- An hour is fine.

- Very well then. I will let them know you're coming. Please, leave the dog. Lexi means a lot to me and for you it's just a dog.

Without saying anything else, Liam turned around and left. He went to see April and June, angry and disappointed. It was a nightmare. The love of his life was gone, his future was scattered into a million pieces presenting only a shadow of a life. There was no happiness, no purpose, no love, only loneliness and pain.

He was walking quickly trying not to use his vampire speed in front of all those people and all he could think of was how much he just wanted to die.

- She'll move in here for a while if that's OK – Liam said to the twins when they opened the door.

- Why? What's happened?

- She knows everything. She read her old diary and now she's afraid of me. She's packing her stuff as we speak and will be here shortly as she has no other place to go. April, this is not Hayley, now I'm sure of it. I don't know what's happened and who you brought back to life but trust me, she's not your sister.

- Like you said, someone may lose their memory but their personality should stay the same. I trust your instincts Liam and if you say this is not Hayley, I believe you. You talked to her much more than me or June and you lived with her for a few weeks and had a chance to get to know her. But I can't just send her away, to be on her own without any family or friends. She can stay with us for now and we'll see what she decides later. Are you going to be OK?

Liam looked at April with his tired and sad eyes.

- No… I don't think I will ever be OK… I need to go now before she gets here. I'll talk to you later. Thanks for your help.

Shortly after they closed the door after Liam, they were opening them for covered in tears Hayley. She was dragging a small suitcase behind her and nothing more. June took the baggage and put it in one of the spare rooms upstairs. April made a cup of camomile tea to help Hayley calm down and relax.

- I can't believe this is happening to me – she said sitting at the table and nervously rotating the mug with her fingers - Why isn't my memory coming back? Why am I so different? That diary… It sounds nothing like me. I know you try to shelter me from the truth but now that I know so much, could you please finally tell me what's happened to me? Why did I wake up wet and covered in sheets and towels? If I really was a vampire once, why am I no longer one? How much has happened but was not written down in that diary? Please, I need to know.

- Can you take any more of unbelievable and unreal? - April looked at Hayley serious and concerned.

- I honestly don't know. Try me.

- Very well… OK… So here it goes… You died and I brought you back to life with my magic.

Hayley was looking at April without a word. The mug started burning her hands but she couldn't move.

- I died? How?

- We don't know. Listen… We've started to believe that you're not really Hayley. I'm afraid something went wrong and instead of bringing back Hayley, we brought you.

- So… Who am I?

- We don't know.

Hayley looked at her red and sore hands.

- Let me get you some ice – said June and approached the fridge.

- I'm sorry Hayley, I know it's all very confusing…

- Confusing? You have no idea how I feel right now. 'Confused' is a hell of an understatement.

- I know.

- Is there anywhere I can go and be left alone? I don't want to hear any more nonsense.

- First room upstairs on the left would be yours. Your stuff is already there.

Hayley got up and went upstairs with a bag of ice in her hands. She closed the door and sat on the bed. Nothing made any sense and the more she was told, the more frightened she was getting. A vampire husband, a witch sister, death and amnesia… It was impossible that it was really her life. It sounded so unrealistic, so bizarre and unbelievable. She dropped the ice bag on the floor, took her face in her cold hands and started to cry.

Liam came back home and was surprised to discover that it was not empty. Isabella was sitting on the floor in front of the fireplace, playing with Lexi.

- What are you doing here?

- April told me everything. I thought I'd pop in and check up on you and Oliver was happy to help me with that. How are you feeling, brother?

Liam sat on the floor next to Isabella and started staring at the dancing flames.

- I could use an endless list of adjectives describing every negative emotion and feeling that you can possibly imagine. I was patiently waiting for Hayl... For that girl to get her memory back but recently it's become clear to me that she was just a stranger. I remember when I first met Hayley – he smiled gently - Even after that attack she felt safe with me and wanted to get to know me and was eager to give me a chance to prove to her that I was a good man. But this girl... After a couple of months of living together she couldn't even look me in the eye. I know she's somebody else, I am sure of it.

- So what is going to happen now?

- April will figure something out. She's a very smart and powerful witch and if someone can fix this and bring real Hayley back it would be her... But the truth is that... I don't really think it's possible anymore... When Hayley died I was devasted but I kept hoping she could be brought back, that hope was the only thing keeping me alive. Now... Now I don't think she's anywhere out there and that she's truly gone for good... I would do anything to stop feeling the way I feel, Isabella. I would make a deal with the devil to bring Hayley back, I would pay any price to turn it all back. I would sell my own soul if that could change anything.

Isabella's heart was breaking like never before seeing Liam like that. He has never been in such despair and it was killing her that she didn't know how to help him.

- April can do the spell and go to Leah but can she go anyplace else? Can she explore other afterlives?

- I don't know. Nobody knows about any other places. There's heaven and hell for people and there's some third place for the witches where their magic is still working and they can freely communicate with other living witches. We don't know where vampires go after death. But what if… What if there was a way for me find out…

- What are you talking about?

- What if I died temporarily?

- Are you insane? That's impossible! If you die, your body will turn into ashes and that's it! You'd be gone for good.

- We don't know that. I bet April can cast some spell to prevent that.

- You can't do this, you risk too much Liam…

- What exactly do I risk, sister? A meaningless, shallow, empty eternity filled with loneliness and pain? I don't want to live like this. I can try to bring Hayley back and if it works that's great, if it doesn't then death would be the best thing that can happen to me right now. There is no happiness lying ahead, Isabella and I can't live like this any longer. If my plan fails… You need to let me go sister, you need to let me do this.

Liam didn't even have tears in his eyes, he clearly made up his mind and his decision was final. There was nothing Isabella could say now that would make him choose differently.

- I can't believe you want me to agree to this, brother. How can I possibly let you do this?

- Isabella, the truth is that I don't need your permission and I don't need your help. Whatever you do or say, it won't change anything. I am just being honest with you hoping you'd understand and I think you should appreciate my honesty and respect my decision.

- I think it's a terrible mistake but like you said I cannot stop you, so do whatever you want but I will not give you my permission to die.

- Very well. I will call April now and ask her to come over. You can ask Oliver to take you home if you want but it would mean a lot to me if you stayed.

April and June came over thirty minutes later intrigued by Liam's idea.

- So – April started when they all sat down in the living room – You have two options here. I can try to bring you back like I tried before with Hayley but we already know that there is fifty percent chance that you may not return… Or you can die wearing my ring. June wasn't brought back to life immediately which means it will give you some time to search for Hayley. But… The chances are that you may just die and never return, I don't know if this ring works the same on vampires as it does on people.

- I know but I am eager to take that risk.

April took her ring off and handed it to Liam. It fit his pinkie.

- Now lie down on the floor. It will be quick and painless, I promise, you won't feel a thing.

- How can you be so sure – Isabella asked – have you killed someone before?

- Isabella, stop – Liam said calmly – Whatever April has prepared for me, I'm not afraid. I'll be fine.

He kissed Isabella's forehead and looked her in the eye.

- I love you.

- I love you too, brother.

The moment Liam lied down on the floor, April quickly cast the spell and he died. It was as peaceful as she said it would be. He was lying on the floor, motionless and he's heart just immediately stopped beating.

- Oh my God – Isabella said through her tears – He really died.

- But he didn't turn into ashes and that's a good sign. Let's give him one hour. After that, I'll try the same spell I tried on June to wake her up.

Liam woke up surrounded by fog and twilight, lying on a narrow path surrounded by tall bushes. He got up and looked around. The sky above was heavily covered with dark clouds, it was cold and perfectly quiet. Suddenly, he heard a loud growl and felt an overwhelming fear. He knew something was chasing him and he needed to run but it didn't take much time for him to realise that he was in some kind of a maze, possibly with no exit. He tried to calm down and think but the fear was controlling him, making him run. After a few minutes that seemed to be endless, there was silence again so Liam stopped. Nothing was chasing him anymore. He tried to climb the bushes but he couldn't as the branches were too soft to stand on them, but when he tried to get through them, they seemed to be too strong and too hard to break through.

- What is this place?

Every now and then, he could hear others screaming and crying for help somewhere nearby but he didn't see anyone.

- Hayley! - he yelled as loud as he could - Hayley!

Then, he heard the growl again and started to run in fear although he didn't want to. After a few more steps, he woke up in his house with April kneeling over him.

- Is that you? - April said looking at Liam unsure.

- Yes, April, it's me. It worked.

Isabella ran over and put her arms around him.

- I'm so glad you're back, you idiot. Don't you ever do that to me again. I really hate you right now.

- Did you find Hayley? - June asked with a note of hope in her voice.

- No, I didn't see anyone.

- Where did you go exactly?

- I don't know. It looked like a maze and there was something following me around and I just knew I needed to run.

- Hell… - June said – That was hell. This is what Jack told me, that something was constantly chasing him and he needed to run.

- It definitely felt like hell. But there were moments when I could stop. I tried to get through the bushes or climb over it but I couldn't. There was no way out of that maze. I called Hayley's name but she didn't respond.

- OK… - said April - Now that we know where she may be, I can go and find her.

- You want to go to hell?! - June asked surprised

- Liam has just been there, I'll be fine.

- But he came back because you were here. We need you here with your magic in case something goes wrong and who will help you if you're in there?

- So what are you suggesting?

- Send me instead.

- And how am I supposed to do that? Liam went to hell because this is where he would go after death. If you die, you'll go to heaven, we already know this. I, however, can choose where to go without actually dying. It will be the same spell I use for meeting Leah, I will just choose a different destination.

- And are you sure it will work?

- I'm sure. I'll be fine June, trust me. Liam, can I have some salt and candles? I need to prepare the spell.

Liam brought April all ingredients as requested. They removed the rug from the living room and pushed the furniture aside to leave an open space in the middle of the room. April created a circle with the salt and lit four small scented candles.

- OK… As I don't belong in hell, I think I should be free to move around, especially that technically I won't be really dead. But… If something goes wrong and I die or don't come back within an hour, call Sarah. She'll know what to do.

April lied down on the floor, closed her eyes and started whispering the spell. After the third time, all four candles lit a bit brighter and April passed out. She woke up on the path inside a maze, exactly like Liam had earlier.

- Hayley!

As nobody responded, she started walking ahead. She could hear someone crying nearby and she could hear the growling but she was not afraid. She knew nothing was chasing her and she was safe. She didn't belong in hell, she was just passing by.

- Hayley! - April yelled again.

She was walking ahead and calling Hayley's name every few steps.

- April?!

She recognised that voice. It was Hayley, she was sure of it.

- Hayley don't move! I'm coming for you.

April started moving across the maze, through the bushes.

- Hayley, talk to me, where are you?

- April! Hurry up!

April started running faster but then suddenly she woke up. She saw Sarah kneeling over her.

- Damn it! Why did you call her?! I needed more time.

- More time? - June said angrily – You were gone for nearly two hours. You said yourself to call…

- I know what I said.

- Why are you so angry?

- Because I found her, I found Hayley. I could've brought her back with me if you had given me more time.

- Bring her back? How? - Liam asked – Don't you need her body in order to do that?

April looked at him surprised.

- You're right, I have completely forgotten about that.

- So where is her body? - Sarah asked.

- Occupied by someone else.

- What? Who?

- We don't know that. Whoever is in that body suffers amnesia and doesn't know who she is. Don't even ask me how that happened as I have no idea.

- So what are we going to do now? - Liam asked – We can't just kill that girl to get the body back.

- No, we can't… We need to get a new body.

- How? Where?

- I don't know.

The girl inhabiting Hayley's body heard the twins leaving the house in a rush and she was glad they left her alone. She put her face on the pillow, covered herself up to her ears and cried until she fell asleep. Although it was still morning, she felt unusually exhausted.

She woke up a few hours later cover in sweat.

- Oh my God.

All those emotions accumulated throughout the past two days jogged her memory. She remembered everything, her life before she died, the moment of the accident, waking up covered in sheets and everything that happened after that. She wanted to go back home but she didn't have any money for a taxi and although twins left their car, she didn't know how to drive. She couldn't call her real husband as he would never believe her, she sounded different not being in her own body. She couldn't show up looking like that, she needed a miracle and the only miracle worker she knew, was the one who brought her back to life. Unwillingly, she eventually sent April a text message: '*I need your help.*'

April came back home as soon as possible. She was constantly thinking how to get a new body for Hayley and she couldn't wait to get her sister out of hell. It was truly breaking her heart knowing that Hayley was suffering in hell all that time they thought she was safe with them.

- What is it? What happened? - April asked the moment she walked through the door.

The girl was walking nervously around the room, biting her nails.

- My memory is back, I remember everything and I need you to take me back home and make my husband believe it's really me. You're a witch, I bet there is something you can do.

- That's great news! So, who are you?

- My name is Megan Woods and I'm from Snowmass Village. Last thing I remember was getting hit by a car when I was walking back home from the store.

- So you died… But it doesn't explain how your spirit ended up here.

- I don't know, I don't understand any of this. April, I know there are many unanswered questions here but all I really want is to go back home to my husband. I just want to go home. Can you help me?

- Of course, that village is only ten miles away, I'll drive you there.

Megan put the shoes on and was ready to go. She didn't take the suitcase as nothing in it truly belonged to her. The girls got into the car but April didn't start driving.

- What's wrong? Why aren't you driving? - Megan asked impatiently.

April took her cell phone and dialled Oliver's number.

- Oliver, get everyone and meet me on the cemetery in Snowmass Village, we got the body. I'll be there in half an hour.

April disconnected and turned the engine on.

- What was that about? - Megan was getting anxious. - What's going on? What do you mean you have the body?

- I found my sister, real Hayley but I can't bring her back because you're in her body. Now, that we know who you really are, I can get you back to your own body and bring Hayley back to hers. So… We'll find your grave and… Well… Dig your body up.

- Are you insane?! You cannot do that!

- So you think you can just show up home looking like this and convince your husband you are in fact his dead wife? Do you really think he'll buy it? Even if I made him believe you, do you really want to spend the rest of your life looking like someone else? There is no going back home in this body, Megan. It just won't work.

Megan didn't say anything. She knew April was right, showing up in her own body was her only option. It would still be impossible to explain how she came back from the dead but it would be much easier than showing up looking like a complete stranger.

- So how are you going to do this? - she asked nervously.

- Don't make me try to explain the whole process to you. I can only assure you that it will be painless and you have nothing to worry about. Trust me, I can do this.

- Have you done it before?

- No… But it doesn't change the fact that I know exactly what to do and I know it will work. Like I said, don't worry, by the end of the day, you'll be sleeping in your own bed being one hundred percent yourself. I promise.

It was nearly four o'clock in the afternoon on the first week of March. Sun was painfully reflecting on the snow which covered the whole cemetery with a deep white layer. The place was completely empty and perfectly quiet. April and the rest of the pack was standing next to a tall family grave. The large engraved letters said 'Woods' and there were three names listed underneath.

- It's so creepy to look at my own grave – Megan said – I can't believe it's all really happening.

- Don't worry – April said with a gentle smile. - You'll be back to normal soon.

- Right… It depends on how my husband is going to take it, I mean… I was dead for over two months and I died on Christmas Eve… I can't even imagine what he's been through.

- He'll be happy to see you, I'm sure of it.

April had a look around to make sure nobody was there. It was unusually cold that day and clearly nobody planned an afternoon trip to the cemetery. She raised her hand and the entrance to the grave broke into pieces. Oliver and Liam took the coffin out and carefully put it on the snow, the shattered bricks disappeared in the deep snow underneath. Everyone took a step back as April approached the coffin.

- Megan, there is no place for you to lay down so I need you to stand still, OK?

Megan nodded although it would be difficult to stand still as her whole body was shaking not because she was cold but because she was so terrified of what was going to happen. April opened the coffin. Megan's body didn't look fresh so her first spell was to make it look normal. Then, she took Megan's hand and she also took the hand of the body lying in the coffin. April closed her eyes, took a deep breath and started chanting: '*Has animas transferre de corpore in corpus.*' Suddenly, Megan passed out and Liam caught her right before she dropped on the ground. April whispered the spell a few more times and looked at the body in the coffin but it was lying as still as before.

- Come on Megan, wake up. - she said impatiently.

Everyone was looking at the body expecting to see some signs of life. April put her hand on Megan's head and started chanting again.

- I can hear the heartbeat – Liam said.

In that moment Megan woke up and sat straight. She looked at her own hands and started crying and laughing simultaneously.

- It worked! I'm back!

- Come one – April said smiling – Get out of that coffin and let me take you home.

Liam took the jacket off Hayley's body and gave it to Megan as a simple black dress was the only thing she was wearing.

- Take it, we don't want you to freeze to death now that you're alive again.

Megan took the jacket with a hesitation. She was careful not to touch Liam's hand. The fact that he was a vampire was still terrifying her and she wanted to be as far away from him as possible.

- Thank you – she whispered and looked at Liam for the first time since she read Hayley's diary - And I mean for everything not just the jacket. I really appreciate what you've done for me.

He smiled gently not saying anything. Knowing how afraid she was, he knew it must have been really difficult for her to even talk to him but he appreciated the effort.

- You are very extraordinary people – Megan said looking at them all - And despite everything that's happened, I am happy I met you. You helped me come back home and I will always be in your debt. Thank you.

- Let's go Megan - April said and started walking back to her car. Oliver teleported back with the others, living them two alone on the cemetery.

They didn't need to drive for too long. The village was small and Megan's house was literally just around the corner. April parked two houses away from the address Megan gave her.

- I wish you all the best, but I'll wait here in case your husband freaked out and you needed my help.

- Thank you April. For everything.

- I'm glad you're OK. Here's my number, if you ever needed me, don't hesitate to call me.

- Thanks and good luck with bringing your sister back.

- Good luck to you too. Have a nice life, Megan.

- Thanks.

But Megan didn't move. She was still sitting in the car and looking at the front door leading to her house.

- What's wrong?

- What am I going to tell him? - Megan sounded nervous – There is no believable explanation of how I got back to life and I definitely cannot tell him the truth. What should I tell him April?

- I think you shouldn't give him any explanation. Just tell him that you woke up and came back home and you don't know what really happened.

- You're right… I can tell him that… What if he freaks out and lock me out?

- Megan, you worry too much. Just go and see instead of wondering what may happen. Go see your husband, I bet he'll be happy to see you.

Megan took a deep breath and finally got out of the car and ran quickly home. She knocked on the door and waited a few seconds before her husband opened. He was looking at her completely paralysed, not moving or saying anything for a few seconds. Then, he burst into tears and hugged Megan tightly. They were standing like that for a minute before they both went inside and closed the door. April smiled and turned the engine on. Her work for the day was not done yet, there was one more person who needed her help and although she was already exhausted by the spell she cast on the cemetery, she needed to find extra strength for her trip to hell and back.

- She looks so peaceful – June said looking at Hayley's body lying on the sofa - As if she was only asleep.

- Where is April? Why is it taking her so long? - said Liam walking nervously around the room.

Suddenly, they heard April parking the car on the driveway.

- OK, let's do this – she said when she entered the house.

She didn't take her boots off and she dropped her jacket on the floor without even stopping for a second.

- April, are you OK? You look pale and tired.

- I'm fine.

- April I know you are under a lot of pressure to get Hayley back and I want to see her as bad as you do but we don't want you to get hurt in the process. If you're too tired to do the spell, take a nap…

- I'm fine, June. Hayley's been in hell far too long now and we can't let her suffer any longer. Don't worry about me.

April started preparing the room for the spell but this time she made a bigger circle as Hayley was supposed to lie in it with her. She lied down on the floor and Liam gently put Hayley's body next to her.

- Good luck – he said with a gentle smile though he still looked worried.

April took a deep breath, closed her eyes and began the spell. A few seconds later, she was back in the creepy maze. She got up and started running ahead calling Hayley's name every few steps like she did before.

- April I'm here!

April started running across the maze cutting her hands and face on the bushes. She found her at last. There she was, standing on the path, breathing heavily, with her red eyes wide open and sweat running down her temples.

Hayley wanted to feel happy and relieved seeing her sister but she couldn't, hell did not allow any positive emotions, they didn't exist in that terrible place.

- I can get you out of here – said April and approached Hayley trying to reach her hand.

But before she managed to do that, a pair of two people showed up between them. They looked like a wealthy couple back from the fifties. The woman was wearing a polka dot dress and a pearl neckless and the man was wearing a three-piece dark grey suit with a striped tie and a hat. They both looked handsome and friendly.

- Forgive me young lady – man said – Unfortunately, you cannot take this soul from here.

- No, please, I'm begging you…

- You shouldn't be here – woman said smiling – Goodbye.

April woke up in the living room surrounded by everyone.

- Damn it! - she yelled angrily.

- What's wrong?

April got off the floor and sat on the sofa completely exhausted with her head thrown back.

- Bloody demons won't let me take Hayley back.

- What do you mean? What happened?

- I was about to take Hayley's hand and get her home but the demons showed up between us and kicked me out.

- You saw her? - Liam asked with a hint of hope.

- I did.

- Is she OK?

Liam asked that question and realised how stupid it was. Of course she was not OK, she was in hell.

- Don't answer that – he added quicky.

- So what do we do now? - asked June.

- I don't know, they won't listen to me, they didn't let me talk so I couldn't explain why I was there.

They all looked at Hayley's body still lying on the floor completely motionless. It seemed like there was no hope left now. They knew where Hayley was but they couldn't get her out and it was worse than not knowing anything at all.

- Let me talk to them – Oliver said unexpectedly.

- What's the point of sending you there? They won't talk to you.

- They will talk to me

- How can you be so sure?

- Because I've been delivering souls to hell for decades so they know my name down there. If they are eager to talk to anybody it would be me.

- Maybe you're right… Maybe it's worth giving a shot. But I can't do this right now, I'm too tired, I won't be able to sustain the spell. We need to wait.

- Then teach me. Let me know the right words and I can do it myself.

- April, can he do it? - June sounded worried – Is it safe? I don't want him to get hurt.

- Don't worry about me Love – said Oliver with his charming smile – I don't belong in hell so they won't let me stay there. If I'm wrong, they will just kick me out like they did with April.

- Give me a piece of paper and a pen – said April - I will tell you exactly what you need to get there and back.

April wrote the words and handed it to Oliver.

- This is your ticket to hell and back. Good luck.

April lied down on the sofa and instantly fell asleep. She has never been so tired in her entire life. The spells she performed that day left her barely alive and she needed a proper rest. Oliver stared at the piece of paper for a couple of minutes, repeating the spell over and over again until he knew it by heart.

- OK, I'm ready – he said and lied down in the circle next to Hayley.

- Be careful – said June.

- I'll be fine and I'll bring her back – he added looking at Liam - You have my word.

Oliver closed his eyes, took a deep breath and cast the spell, carefully repeating the words April wrote for him.

- I'm going to eat something – said June and started heading towards the kitchen – Do you feel like having a pizza? - she added looking over her shoulder.

- You just made me realise how hungry I am – said Isabella - Let's order something nice. I bet Hayley will be hungry too.

– I'm not hungry – said Liam, sitting on the floor, staring at Hayley and impatiently waiting for her to wake up.

- Get yourself something to do. - said June - April was gone for a couple of hours and didn't do much on the other side, Oliver went to hell to negotiate with the demons so I assume it's going to take a while. Looks like a few minutes in hell is a few hours in real world.

But Liam didn't move, he didn't want to leave Hayley's side, he wanted to make sure he was right there when she's finally back and he didn't want to miss that moment.

Oliver woke up in the maze surrounded by fog and silence.

- I want to talk! - he yelled not wasting a single minute.

A nice good-looking young man showed up right in front of him. He was wearing a suit and a tie, looking very smart.

- Mr Fox, what a surprise. To what do we owe this pleasure?

- You put on your human face for me, how nice – Oliver said trying to sound friendly.

- Well, I didn't want to scare away my guest. So what brings you here?

- I'm here to collect.

The man laughed.

- Collect? You deliver to hell, not collect from it. Don't be ridiculous, Oliver.

- I thought maybe you could make an exception this one time. I'm here for Hayley Anderson.

- Another one in just one day? She must be very popular, you're not the first one trying to steal her away.

- So what's it going to be? Can we make a deal?

- We already have a deal in place, Oliver.

- You're right, but I've delivered a countless number of souls throughout my whole life so maybe you can give me one soul in return.

- You are already getting something in return, Oliver. When was the last time you needed to see a doctor?

- I see your point, but maybe we can make a new deal, maybe there is something I can offer in return for Hayley. She doesn't belong here.

- Of course she does. She's in hell because she deserves it, she's a vampire. And what's even worst, she's a vampire by choice.

- But she's one of the good ones.

- Is she really? Please, correct me if I'm wrong but I believe she killed someone.

- To protect her sister.

- Protect? At that point her sister was already dead. It was a revenge, she was protecting no one.

- Right… But maybe you can give her another chance. She's been in hell for months now. We're talking about one sin here so hasn't she paid for it already? Give her another chance, let her come back as a human and if she does something bad again, I will deliver her soul here myself. How does it sound?

The man was looking at Oliver, thinking intensively.

- Very well, we can make a new deal. I can give you Hayley back but there is a price to pay for her soul. So how much are you willing to give in return?

- Just tell me what you want.

Oliver and Hayley woke up a few hours later. All three girls were sleeping on the sofas in the living room and Liam was sitting on the floor staring right at the bodies in the circle, waiting impatiently. He got up promptly when he saw Oliver and Hayley opening their eyes. His hands were shaking as he was helping Hayley get off the floor and his heart was beating fast. He was looking at her with fear, hope and uncertainty, hoping for the best but preparing for the worst.

- Please, say something – he said quietly, holding Hayley's hands and looking her right in the eye.

But Hayley didn't say anything. Instead, she threw her hands around Liam's neck and started to cry.

- You did it - said June and gave Oliver a quick kiss on a cheek - Are you OK?

- I'm fine. I told you, you had nothing to worry about, everything's OK.

- Well done Oliver. - said April rubbing her red and tired eyes - And thank you.

Once Hayley let go off Liam she hugged her sisters tightly, happy to see them again.

- Welcome back – Isabella said with a smile – We missed you.

- Good to have you back, sister – said April – how are you feeling?

Hayley reached for a tissue and wiped the tears. She looked around the room at all those familiar faces of people she loved so much. She smiled and tears came to her eyes again.

- I'm OK – she said crying and smiling simultaneously – It's good to be back.

- I can't even imagine what you've been through – said Liam and put his arm around Hayley.

- I really don't want to talk about it. I'd rather listen to you, I bet there is a lot I've missed. Tell me everything!

Hayley was sitting on the sofa cuddling up to Liam and listening to April talking about the hunter, the evil witch and Megan. She was trying to stay focused but every now and then her mind was taking her back to the maze and the fear was making her restless. She remembered vividly what hell was like and the terrifying images were still lingering in her mind.

- April I think it's enough for today – said Liam – We should let Hayley take some rest. There will be time for stories later.

- Right, sorry, how silly of me. Have a goodnight sleep Hayley and we'll see you later. Come over whenever you're ready.

- I will be there as soon as I can. - said Hayley with a vague smile.

She was very tired but had no heart to ask her sisters to leave. She felt relieved when Liam read her mind and said aloud what she wanted to say for the past half an hour. She brushed her teeth and quickly changed into her pyjama. She dreamt of a hot relaxing bath but more than that she wanted to sleep. It was late at night and the new moon was showing high on the starry sky. Hayley went to bed squeezing between Liam and Lexi. She fell asleep immediately, feeling safe and happy, lying in her own warm and soft bed. Liam cuddled his face into Hayley's hair and held her tightly in his arms. Now he was sure it was truly her as the gaze he missed so much was full of love once again. He was happy Hayley was human again and had a chance for a normal happy life, away from merciless vampire hunters and hateful witches. Whether she was a human or a vampire, he worried about her just as much, but she was clearly happier as a human and Liam wanted to see her happy more than anything. They both have been given a second chance and they wouldn't make the same mistakes again. April's magic could keep Hayley young and healthy so she could be with Liam forever. Turning her into a vampire was a mistake, she hated her life and ended up in hell and that could never happen again.

June asked Oliver to stay with her instead of teleporting back to his house. She was not tired and wanted to talk to him alone. When April went to her bedroom upstairs, they stayed outside sitting on the porch swing despite freezing cold.

- So tell me, what did they want from you?

Oliver didn't answer.

- Come on – she insisted – I'm not stupid Oliver, I know they wouldn't just give Hayley back to you without wanting anything in return. Be honest with me, what did they want?

Oliver knew there was no point in trying to avoid that conversation. June was very stubborn and she would not stop asking. And he wanted her to know, he wanted to be honest with her and be able to confine in her.

- You're right… They didn't want to give her back so I made a new deal with them… My previous deal with them has been void.

- What does it mean? - June furrowed her brow.

- It means that I don't work for them anymore.

- That's good then, you're free, right? Isn't it what you wanted?

- But it also means that they have taken my powers away and I'm no longer protected by magic.

- So what are you saying?

- I'm saying that I'm not a witch anymore, now I can just grow old and die, I'm just human.

June looked at Oliver shocked, unsure what to say.

- That's OK June, I don't regret what I've done, I'm happy I could help Hayley. I just need to adjust.

- It won't be so hard.

- You think? I won't get paid by the witches anymore so I need to find a proper job but I'm forty and I have zero experience in anything so that's not going to be easy. And I can't teleport anymore so if you have any holiday destination in mind we need to travel there like everybody else.

- It's going to be OK. I wasn't with you because of your powers, I was with you in spite of them. The only thing pushing me away from you was your 'job' and I tried really hard to accept it but now it's not an issue anymore. I'm glad you're free from your responsibility towards the witches or hell or whatever it was. You can lead a normal regular life with me, I can help you. This is the only thing in which I am better than you – she added with a smile – Everything is going to be OK, trust me.

Oliver looked at her with his tired eyes. The spell he has performed that night consumed all his energy.

- Thank you Love. Now, let's go to bed. I feel like I'm going to pass out. I don't remember the last time I felt so tired.

- That's normal – June smiled – Everyone feels that way when they go to hell and back.

Oliver laughed at June's joke, put his arm around her and they both slowly went upstairs to June's bedroom as Oliver was too tired to go back to his own place.

June was lying in bed watching Oliver sleeping. She couldn't fall asleep thinking about their future together. She knew it was going to be hard to get Oliver live an ordinary life. In the morning they would ask April for the ring protecting him from illness and passing time but would he ever get used to the fact of being powerless? June rolled on her other side and before she closed her eyes she saw her ruby pendant lying on the bedside table and slightly glowing red. She smiled and closed her eyes. *'Not so ordinary after all'*

When Hayley woke up in the morning she was alone in bed and Liam was downstairs in the kitchen preparing breakfast. She looked at the clock, it was nearly noon. She stayed in bed a bit longer, staring at the ceiling, thinking about her time in hell. She was glad to be back as a human and given another chance. She was so happy seeing her family again, feeling warm, safe and loved. For the past few months all she could have thought of was Jack and how much she regretted killing him. Now, she could be happy again, living a brand new life the right way, exactly as she should have.

She got up and went downstairs. Liam was done with the food now and the table was full.

- Good morning – he said with a smile – Or maybe afternoon would be more accurate. Did you sleep well?

Hayley walked up to Liam and put her hands around him.

- I love you so much – she whispered into his ear and kissed him.

- I love you too.

- I saw some new photos on the wall.

- These are not your memories, they don't need to be there.

- Let's take them down then so they don't keep reminding me of the time when I was away, although… I don't think I will ever be able to forget.

- Try not to think about it anymore. You're back now and you will never see that place again, you don't belong there. It's all a part of your past now and you don't have to re-live it every day.

- You're right, it will never happen again. I'm sorry I seem so off.

- Don't apologise Hayley, you have a good reason to be this way. I've been there too, I've seen it and I know how horrifying that place was.

- I can't believe you risked your own life for me just to see if I was there.

- Hayley, my life without you… - he paused - It was not living, it was existing, it was my very own hell on earth, so I was not really risking anything as it couldn't have been any worse.

Hayley reached her hand across the table and grabbed Liam's hand.

- So I can say now that you literally followed me through the gates of hell.

Liam smiled.

– It's good to have you back. I missed you so much.

- It must have been very hard for you to see Megan's negative reaction, after all… She looked like me.

- It was painful just for a second, then I was just sure it was not you. With your memory or not, I know you wouldn't just freak out like that.

- You're right, I probably wouldn't…

- Hayley… There is something you should know… I just want to be completely honest with you.

- OK… – Hayley looked at Liam expectantly and with growing anxiety.

- You see… I was very heartbroken and depressed without you – he said staring at his plate and playing with the fork nervously – But fresh blood made me feel better. I found a way to keep my mind busy and give myself a tiny bit of happiness just to keep myself alive.

She looked at him shocked and speechless.

- Did you… - she said stuttering – Did you kill someone?

- No! - Liam responded quickly looking Hayley deep in the eye – No, I killed nobody, I swear. You need to believe me.

- I believe you. It's just… The way you started this conversation got me really nervous and I thought… Never mind – she smiled – That's fine Liam, I'm not angry.

- Really? - Liam was truly surprised – I thought you would be mad.

- I was a vampire once too and I remember exactly what it felt like. If you hadn't stopped me there in Rome, I would've bitten that girl. And if you say that it was the only thing making you happy and you didn't kill anyone then I'm fine with it.

- You're amazing, Hayley. I'm happy you're forgiving me my awful behaviour and I promise it won't happen again. Now I have you and you give me all the happiness in the world and I don't need anything else.

- Good, I want you by my side at night and not somewhere out there, chasing some strangers like some vampire.

- Very funny – Liam added with unhidden amusement.

- OK, it's time to call June and April now – said Hayley as she started tidying up the table - They wanted to talk to me today. I also need to talk to Oliver and see what the price was for my soul.

- Price?

- I don't think they let me go just because Oliver asked them nicely. I bet they wanted something in return and he obviously gave it to them.

- You're right, I didn't think about it. Call them all and get them here. Let's have a nice family Sunday afternoon. I'll order something to eat.

- But please order some normal takeaway and not someone you can bite.

- Would you cut it out? It's not funny anymore.

But he smiled anyway when he was leaving the kitchen.

As Hayley was waiting for her guests to show up, she approached the wall by the stairs and took down the photos of Megan. She got sad seeing herself in these photos but knowing it was not her.

- There are other photos on this wall worth your attention, you know? – Liam said standing behind her with his arms crossed and leaning against the wall– There are so many amazing moments worth re-living, you don't have to focus on those few ones not relating to you.

- There's our wedding day and Hawaii and Cuba… I've had so much fun with you.

Hayley went to the kitchen and threw the photos to the bin.

- Let bygones be bygones – she said and went to open the front door as her guests were already outside.

They all spent a lovely afternoon at home sitting by the fireplace and reminiscing. Hayley was sad that she missed Christmas and New Year's Eve. It was her favourite time of the year and she couldn't believe she literally spent it in hell, away from everyone she loved.

- So what do you plan on doing now? - asked June.

- I just want to spend some quality time with Liam and Lexi, relax and chill and then I'll go back to work. God knows how I'm going to explain my disappearance to my clients… I bet they won't be interested in coming back to being my patients and I would need to wait for some new ones.

- Either way, you'll be fine – said Oliver with an encouraging smile.

- Thanks Oliver, by the way, I haven't had a chance to thank you for saving me. I would never forget what you've done for me. Thank you.

- No problem Hayley, I'm glad I could help.

- So what was the price? What did they want from you in return?

Oliver hesitated. - They took my powers away. It looks like I'm not a witch anymore.

- Wow… I didn't know they could do that. I'm really sorry.

- Don't be, I can live with that. I'm just glad you're back.

- April, is there a way to check how much magic is actually left in Oliver? I know he feels powerless and he can't teleport anymore but I don't think he's human.

- June, what are you talking about?

- My neckless still glows when Oliver's around.

- Does it really? That's interesting…

- Give me your hand – said April and approached Oliver.

She closed her eyes and stayed quiet and focused for a few seconds.

- I can't feel anything – she said and let go off Oliver's hand – I'm sorry, I don't know why the neckless still reacts to you but I can't feel any magic. Maybe it's supressed somehow… Maybe it's dormant and will reappear one day… I really don't know.

- That's fine April, I don't need it. You honestly need to stop worrying about me and feeling sorry for me. The price I paid for getting Hayley out of hell was extremely low and I'm glad they claimed only my magic and not my life. Let's not dwell on this anymore, I don't regret it and I would do it again for anyone of you without hesitation. Now, where are those pizzas you ordered? I'm getting hungry. There! Right on time – Oliver added when he heard the doorbell.

He got up and opened the door. But it was not a pizza guy.

- Megan? - Oliver said surprised – What are you doing here?

- I came by to see you. I wanted to meet Hayley and give her back her jacket. Is now a good time?

- Sure, come on in.

Oliver let Megan through and led her to the living room where everyone was gathered.

- It looks like you're having a family gathering, I don't want to interrupt.

- Don't be ridiculous, have a sit and I'll get you something to drink.

Megan sat on the sofa next to June and looked around the room, stopping her gaze on Hayley.

- It's nice to finally meet you Hayley, I feel a bit weird now having lived your life for those few weeks.

- It's nice to meet you too. I've heard so much about you.

- Well… I bet not all of it was good, was it? The way I behaved…

- Don't worry about that, we understand how difficult it must have been for you.

- But I still owe you an apology – she said directing her gaze at Liam - I can justify my act by saying that I was overwhelmed after reading that diary, which I also apologise for, by the way – she added looking at Hayley – But the bottom line is that you have been good to me and made me feel like home although you suspected something was not right. I saw you were a good man but I treated you like a monster and it was unfair. I'm sorry Liam.

- I appreciate that Megan and the fact that you came back here today says a lot about you.

- So how was your return home? - April asked – How did your husband react?

- He was so happy to see me. At first he thought I was a ghost or an illusion, that I was not real and his broken mind was playing tricks on him. He didn't ask any questions and was just happy he could see me and hear my voice again. He didn't want to talk about Christmas or my funeral. He started freaking out though when we went out together for a walk with our dog and he saw me interacting with other people. Then, he realised that I was truly back in flesh and blood and I was not just a ghost. He asked me eventually whether I remembered anything about afterlife or how I got back and if I saw God but I told him that I didn't remember anything and I didn't want to talk about it anymore and just wanted to come back to living my life. So he stopped asking and just let it go. Yesterday, we went to the cemetery and fixed my parents grave. I could say that my husband was deep in thought trying to find any logical explanation but he didn't say a word. I can't even imagine what theories must be running through his head. But I decided not to talk about it and just leave it in the past.

- I'm glad you're back to normal now – said April – After everything you went through, you deserve a long and happy life.

- If I may ask – Megan started hesitantly, looking at Hayley – What really happened to you? I know you don't know me at all but I feel like I knew you my whole life and I really want to know what happened.

Hayley hesitated with an answer. She didn't want to talk about her time in hell, especially with a stranger.

- I died but my sister brought me back to life, that's all.

- Do you remember anything about afterlife?

- No Megan, I just remember waking up.

- Oh… I hoped that maybe you could tell me something, assure me there was a real heaven.

- I can assure you that – June said – When I died, I went to heaven and it was beautiful and I felt amazing.

- Really? - Magen asked surprised – You died too? Did you all die at some point in the past?

- No – June laughed – We're not that crazy.

- Right – April added sarcastically.

- Thank you June, it really means a lot to me. I was afraid that after death I would just come back as someone else, like I did… But now I can hope that there is a beautiful paradise waiting for me and that I will see my parents again one day and everything will be perfect… I think I'll be going now – Megan said getting up from the sofa – It was really nice to see you alive and well Hayley. Here's your jacket – she added pointing at the bag standing on the floor by the sofa – I guess you may need it, the winter has not ended yet.

- Thanks Megan. It was nice of you to come over and check up on us. I'm glad your life is back to normal, you deserve it.

- It's not really back to normal. I mean… I have a witch on a speed dial in case of an emergency. - she added gazing at April with a smile.

- I hope you will never need my help though. - said April – But if you do, don't hesitate to call.

- Thanks April. Thank you all for everything. Enjoy the rest of your day and feel free to visit.

- Some day – said Hayley with a gentle smile.

But in many cases 'some day' really meant 'never' and Hayley knew that. She knew Megan was a lovely person and she wished her all the best, but she didn't want to see her ever again. It felt weird knowing that Megan lived as her in her own house and now that she knew her real face, it was even harder to accept that fact and overcome it. She didn't blame her for anything and whatever has happened wasn't her fault but for some unknown reason, she didn't like Megan and wanted her to stay away from her and her family. She didn't need her to keep reminding Hayley about her time in hell. The images filling up her head were more than enough.

Chapter 16

Hayley spent the whole next week on relaxing and enjoying her time with Liam. They were snowboarding, skiing and hiking. Every evening, they had their movie marathon cuddling on the couch by the fireplace. They were appreciating every single minute spent together, happy like never before.

On Saturday evening they were getting ready for their dinner at April and June's. They didn't know what the twins had planned for the weekend but Hayley and Liam were asked to dress smart so Liam put on his suit and Hayley was wearing her elegant black dress and pearls. When they opened the door Hayley was stunned. The whole house was decorated with Christmas decorations. There were garlands and Christmas lights all around the house. In the living room in the corner, there was a six-foot Christmas tree and it was not decorated in red and gold like Hayley's tree, this one was full of colours, without any pattern or harmony maintained and yet it looked exceptionally beautiful.

- Oh my God – Hayley said shocked and amazed - What is all this?

- Well – said April – You were so sad you missed Christmas so we thought we could re-do it for you.

- In March?

- Yeah, why not? Merry Christmas, Hayley.

- You're insane!

- Don't you like it?

- Of course I like it. I love it!

- Great! Make yourself at home, we will go grab the turkey, it should be ready now.

- What a surprise - said Liam handing over a glass a champaign.

- I'm speechless. - said Hayley admiring the Christmas tree - I didn't see that coming, Christmas in March, who does that? Look at this tree Liam, this is how we did it when the twins were kids. There were no rules so we could put on the tree whatever we wanted, starting from various Christmas decorations and ending with toys, sweets, key rings, pendants... Whatever could be hung. Every year the tree looked chaotic and utterly terrible and I loved it. I can't believe they did it the same way now, it makes me nostalgic. Did you know what they've planned?

- No, I had no idea. They probably didn't fill me in knowing that I wouldn't be able to keep a secret.

- Come on guys – said June – Dinner's ready.

They spent an amazing evening singing Christmas carols and opening presents although Hayley was the only one receiving all the gifts. Christmas has never been so perfect and even though it was celebrated in March, it was the best Christmas she has ever had.

- Thank you girls – Hayley said when they were sitting in the living room completely stuffed after dinner – It was an amazing evening, I had so much fun.

- 'Was' you said? This day has not ended yet. - said June with a smile.

- I know but it's already nine o'clock and I was ready to go home. Do you have anything else planned?

- Well... Obviously, after Christmas... There's New Year's Eve.

- Are you serious? You want to do the New Year's Eve tonight?

- Of course, we're going out!

- Dancing?- asked Hayley with a hint of hope.

- Absolutely. What else could we do on New Year's Eve?

They all went out to enjoy live music in the local pub. It was not so crowded and there was plenty of space for dancing. Hayley was wearing her winter boots along with her fancy black dress looking funny and inappropriately dressed for Saturday dancing in a pub, but she didn't care. She didn't care where she was and how she looked. She didn't care about people laughing and pointing their fingers, they didn't exist in that moment. She was so happy dancing and singing, surrounded by those she loved the most. She wanted that night to last forever and despite being tired and overeaten, she didn't want to leave the dance floor.

- Where are you taking me next? - Hayley said with unhidden excitement when they left the pub right before midnight.

- Embrace yourself for the fireworks display.

They all reached Oliver's house only a few minutes before midnight but everything was ready and all they needed to do was to light a match. They counted down from ten and the show started. The fireworks were beautiful, illuminating the night sky for nearly five minutes. They burnt with coloured flames and sparks, some disappeared promptly but some lasted for a few seconds, slowly dying out as the sparks were falling towards the ground.

- Happy New Year! - June said and hugged her sister tightly. - Enjoy your new life, Hayley.

- Thank you June. Thank you all for organising all this for me, you have no idea how much it means to me. I can't wait to put on the wall the photos I've taken today. This was an exceptional Christmas and New Year's Eve and I will carry this memory forever.

Oliver was sitting on the bed with a laptop on his lap, late at night, unable to fall asleep.

- What's wrong? - asked June when he sighed loudly clearly annoyed.

- I'm looking at flight tickets. I didn't know how ridiculously expensive they are.

- Tickets? Where?

- Anywhere. I just wanted to go somewhere with you, show you some beautiful places but it looks like it would cost us a few hundred dollars and take us a few hours just to get anywhere. Did you know that a flight to Europe may take like fifteen hours?

- I know, that's why I don't travel. But that's OK Oliver, I don't have to see the world, I'd be happy to go hiking with you or skiing, we can stay local and still have fun.

Oliver didn't say anything. He was staring at the screen looking sad and disappointed.

- You miss it, don't you?

- Miss what?

- Teleporting.

- I don't regret anything, June

- This is not what I asked.

- Yes… I miss it. But it's not a big deal June, I can live with my decision.

- I'm sorry Oliver. It was unfair, Hayley is my sister and it should have been me or April making that deal, not you.

- Hayley is my friend, she's also my best friend's wife and your sister. I told you, I don't regret anything. Besides, demons wouldn't make any deals with you, they sent April away nearly immediately, they didn't want to talk to her. There was nothing you two could've done. Don't think about it anymore. What's done is done and there is no point to dwell on it.

- You're right. Now shut down the laptop and try to get some sleep. Now is not the time to think about high prices and long journeys, but if you can't sleep, go and grab the game pads, I will kick your butt in a shooter game.

The next morning when June was at work, Oliver was working on his CV. The vision of his future didn't look good. He never really worked anywhere, he knew nothing about repairing stuff or customer service. He was in his forties and his CV page was blank.

- McDonald's – he said to himself with tears in his eyes – That's my only option… Where else can I go?

He was staring at the blank page for a while, completely motionless.

- I'm useless! - he yelled and threw his laptop against the wall breaking it.

- Damn it! - he yelled again seeing his laptop broken and a small shallow hole in the wall.

That day couldn't get any worse. He couldn't remember the last time he felt so miserable. He knew June would worry and that thought was making him feel even worse.

- I can help you – suddenly Oliver heard a voice and panicked as he didn't know anyone else was there. He got up quickly and looked around.

A young man came out of the kitchen and sat on the couch, looking at Oliver with a smile. Oliver's never seen that man before but he knew exactly who he was. The man looked average and he would not stand out from the crowd in his plain black sweatshirt and jeans.

- What are you doing here? Our deal is over, go back to hell. - said Oliver looking angry and sad.

But the man didn't feel like leaving and he just sat back comfortably, with his gaze focused on Oliver. The smile on his face made him look creepy rather than friendly.

- I can see you are struggling. It is not easy to start a normal human life after decades of what you've been doing so far - his voice was calm and friendly, making Oliver believe the man really cared about him and truly wanted to help - You knew it was going to be difficult, we warned you.

- I'm fine. Don't worry about me.

- But you have a choice, you know? We can turn it around for you. We'd be happy to see you back in service, Oliver. You can have your powers back, you can be the man you've always been, you can return to the life you know. All you have to do is ask.

- At what price? - Oliver didn't hide his interest as demon's offer sounded very tempting.

- Like I said, we can turn it around.

- You want Hayley back, is that it?

- Yes.

- I could never do it to her, she's my friend. - Oliver sounded sad and frustrated again.

For a second, he truly believed there was another option for him and the demon came back with a solution to all his problems, but now he knew he could never agree to an offer like that.

- Is that the case really or are you just afraid what others would think of you? I am willing to help you, Oliver. You can get what you want and no one has to know the truth. We can send another witch for Hayley, it doesn't have to be you. Your friends would never know you had anything to do with her death.

Oliver was staring at the floor, deep in thought. Demon's magic was working on him. He wanted to be himself again, he wanted to live his life the way he knew best and he was not ready to face the future where he would be working ten-hour shifts.

- What future awaits you, my friend? - demon continued - Working nine to five Monday to Friday for little money, is that what you really want? We can offer you much more for your services, Oliver. No old age, no sickness, no pain…

- No… No, I can't do this…

- You're making a terrible mistake.

- Maybe I am, but I can't send my friend back to hell, she doesn't deserve it.

- So you truly care about her then, don't you? - The man looked surprised.

- I do, yes. I care about her and I care about the ones who love her.

- Very well then. - the man slowly got up from the sofa - You had your chance for a better life and you rejected it. You made your choice Oliver, once again. I wish you all the best, my friend. Try to stay alive.

The man disappeared living Oliver alone. He was staring at the spot the demon was standing a second before. Then, he looked at his laptop lying on the floor by the wall and sighed loudly. He didn't have the strength to deal with it just yet.

- How was your day? - asked June kissing Oliver on a cheek.

She cheerfully passed him by and walked into the living room.

- What's happened? - she asked looking at the broken laptop and damaged wall.

But Oliver didn't respond. He picked up the laptop and put it on the coffee table.

- I need a new laptop, this one isn't working anymore.

- I can see that. Oliver, talk to me, what's happened?

- I wanted to look for a job today, but my search ended with a blank CV page so I got a bit frustrated and I threw my laptop. It was a stupid thing to do, I know, but... I have no idea what to do. I'm stuck, June.

Oliver looked miserable and it was breaking June's heart but she didn't know how to help him.

- You don't have to do this right now, Oliver. We can come back to that job search later, we'll figure something out. Give yourself a bit more time to adjust.

Oliver sat on the sofa throwing his head back.

- Time... - he repeated quietly - I don't know how much I have left.

- Don't worry, April can bring you back if something happens to you. I'm sorry that her ring doesn't work on you.

- That was the part of the deal. Demons are not stupid, it wouldn't have made any sense if they had taken their protection away but then let April protect me with her magic. A simple human life… That's all I have.

- That's truly admirable – someone said suddenly.

The same young man appeared in Oliver's living room for the second time that day.

- Don't worry June – said Oliver looking at her terrified face – He won't hurt you.

- Who is it? - she asked with her breaking voice although she already knew the answer. She could feel a terrible cold and emptiness emanating from the man and it made her feel scared and sad. He looked perfectly normal and yet, it was easy to tell he was far from human.

- Do not fear me – the man said with a gentle smile – I'm not here for you.

- Why are you here? – Oliver asked with unhidden annoyance, getting up from the sofa – I told you, I won't change my mind and I have nothing more to say to you.

- I know. Despite your suffering, you're still persistent. I have a new deal for you, my friend. It has nothing to do with Hayley this time or anyone else as a matter of fact. It's only about you. However, I'd like to see what your girlfriend has to say, I know her opinion is important to you.

Oliver didn't say anything. He was just staring at the demon impatiently waiting to hear about a new deal.

- You are a true hero – demon continued and sat on the other sofa opposite to Oliver and June – You saved your friend even though you knew the price. Today, when I offered I could turn it all around, you said no. You can see your meaningless future and yet, you still say no to my deal. You are a truly valuable person, selfless and carrying and I would like to reward you for this.

- Why would you do that? - June sounded genuinely surprised – You're a demon.

- Which means I punish bad people but I am not bad myself. I may not have a heart or a soul and I don't have compassion for humans but I do understand good and evil, I know what's right and wrong and I can base my decisions on this knowledge. I am sure that rewarding Oliver would benefit us all and it is a good decision to make an offer like that.

As June didn't comment on that, feeling very uncomfortable talking to a demon, the man directed his gaze at Oliver and continued:

- We need you Oliver, probably as much as you need us, truth be told. So… We'll be happy to go back to our previous deal. You can have your life back and work for us again. Everything would be as it was and we don't want anything extra in return. What do you say?

- He says yes – June said not giving Oliver any chance to react.

- Are you sure? - asked Oliver with a note of hope in his voice – You didn't like that about me.

- But I can't stand seeing you so miserable. I would agree to anything just to see you happy again. You have been looking for a job for a few hours today and that left you completely broken. What's going to happen once you go to a job that you hate? How can you be working behind the counter or in the factory with all these normal people knowing that not that long ago, you have been an immortal witch who could teleport and go to hell and back to help his friends? You don't belong any place else Oliver so if the key to your happiness is to go back to what you used to be, then so be it.

Oliver smiled and stroke June's face with his fingers.

- Thank you – he said quietly – You have no idea how much it means to me.

He approached the demon.

- Looks like we have a deal – he said with a smile and reached his hand out.

- Perfect – said the demon and shook Oliver's hand.

June saw a pale orange and yellow light passing through their hands. Oliver's breath was shallow and rapid as the power was passing through his body. Suddenly, the light disappeared and the demon let go off Oliver.

- Pact has been made – he said - Welcome back Oliver Fox. Your first order should come through shortly.

He smiled again and disappeared.

- I don't get it – said June – it was a demon from hell and yet… He was nice and helpful… Shouldn't he be all evil?

- Not exactly, you see… It's just their job to punish bad people for their sins but they are not evil themselves… Although… They seem to enjoy what they do.

- They are weird creatures. I hope they won't come over too often.

- Hopefully, you will never see them again.

- So how are you feeling? Better?

- I feel great – Oliver said with his usual charming smile – Thank you, Love.

- For what?

- For letting me do this.

- Yes, well… This is not the best solution and I am not particularly thrilled about it… But I'm glad to see you happy again.

Oliver kissed her gently but then reached to his pocket and unfolded a piece of paper that was in it.

- Let me guess – said June – You need to go now.

- I'm sorry, Love, duty calls. But I'll be back soon and I hope you'll wait here for me.

- Go – she said with a gentle smile – I'll wait for you.

Chapter 17

April was sitting in her bed nervously biting her lower lip. It was late at night and although she really wanted to, she couldn't fall asleep. Finally, she reached for a notepad and a pen and started to write:

March 30th

I've decided to start a diary just like Leah did centuries ago. I have never thought about doing so as I've seen no point in writing down my emotions and feelings but I have nobody to talk to and I hope this technique may help me deal with what I've been going through.

I should've started this diary over a year ago when I've discovered my powers for the first time on that boat to Hawaii. I must say I felt great when I discovered I was a witch. Magic was fascinating and exciting and I couldn't wait to see what I was truly capable of. My time in New Orleans was like a dream come true. Witches were very friendly and helpful and it felt like home. I was so happy, eager to learn, working hard trying to memorise as many spells as possible, checking my limits, constantly longing for more. At first, I thought I was always that strong and I could do as much as any other witch... But recently I've started to doubt that...

When I first saved June I thought it was normal for a witch to perform a spell like that but then I was told it was not the case and apparently what I did was very unique and extraordinary. That's fine though as all witches have their special gifts. Mine obviously was resurrection. And even though that spell drained me from my powers for a few hours and I felt completely exhausted, the next day I felt even more powerful as if I've pushed my limits by crossing the line with such a powerful spell. Since that incident, I've felt stronger than ever.

When Hayley died and her body turned into ashes, Leah told me that there was a way to turn those ashes back into a body but such spell required huge amount of power. There was no other witch willing to help me, even Sarah was unsure and hesitated saying that such spell could kill us both. I tried myself with small animals first. I spent hours in the Bayou, burning dead rats and trying to make them whole again but it was not working too well at first. But with time, I managed to achieve success, that's when I asked Liam to let me try the same spell with Hayley. And I did it, I fixed her body perfectly which was a huge achievement. Later that day, when I tried to bring Hayley's spirit back to her body, I felt I was too weak to do it but I didn't want to give up. I channelled Liam and his power strengthened me and although I used most of it performing the spell, some power stayed in me and made me stronger. I nearly died that day trying to bring my beloved sister back to life. I still don't understand what went wrong and why it was Megan and not Hayley who woke up that day in Aspen. Was it because Megan died the same time I was performing that spell and her spirit was the closest one to the world of living? Or maybe it was me who did something wrong? I guess I'd never know...

Performing that spell made me stronger again and left me with enough power to perform another spell a few weeks later – I moved Megan's spirit back to her old body. Apparently, this is a very difficult spell requiring a lot of power and Leah was shocked knowing that I did it all by myself without anybody's assistance.

I can feel power in me and I am perfectly aware of how strong I've become. I can do things that no other witch can do and it feels great but at the same time it's very scary. It frightens me and now I'm afraid to discover what I'm truly capable of. With this power come emotions that I find difficult to control. I was thinking about coming back to New Orleans and having my revenge on the coven. I feel stronger than ever and I know I could do terrible things. I'm strong enough to burn that city to the ground with all traitorous witches trapped in it. I hate Iris for how she felt about killing Hayley. Maybe she was a vampire but she was also my sister and she did not deserve to die. They were supposed to protect her! I brought her and Liam to the city giving them hope they were safe there with a friendly witch on every corner. And Hayley died there... I was supposed to protect her, the witches were supposed to protect her and we've failed. I thought Iris was my true friend, I treated her like a sister and I trusted her completely but when I came to her covered in tears, asking for help, she saw nothing wrong with Hayley being dead. If it hadn't been for the fact that Emma killed June too, the witches wouldn't have done anything. They punished her for killing June but not for killing Hayley. They broke my heart that night and I hate them all for it. The anger I feel is overwhelming. Every now and then, I walk around the city at night looking for a fight. When I come across someone who wants to harm me, I hurt them. I don't want to kill anyone and I'm trying to be careful but God knows when I'll accidentally cross the line. I left so many people terrified, covered in tears, begging me to stop... I was the one calling Liam a monster for feeding on those girls in the bar but at least he was not hurting anyone. They were drunk, completely unaware of what was going on. Maybe he is a monster for what he did but am I any better? I'm afraid to admit that maybe I'm even worse...

I'm scared and I wish I could talk to someone about it but I don't want to worry my sisters. They have been through so much recently and they don't need any more problems now. I could talk to Leah but every time I tell her what I've done she's left even more shocked than before and it makes me even more scared. But what if my power finally consumes me? What if it becomes too much for me and I won't be able to control it? What if I kill someone? I'm afraid and alone and I don't know what to do. Is there anyone out there who can help me? And if so, how do I find them?

April put the diary aside, turned the lights off and lied down in bed but she stayed awake for a while thinking, unable to fall asleep. After three o'clock she finally gave up and went downstairs for a cup of camomile tea hoping it would ease her mind. June was sleeping at Oliver's that night so April was all alone. When she came to the kitchen and turned the lights on, she noticed a man sitting at the table, looking at her with a gentle smile. April raised her hand to cast the spell but the words trapped in her throat.

- Don't be afraid April, I'm not going to hurt you – said the man.

He was tall, with dark eyes and perfectly black hair tied back in a short ponytail. He was wearing a suit but no tie and his slightly unbuttoned shirt gave him a bit more casual look. He didn't look dangerous or scary but the fact that he was inside April's house in the middle of the night scared her a lot. The way he stopped April from performing the spell assured her the man was a witch.

- How do you know my name?

- I know everything about you, in fact, I know more than anyone else.

- What do you want? - April asked still standing by the kitchen door.

- We need to talk.

- Who are you? - she asked trying to hide her fear in a confident tone of voice

- A friend.

- Do you have a name?

- No.

April looked at the man suspiciously, trying to decode his thoughts.

- Are you a witch?

- Maybe. Is it important? Does it matter who I am?

- I'd like to know who I'm dealing with.

- I'm your friend and I'm here to help you, isn't that enough?

- Help me? - she furrowed her brow – I don't need help.

- You don't need to lie to me April, like I said, I know everything about you. The power that you possess is overwhelming you and it may seem it's too much for you but it's only because you don't control it. But I can help you with that.

- How?

The man got April's interest now. He sounded genuinely concerned and considering how much she was worried and frightened, she wanted to see what he could do for her.

- I can help you gain full control over your power, I can help you get even stronger and utilise your full potential the way you want to. But I'd like something in return - an access to your power. I would partially use your power and in return I would share my knowledge and experience with you.

April snorted.

- So you want to help me only because I can make you stronger, is that it?

- No April, I want to help you because I hate to see you struggling. You should use this power and not let it slowly kill you. I can feel your fear but you shouldn't be afraid. Yes, I will get something in return but it won't affect you much. You can gain so much for such a small price.

April didn't know what to say. She wanted some help, she needed it but how could she trust that man? A total stranger with no name, sitting in her house, hiding in the dark.

- I need to think about it – she said leaning against the wall with her arms crossed on her chest.

- What is there to think about? You need help and I'm here to help you. You have nothing to be afraid of, as powerful as you are I wouldn't even dare to stand against you. You are far more valuable as a friend so why would I want to be your enemy? You want to burn New Orleans to the ground? Fine, I can help you with that.

- How do you know about that?

- April, you can trust me. Come here, give me your hand, I'll give you a sneak peek of what you can have.

The man got up and reached his hand out but he didn't approach April so as not to scare her. She hesitated for a second but slowly moved forward. The moment their hands touched, she calmed down and relaxed. She was not afraid anymore, either of that man or the power she felt. She smiled and breathed a sigh of relief.

- How did you do it?

- We did it together. This is what it feels like when your magic doesn't control you. And you can feel this way all the time, I have a power that would help you control yours.

April took her hand back and the fear returned instantly.

- What do you need me to do?

The man reached his hand out again and with a simple spell created an open wound inside his palm. It was clear he wanted April to do the same. Once their hands touched again April felt calm immediately. Her head filled with spells that she didn't know before. Everything that man knew about magic, she knew now too. The magic was no longer consuming her but she could still feel it, dormant, ready to be used. The man let go off April's hand and their wounds healed instantly.

- We're linked now – he said – You have all my knowledge now and my power is helping you. Now, I also have access to your power but don't worry, you won't feel any difference, it won't make you weak.

He watched April as she was standing in the middle of the kitchen, smiling, feeling calm and happy.

- I need to go now, if you ever need me again, call me out in your thoughts and I will come to you.

- And what should I call you?

- A friend – he added with a smile and disappeared.

April turned the lights off and went back to bed as she didn't need her camomile tea anymore. She fell asleep with a smile on her face, feeling better than ever.

The next morning April knew what happened last night wasn't a dream. She hasn't felt that good for a while. No fear, no sadness, she was truly happy. There were no limits to what she could do now, she was sure of it, she could feel it. Whatever she thought of doing, a right spell came to her head right away. She could finally teleport just like Oliver, she could make herself invisible or appear anywhere without even physically leaving her bed. She smiled thinking about June and the idea of how many banks she would rob if only she knew her sister could make here invisible and teleport her to any vault. She would be the mastermind of a crime and probably Isabella's number one bounty.

April was truly limitless now, she could do whatever she wanted, she could make all her dreams come true. She thought about Iris and the other French Quarter witches. She was ready to face them all now, powerful, invincible and fearless, and she could kill them all if she wanted to. Her head was full of amazing spells and she couldn't wait to put them into use.

April sat on her bed, reached for her diary and started to write:

March 31st

Yesterday, my life has completely changed and I am no longer the same person, I am someone totally different. This one man has fixed everything for me. He has given me the strength to control my magic and I must admit I have never felt better. I don't know who he was and what exactly it is that he did but he gave me exactly what I needed, what I wanted so desperately. He knew my fears and my desires. He is my saviour and I don't even know his name. I hope Leah has some answers. I know I could call him in my thoughts and ask all the questions, but I got the impression that, for some reason, he doesn't want me to know who he is.

I feel amazing and I didn't pay any price for it. That's what makes me a bit restless as I know everything has a price... But I won't worry about it today. I want to enjoy my new self knowing there is nothing impossible for me anymore. God knows how long it will last.

Later that day, April prepared the spell to see Leah. She wanted to talk to her, ask her about the mysterious man, hoping she would know him. They sat down in the wooden hut as usual, away from curious witches and unwanted eavesdroppers.

- I'm glad to see you happy again, April. You've been so miserable recently and with everything bad going on in your life I couldn't blame you. It hurt me that I couldn't help you, couldn't find any words of comfort. So what's changed? What good news are you bringing me today?

- Well… I met someone. A man. He came to my house and offered help. He knew everything about me, he knew I was struggling with my powers and he helped me.

- Who was he?

- I was hoping you would know that. He never told me his name. He appeared out of nowhere and then just disappeared. I assume he can teleport like Oliver. He had great knowledge and experience although he couldn't be more than forty. But maybe he was delaying his age… I don't know, it's hard to tell.

- What did he look like?

April described the man with detail and repeated everything he said, word by word. She was observing how curiosity showing on Leah's face was slowly changing into fear as April told her about the blood pact they've made. Leah was looking at April with horror, her eyes were wide open her jaw was down.

- Leah, are you OK? What's going on?

But Leah didn't say anything and just kept staring into April's eyes with growing fear.

- Oh my God – she finally whispered – What have you done?